Joan Fallon, author of *The Only Blue Door*
…a perceptive look at modern Britain…A page-turning story which leaves you wanting to read more.

Jackie Hayden, author *My Boy: The Philip Lynott Story*
Carew's fluid flab-free writing style tows you along the highs, lows and uncertainties of Claire's life

Dani J Norwell, author of *Most Unlikely*
I love a good metaphor and this story is built on one.

Books by Susan Carew

Beyond the Waves series
Take the Plunge
Beyond the Buoy

Beyond the Buoy

Susan Carew

Copyright, © Susan Carew 2024

The right of Susan Carew to be identified as the author of this work has been asserted in accordance with the Copyright, Designs and Patents Act 1988.

All rights reserved. No part of this publication may be reproduced, stored in or transmitted into any retrieval system, in any form, or by any means (electronic, mechanical, photocopying, recording or otherwise) without the prior written permission of the publisher. Any person who does any unauthorised act in relation to this publication may be liable to criminal prosecution and civil claims for damages.

This is a work of fiction. Any resemblance to actual persons, living or dead or events locales is entirely coincidental or used in a fictitious manner.

ISBN: 978 -1-7390922-0-7

First published in 2024

Cover design by Kari Brownlie

Cover design copyright © Susan Carew

To Mammy, still missed

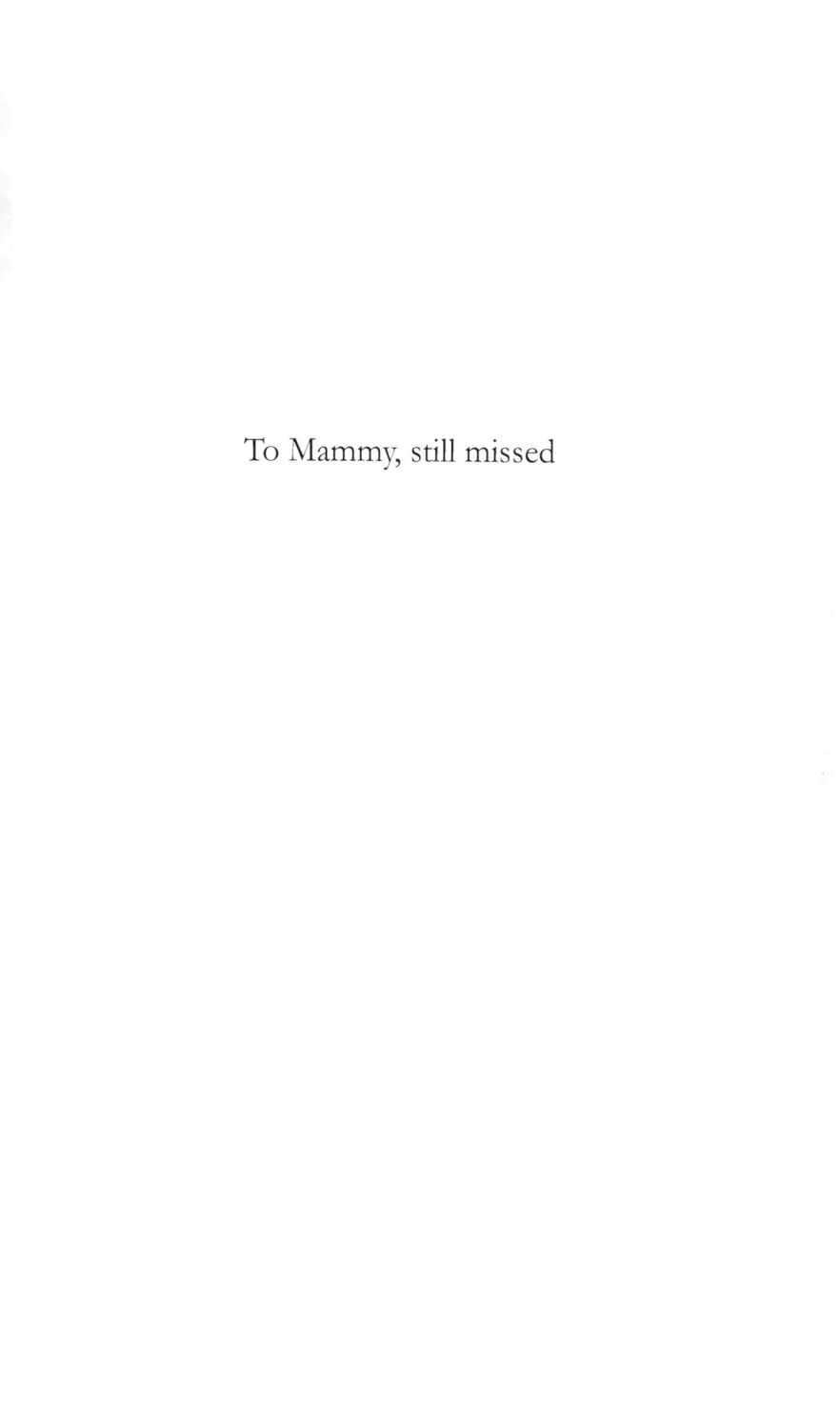

Prologue

Late Autumn

The buoy bounced in the sea as Claire struck it. 'Come on, Mark! I know you can do this,' she said, encouraging him forward. The sea was grey and murky. It had taken all her powers of persuasion to get him to swim today. Since his arrival in England from the shores of Spain he'd been none too impressed with the temperatures of the air nor the water. Whilst Claire was a proficient and avid swimmer, the same could not be said of her partner. She watched him as each arm raised and slapped into the choppy waves. *I hope he's going to be okay, he looks as if he's struggling. Perhaps we should call it a day.* Mark stopped and was treading water. 'Are you all right?' she asked.

'My goggles are leaking. I'm just tightening them,' he said, and snapped them back into place before continuing.

Mark was still some way from the buoy and now Claire knew it was a mistake to push him. She looked up at the sky; it was threatening to rain. Decision made, she began to swim to Mark. 'I think we should stop now. You've done really well, but the conditions aren't great and you're not exactly used to this type of sea. The last thing I want is to put you off swimming altogether.'

'I am cold,' he admitted. 'Another day though, hey?'

'Definitely.'

They waded through the shallows to the place where they had left their belongings. Changing quickly, Mark pulled on a jumper and got out a thermos flask. 'Here, I brought along some coffee, that should warm us up. I've got some chocolate if you want as well.'

'You're a star.' Claire was cold now too and a hot drink was just what she needed. She raised her mug to Mark and he filled it. She smiled at him.

'What?' he asked.

'This is nice, I'm having a good time.'

'Freezing on a British beach. You have some funny ideas about enjoying yourself.'

'No, not that, silly. I mean being here with someone who is thoughtful enough to remember to bring along post-swim provisions.'

'It's only coffee and a Mars bar.'

'It's more than that. It shows you care, and I know the last thing you wanted to do today was to go swimming in the English sea. But you did it to make me happy. That's true love and well, there have been times in my life when I never thought I'd ever find happiness with someone again. Meeting you, it's changed everything. You've restored my faith in love, Mark Fraser. And let me tell you, I was a tough nut to crack.'

'I don't know about that. I think when you meet the right person it isn't hard work, it just clicks – feels right.

If I'd been told a while ago that I'd leave Spain and settle back in the UK, I would have thought they were mad. Never in a hundred years could I have imagined it, but for you, for us, it's not a bother at all.'

They snuggled closer to each other, content to be together and watch the sea.

'It's a shame though,' Mark said, 'not to have got to the buoy. I really thought I could do it. Since we got together I've been working on trying to be a better swimmer, but it's further out from the shore than it looks.'

'Everyone says that, but don't worry. You've done so well to improve the way you have and with practice you'll get there.'

'Past the buoy?' He chuckled.

'Let's not get ahead of ourselves. You're safe enough up to the buoy, but beyond it, well, you never know what's out there. You'd need to have support and not go it alone, that's for sure.'

Mark said, 'I'll keep working on it, might need to get a wetsuit though. I'm bloody freezing! Let's make a move. It's a busy day for me tomorrow.'

'Has it been difficult fitting into a new job?'

'Nah. One hospital A&E is much like another, although it will feel a bit odd to be using my mother tongue at work again after all these years.'

'Thank you,' Claire said.

'What for?'

'For uprooting your life to come and live with me like this. I want you to know how much I appreciate it.'

'It's what we do for the people we love. And, as I said, work is work wherever you are in the world. It's the person you're with that makes it special.' He leant down and kissed her lips. 'I know a very nice way of warming up, but I think it should be done in the cosy warmth of the bedroom.'

Claire giggled. 'Sounds good to me.'

Chapter One

Early Spring the following year

'Oh yes, that's good. Just there… arrrrhh.' Claire shivered as the masseuse hit the spot on her neck that had been giving her trouble for weeks. She'd assumed it was due to spending so much time in front of a computer, but when the therapist told her she was very tense and asked if she'd been stressed recently, Claire had to admit that yes, she had been. How long had she been carrying around doubts about her relationship with Mark before she'd acknowledged them herself, let alone voiced them out loud?

'Your shoulders are very knotted. I'll spend some extra time on them. Is the pressure okay?'

'Fine,' mumbled Claire, her head squished into the face-shaped hole in the massage table.

'I'll use some lavender essential oil to help with the de-stress.'

Claire uttered something inaudible. She was so blissed out, the masseuse could smother her with butter for all she cared. She'd forgotten how good a massage could be. Why hadn't she thought of doing this ages ago? She zoned out, the tinkling background music and the rhythmic hand movement on her back lulling her to almost unconsciousness. She lost track of time and when the masseuse wrapped her in a blanket and whispered for her to get dressed in her own time, she could barely believe an hour had passed. She lay there not wanting to move. However, knowing the next client would be waiting, she forced herself to get up.

Blinking in the light, Claire made her way back to their room. As she let herself in, she could hear Mark in the bathroom. 'Hello!' she announced.

'Just in the shower. Be out in a tick,' Mark called back over the din of the water.

Claire flopped onto the bed. She could fall asleep right now. Today's back massage had been the last in a line of treatments she'd had during the past two days at the spa hotel they were staying at. She was so relaxed she felt as if her bones had melted. Perhaps it had been a mistake waiting until the last evening to go out for a posh meal. The way she was feeling, she wouldn't make it past the starter. She yawned and closed her eyes, drifting off into a light sleep. The next thing she knew Mark was tickling her under her chin.

'Come on, sleeping beauty. Time to put your glad rags on.' Mark stood over her, wearing a suit and smelling discreetly of cologne.

'You're already dressed.' She looked down at her

dishevelled robe.

'Yes, so you'd better hurry. Our reservation is in 45 minutes.'

'So soon?' Claire was aghast; she still had to shower.

'I'll wait for you in the pub across the road,' Mark said.

'That dive? Why not the hotel bar?'

'Bit too stuck up for my taste. The landlord in the pub's a friendly bloke. I'd rather spend time chatting to someone genuine than be on my best behaviour downstairs.'

Claire thought the hotel staff had been lovely, and she certainly didn't think the atmosphere was anything but friendly. Mark blew her a kiss and was gone.

Claire hurried across the road; getting ready had taken longer than planned and they were going to be late for their dinner reservation. Entering the pub her eyes swept over the bar, looking for Mark. She couldn't see him. Had he got fed up waiting and gone ahead? Then she heard a man curse. She looked for the source and saw Mark in front of a slot machine. As she watched he gave it a thump and turned away, his expression one of thunder. He saw Claire and put a smile on his face.

'Everything okay?' Claire asked.

'Yeah. Why shouldn't it be?'

Ignoring the tone, Claire said, 'Sorry I'm a bit late.'

'Well, you're here now. Shall we go?' Mark took her

elbow and hurried her out. The restaurant was close by, and they walked in silence. Mark only spoke when they went in, to give his name to the maître d'. Once settled in their seats he smiled at Claire, and looking about the place he said, 'This is nice, isn't it?'

Claire took his hand. She didn't know why he'd been so angry earlier, surely not because she'd been five minutes late? But she was determined the evening should go well. 'It's lovely, very romantic. And this time together has been great. I really think we needed to reconnect; you've been so busy with work. I feel as if we haven't had a decent conversation in months.'

The menus arrived and Mark uncoupled his hand from Claire's to take his. She noticed he hadn't commented on what she'd just said and now seemed engrossed in reading. The waiter listed the specials of the day. Claire listened, but Mark wasn't paying any attention. He bellowed out his order and looked at Claire expectantly. 'What are you having?'

'Er, well, I haven't decided yet. I thought the specials sounded nice, maybe the duck.' – looking up at the waiter. 'Can you give us a few minutes while we decide?'

'But of course, Madam,' the waiter replied, giving her a charming smile, which vanished as soon as he looked at Mark. 'Please let me know when you're ready.'

'Mark,' Claire said in a loud whisper, as the waiter moved away. 'That was a bit rude. We're not at a fast-food restaurant, you know. What's your hurry?'

Chastened, Mark said, 'Sorry love. You're right. Let's enjoy the experience' – he chuckled – 'and at these prices we want to make the most of it.'

Claire thought it was a bit crass to mention the cost. And Mark's attitude wasn't great, it was if as he didn't really want to be here. It wasn't every day they went to a Michelin-star restaurant, and it had been at his suggestion they come here. Why was he being so disagreeable about it now? It put a damper on the evening from which it didn't recover, and while they attempted to make conversation, it was forced and unnatural. Their plates had just been removed when Mark patted his jacket and said, 'Oh damn! I've forgotten my wallet. You order dessert – I'm not having any – and I'll go back to the room and get it.'

The waiter returned, looking at Mark's retreating back, and Claire felt the need to explain. 'He'll be back in a minute.' She smiled at him. 'Can I see the dessert menu please?'

Some time later, Claire's dessert had been ordered and eaten. She was beginning to get edgy. Where the bloody hell was Mark? It also left her in a quandary. She didn't have any money with her, Mark had said this was his treat, and she'd left her phone charging back at the hotel. How long could she sit here and put off asking for the bill? The evening was ruined. It also occurred to her that Mark's reason for leaving didn't ring true. How had he paid for his drink in the pub if he didn't have his wallet on him? He was acting oddly. Just as she was thinking she'd have to have an awkward conversation with the staff, Mark reappeared. He was flushed and out of breath.

'I'm sorry I took so long. Couldn't find the bloody thing anywhere. I was beginning to think I'd been pickpocketed!'

Relief washed over Claire. 'God, Mark. I was feeling like a right idiot sitting here on my own. I've been getting strange looks from everyone. Can we just go now?'

The bill summoned and paid for, they left. As they exited Mark nodded his head at the pub. 'How about a nightcap before we turn in?'

'I don't fancy one, thanks.'

'Ah, go on. Be my way of apologising.'

'All right then,' Claire said, reasoning that they could salvage something of the evening.

At the bar the landlord came over to them. 'Back again?' he said to Mark. 'Trying to win back your losses?' He sniggered. 'Need more change for the fruit machine?'

Chapter Two

Claire leant back in her chair and stretched. She'd spent the best part of the afternoon working on the accounts of one of her company's top clients. It required her utmost concentration and thus far had been a good distraction from the events of their trip. Glancing at the clock she reasoned she'd put enough working hours into the day. She rolled her neck and decided what she needed was a swim. It wasn't a swim club night, but a gentle workout and a chinwag with her best friend would sort her out. She gave Alison a call and they arranged to meet for a swim.

She flung her sports bag onto the passenger seat, got in and was momentarily perplexed as to why her feet wouldn't reach the pedals of the car. Laughing at herself, she remembered, Mark hadn't wanted to ride his bike into work because of the recent bad weather and had been borrowing her car. The inside of the windscreen was smeared with grime, so she reached into the glove compartment for a cloth. As it opened a shower of papers fluttered out. Puzzled, she picked one up. A used scratch card. Leaning across to get a better look she picked up a few more; there were dozens of them. What the hell…? she thought. How did these all get in here? The footwell was smothered in tiny silver flakes. Why would Mark buy a load of scratch cards? He'd never shown the slightest interest in them before. She felt a quiver in her stomach as she remembered the incident at the pub with the slot machine. She shoved the cards into her bag. She'd mention it to him later.

———

Claire rustled around in her bag, searching for her Aquarium membership card.

'You haven't left it at home, have you?' Alison asked.

'No, I always put it here. Found it!' As she pulled it out, the scratch cards cascaded to the ground.

'Didn't know you were a secret gambler.' Alison leant down and scooped up some of the fallen tickets. 'Gosh, how many have you got here? These must have cost you a fortune. I hope you won.'

Claire grew hot. Should she deny they were hers? Then Alison would assume they must be Mark's. She didn't want to say anything until she had discussed it with him. It could be something or nothing, although the fear that niggled at her suggested otherwise. She scrambled for something to say. 'Busted!' – she laughed – 'I've been getting a couple of these with the weekly shop. I thought how nice it would be if I won some money and could buy Mark a car, then he wouldn't have to cycle to work in bad weather. Daft, I know. I end up sticking them in the glove compartment in disgust when I don't win. I've had a bit of a clear out and am going to throw these away. There must be a good few months' worth here. I should learn to be tidier.'

Alison looked unconvinced. She handed the cards to Claire. 'You know this kind of thing can get out of control. That's how addictions start. It's not a road you want to go down, and the chances of winning are not stacked in your favour.'

Claire bristled at Alison's suggestion. That's the trouble with good friends, they don't hold back. Snatching the cards, she said, 'I do not have an addiction. Christ, Alison, relax. It's just a bit of fun, two minutes of escapism and imagining having a bundle of cash to splash.' She swung her backpack onto her shoulder. 'Shall we get on and have a swim then?'

'Yeah, I can't wait. I really need to unwind after the day I've had.'

'Work getting you down?' Claire knew Alison's teaching job could be full on.

'Actually no. The opposite, in fact. The deputy head has tendered her resignation and my boss is encouraging me to apply for the position, says I'd be a shoo in.'

'Brilliant! About time that school recognised your worth.'

'Maybe.'

'You are going to apply, aren't you?' Claire was

astonished that Alison wasn't leaping at this opportunity.

'It will mean even more hours and time spent away from home. I'm not sure it's practical with the boys.'

'The boys? Callum is at university, and he's an adult. And Jamie, he's pretty independent and growing up fast. Before you know it, he'll have flown the nest. You don't want to pass up a chance like this. You love that school; you'd make a great deputy. Who knows, one day you could be head.'

'I don't know about that,' Alison said, although Claire could see she was now considering that possibility. 'I suppose it couldn't hurt to apply. I've never given much thought to promotion, just keeping on top of things has kept me fully occupied this past decade.' This in reference to the loss of her husband and bringing up her two sons alone, not to mention a life-threatening accident on holiday a few years before.

'But everything you've done up until now has been for other people.' Claire included herself in this. 'Becoming deputy would be for you. Something to call your own. And the extra money wouldn't go amiss, would it? Look, if you apply and don't get it, you've lost nothing. If, on the other hand, you do, you've given yourself options. You can always change your mind and not accept. Just knowing they think you're good enough will be a confidence-booster.'

'Maybe, I'll give it some thought,' Alison said.

Claire was warming some leftover lasagne in the microwave when she heard the front door slam. Mark came in and seemed to be in a good mood. He gave her a big hug and a kiss.

'How's my favourite girl then?' he said whilst still holding her. 'You look happy and if I'm not mistaken,' – he sniffed her neck – 'you've been swimming.'

Claire laughed. 'Yes detective, I have. I was working on the Rollinson project and was hunched over my computer all afternoon so needed to straighten the kinks out in my shoulders.'

'I thought that was a rush job. I'm surprised you had the time to go swimming.' Mark peered through the glass of the microwave. 'Any lasagne left?'

'Yes, in the fridge. I did a bit more work on the account when I got back. It's more or less done. I have a meeting about it tomorrow, so I'll be going into the office. Okay?'

'What? Oh, yeah, fine,' Mark said, as he heaped a generous portion of food onto his plate. 'I was going to go to the gym anyway.'

'Again? Haven't you just come from there?'

'So? Aren't you going swimming again tomorrow?'

'I suppose so. It's just you seem to spend an awful lot of time at the gym these days. They haven't got a new sexy young female trainer, have they?' She'd intended it as a joke but Mark frowned.

'What's that supposed to mean?'

'Nothing, I'm just being silly. And I think it's great you want to keep fit. You seem to be making friends there too, which is good. I want you to be happy here, to settle in.' She put her arms around him, and he leant into her. She let her head fall against his back and closed her eyes.

Chapter Three

'Mum! Where are my boots? Mum!' The teenage boy's muffled entreaties were lost as his upper body was secreted in the cupboard under the stairs. He rooted around, haphazardly throwing shoes about. 'Mum. I'm going to be late!'

'What is all the shouting about, Jamie?' Alison said, coming down the stairs with a habitual pile of dirty washing in her arms.

'I can't find my football boots. They're not here.' Jamie's face was red from exertion, which highlighted the acne that had recently erupted. He straightened, his arms hanging at his sides.

'I put them outside. They were so muddy I didn't want them getting the other shoes dirty.'

Jamie tutted and stomped to the back door. 'Mum. They're filthy. I can't wear these like this. Couldn't you have cleaned them?' He held the boots aloft with a look of disgust.

'Er, excuse me?' Alison said. 'What did your last servant die of? You're old enough to clean your own boots. Bad enough I have to deal with your football strip.'

'That's why I left them in the cupboard, so I could remember. Now I'm going to be late. I still haven't got my kit ready.'

Alison sighed, 'Your kit is on your bed.' – She held her hands out – 'Give me those. The mud's all dry. I'll give them a quick brush; they should be fine.'

'Thanks Mum. You're the best!' He planted a swift kiss on her cheek and raced upstairs. Alison smiled. It wouldn't be too long before these displays of affection were a thing of the past; best appreciate them while she still could.

'Don't take all day,' she called after him. 'I've got to go to the supermarket, and I need to get back here to do some prep for school tomorrow. If you want a lift, you'd better get a move on.'

'Ryan's picking me up.' Jamie said, thumping down the stairs and clunking his sports bag behind him.

'Who?'

'Ryan, our coach.'

'Oh. You mean Mr Harman.'

'No one calls him that. He's not a teacher, you know.'

'Umm.' Alison decided not to comment. There was no way she'd let any of her pupils call her by her first name. She thought it blurred the lines for a figure of authority to be too pally, though she reasoned that Jamie had a point. Plus, Ryan was only in his twenties, so closer to her son's age than his teachers. He had been a promising young player at a football academy, before a persistent knee injury had put paid to any plans he'd had for being a professional. This hadn't dimmed his status amongst the boys he was coaching though, that and his muscle-bound physique – no doubt envied by her skinny son. Nowadays, Jamie's attention was singularly directed towards his football, and attempts to bulk up to look more like his idol. A car horn beeped, and Jamie ran out, banging the door behind him. No kiss for Alison this time, she noted.

Alison was at her laptop in the kitchen when she heard voices in the hallway. Getting up she saw her son and his coach making their way in. Jamie was shrugging off his jacket. 'Hi Mum. Ryan gave me a lift back. He wants to speak to you.'

'Hello Mrs Harris,' Ryan said, in a tone Alison thought he probably only used for his grandmother.

'You can call me Alison. No need to be so formal, makes me feel old.' She laughed, but noted Ryan's expression, which said, well you *are* old. Changing tack she said, 'I was just about to make a cup of tea. Would you like some?'

'Do you have any Red Bull?'

'No, I'm sorry, I don't buy the stuff.' Alison wrinkled her nose.

'Here you can have mine,' offered Jamie, reaching into his bag. 'I got a couple from the vending machine.'

'Since when do you drink Red Bull?' Alison watched as Jamie handed over the drink, his eyes alight.

'Oh, you know, it helps keep me alert.'

'Alert? You're seventeen, you don't need that amount of caffeine in your system, especially drinking it at this time. No wonder you're up at all hours.'

'It's no biggy, Mrs Harris, I mean Alison. All the lads drink caffeine drinks, it helps with their performance after a day at school.'

'Well, I'd prefer if you didn't drink this at all.' She took the can that Jamie was just about to open away from him. He didn't say anything, but the scowl on his face told her she'd embarrassed him.

'Ryan wanted to talk to you about my training, didn't you, Ryan?'

'Yes. I thought you'd like to know how well Jamie's doing. He shows great potential, and I'd like to see him make the best of his talents. Maybe even try and get him enrolled at a football academy. Normally, he'd be a bit old for that, but I have some influence, and we might be able to swing it.'

'Isn't that great, Mum?' Alison had never seen her son looked so delighted. She ruffled his hair, he twisted away. 'Mum. Don't.'

'Maybe that's something we could look into.' Alison didn't want to raise Jamie's hopes and needed to do her own research before she committed to anything.

'Of course,' Ryan said, 'but in the meantime, we could still work on improving Jamie's general fitness, see if we can beef him up a bit.' As he said this Ryan gently punched Jamie's arm. Jamie laughed and went red with pleasure. 'I'd like him to come to my gym, do some weight training. His speed and stamina are pretty good, but he could do with strengthening and developing his muscles. That's if he wants to compete with lads who have been at the academy a few years.'

'I see,' Alison said.

'I'd supervise everything, and I'd be able to give Jamie a lift there and back. It wouldn't inconvenience you at all.'

'My son is not an inconvenience. I'd be happy to support him if this is what he wants to do' – she saw her son punch the air – 'if he's good enough, *and* his schoolwork doesn't suffer.'

'It won't, Mum. I promise! Not that I'd need A-levels if I become a footballer' – then seeing Alison's pursed lips, he quickly added – 'but I know how important a good education is,' mimicking the phrase so often used by his mother.

Chapter Four

Alison was helping herself to milk for her mid-morning coffee when Mary Griffin, the headteacher, appeared at her side. 'Morning Alison.'

'Hello there Mary. We don't often see you in the staffroom at this time. Would you like a coffee?'

Mary shook her head. 'I see from the timetable that you have a free afternoon.'

'Yes, my class are off to the local wildlife sanctuary and Lydia said she'd be happy to oversee things as not many of her pupils had signed up for it. Brian will be there and we were inundated with offers from parents to help supervise, so I thought I'd take the opportunity of catching up on a few things in the classroom. Lots of old posters and drawings need taking down.'

'Quite. I wonder if you could come to my office then, say around three?'

'Anything wrong?' Alison scanned her brain to think of something that might be amiss.

'Everything's fine. I thought we could have a little chat about your application to become deputy head.'

'Oh right, yeah. That would be great. I do have a

few questions I was wanting to ask you.' Mary didn't say anything. Feeling she needed to fill the silence Alison said, 'So, three o'clock. I'll be there.'

Sitting in the school secretary's office at the designated time, Alison smirked to herself thinking of all the little children who would be here because of bad behaviour, and how nervous they'd be feeling. Mary had been quite the mentor to Alison, and they'd always had a friendly working relationship, but as head she could appear quite ferocious to a small child, should the need arise. Alison could hear laughing from inside the office, and a man's voice she didn't recognise. The door opened and Mary came out. Her smile disappeared as she looked Alison up and down. 'Oh dear. What happened to you?'

'What?' Alison said, then following Mary's gaze she looked down at her top, which was dobbed with red paint and a single piece of glitter-splattered macaroni. 'Arts and crafts' – she laughed – 'what are you going to do? There's only so much paint and small children you can have together in a room before something happens!'

Mary's expression was pained. 'Do come in, Alison.'

Alison followed her and saw an officious-looking man sitting behind Mary's desk. He peered above his glasses and looked her up and down. He was holding a pen and leafing through what looked like a personnel file – Mary didn't hold with keeping records on the computer. She was old-school and proud of it. Alison started to feel uncomfortable.

'This is Sebastian Royce-Gilby,' Mary said. Alison took his outstretched hand to shake. 'He's one of the school governors.' Upon hearing this information, Alison unintentionally gripped his hand tighter; seeing him wince, she quickly released him.

'Sebastian was in the area at a governors' meeting. When he found out one of the candidates for the deputy head position worked in the school, he thought it would give him the chance to meet you informally.'

Candidates? thought Alison; she hadn't been aware the post had been advertised yet. She smoothed down her top, excruciatingly aware of how scruffy she must look. What a terrible first impression. 'Oh' – she squeaked – 'I haven't had time to prepare…any questions.'

'Mary tells me you've known about the vacancy for some time, so I'm sure you've had a chance to go over the job description and think about your application.' Sebastian gave what might have passed for a smile. 'And we're only here for a little chat, nothing to worry about.'

Oh really, thought Alison. So why do I feel petrified then? But she reasoned this wasn't the interview, and it might be a good thing to test the waters before the real thing. More than likely this Sebastian Whatsit wouldn't even be there for that. Feeling comforted by this thought she sat up a little straighter.

'Alison, you don't mind me calling you by your first name, do you?' Sebastian asked.

'Not at all.'

'You've worked at the school a long time, fifteen

years. Why are you interested in being this school's deputy headteacher?'

'As you said, I've been here a long time, learned my craft as a teacher so to speak. I've always been happy at the school, it's like my second home. In fact with the hours I put in, I spend more time here than my actual home!' She laughed, then stopped as she saw his impassive face. 'Not that I'm complaining, it's all part of being a teacher.'

'You do know that along with the added responsibilities of a deputy-head teacher would be longer working hours?'

'Yes, I'm aware of that. The extra income might soften the blow though' – NO! Never mention money in an interview. She scrambled now to recover – 'But of course, that is not my motivation. Teaching is a vocation, at least to me, aside from my boys, it's my life.'

'Umm,' he noted something down. 'Could you describe your strengths as a leader?'

Alison shifted in her seat; this didn't feel like an informal chat. She glanced at Mary, who was scrutinising her lap. 'I think I am approachable; people feel at ease coming to me for advice. I've mentored several new teachers and enjoyed doing so. I'm a good listener, which I believe is essential when you are in a position of authority – it's not enough to only give directives.' She felt pleased with her answer.

Sebastian smiled. 'Where do you see yourself in five years' time?'

'Hurtling towards sixty!' Okay Alison, she admonished

herself, this is no time for jokes. Gosh, look at his face. 'No seriously, within the school. That would depend. If I were to become deputy head, I'd like to think I would have implemented some of the ideas I have,' – she had no ideas, this was pure bluff – 'which I would expand upon in the formal interview. But whatever happens, I'd like to think I'd still be here making a valuable contribution. Whatever my role.'

'Yes,' he said, not giving any indication of what he thought of her answer. 'Can you tell me about a time when you managed a change at the school?'

Alison's mind went blank. The only one that came to mind was when the timetable had been altered, and the start time brought forward by half an hour. Alison had thought it an awful idea. When it was implemented there were so many teething problems the staff had revolted; in fact, Alison seemed to remember being the instigator. She swallowed. 'Do you know, I can't think of anything off hand.' She watched as Sebastian scribbled something. 'I'm sure I could, given more time…'

'That's quite all right, Alison. I think I have enough for now.' He stood up and shook hands with her.

Mary ushered her out and Alison stood by the closed door, leaning her head against it. Her knees were shaking. As she stood there trying to recover, she heard a murmured voice inside say, 'Oh dear.'

Chapter Five

'I swear, Claire, I was torpedoed! What the heck was Mary doing? You think you know someone. That you can trust them, and then they go and behave like this. I feel…I feel' – Alison searched for a word – 'betrayed! Informal chat, I don't think so, and she knew that wasn't the case. You should have seen her, simpering away to Sebastian double-barrelled, and barely able to make eye contact with me. Meanwhile I'm looking like a right twit. I was making jokes. Jokes, for goodness' sake!'

'You do do that when you're nervous,' Claire said.

'I know! And I was nervous. I had nothing prepared; I hadn't given a thought to the interview, truth be told.' She scrubbed at a non-existent stain on the worktop she was standing by. Ever since Claire had arrived Alison had been cleaning, while she barked out the story of her encounter. From experience Claire knew that when her friend was preoccupied or stressed, she took to housework. Judging from the spotless nature of the kitchen and the overwhelming pine smell, Alison was very angry. It wasn't an emotion that Claire was used to witnessing in her.

'What are you going to do now?' Claire asked. 'Are you going to have it out with Mary? Do you know when your real interview is taking place?'

'Never!' Alison sat down and flung the dishcloth onto the table.

'What do you mean?'

'I'm going to withdraw my application, that's what. Obviously, this…charade that Mary organised was to demonstrate that I'm not up to the job. Maybe she wanted to save me the time and bother of doing all the work for the interview.' She pressed her hand to her forehead and sighed. 'It might be for the best anyway. Me as deputy head. What was I thinking?'

'If Mary didn't think you were suitable, why would she suggest you apply? Perhaps she really did think meeting this Sebastian bloke would be a good thing. She might have thought it would help.'

'She got that wrong, didn't she?'

'And as for withdrawing your application. Aren't you giving up a bit too easily?'

Alison shook her head. 'I've done nothing but go over this since it happened, and every time I try to imagine being deputy head my stomach goes into knots. Then, when I think about just carrying on as I am, it's a relief. If the thought of the job alone gets me stressed, lord alone knows what the reality would be like.'

'But that's often the case when you start something new. I bet you felt like that before you became a teacher.'

'Maybe. But I was a lot younger then, better able to bounce back from adversity. It's harder as you get older.'

Her expression was pained. 'I'm tired of fighting it all. Being a single mum and bringing up two boys alone is hard enough. Added to that is the grief of losing Gavin. I think about him every day. That doesn't go away, I've just learned to live with it.'

Claire took this in. These days Alison rarely talked about Gavin. How naïve to think that because of this she didn't feel his loss all the time. 'You should do what's best for you. If you don't want to go for the promotion, don't do it. It's not worth upsetting yourself. You love your job, you're good at it and the children adore you. That's special. A lot of people hate what they do and would be envious. Perhaps it is best to appreciate what you have. Who said it's vital to always keep striving for more?'

Alison touched Claire's hand. 'You always say the right thing. It feels good to talk about it, rather than keeping it all bottled up. Although I have been rather preoccupied about what's going on in my life recently and totally forgot to ask about your spa break. I'm surprised *you* haven't mentioned it before now. How did it go? I bet you both feel better for it.'

'Not exactly.' Claire swallowed. Should she say anything at all given that Alison was going through a tough time? She was still trying to make sense of it all: the scratch cards and Mark's behaviour on their break away. However, she thought she'd go mad if she wasn't able to tell someone about her fears, and if she couldn't speak to her best friend, then who?

Alison asked, 'What is it? Did something happen?'

'Yes. No. I'm not sure, I'm not au fait with these kinds of things.'

'What kind of things? What are you talking about?'

'Gambling.'

'Gambling?'

'I think Mark may have a gambling problem.' There, she'd said it out loud. It stung.

'Blimey. Are you sure?'

'Yes and no.' She told Alison about the incident at the restaurant, and how Mark had disappeared during the meal so he could feed a slot machine.

'So how did he justify that?' Alison said.

'He denied it, kept to his story of going back for his wallet. He said the landlord was joking, that he was referring to earlier on in the evening. But I knew he wasn't. It was such a bullshit lie, but the more I challenged him the more defensive he got. In the end we went to bed, and on the drive home the next morning he put on loud music so we could avoid conversation. We haven't really spoken since. I've been looking on the internet about gambling addictions and he's certainly displaying tendencies: he's not sleeping, and he's stressed all the time, like he has something on his mind. Do you remember me mentioning that to you before? I thought it was down to work, but there's the fact that he's short of money all the time too, asking me to lend him some for this or that. Then I found all those scratch cards…'

'Those were Mark's?'

'They certainly weren't mine. I hated lying to you about that, but I didn't want to say anything until I'd spoken to him. I didn't want to make a big deal of it in case it was nothing.'

'So, have you talked to him about this?'

'No. Out of the blue his attitude has changed. He's been the bright, breezy Mark I fell in love with. His mood has been up and down recently so I didn't want to rock the boat. Looking back now, that could be why he'd suggested splurging on the extra spa treatments and the fancy meal – he'd had a big win or something. Now every time he's out of the house or in another room I'm thinking, "What's he up to? Is he gambling?" That's no way to be, is it?'

'No, it's not. I'm so sorry, Claire. How awful is this, but surely you have to confront him? Maybe there's an innocent explanation.'

'Claire sighed. 'Maybe, but I don't think it's going to be that simple. If I had some sort of concrete proof to present to him, that might be different, but until then I'm stuck.'

※

Claire let herself into the house. It was silent; Mark must be at the gym, she reasoned, or was he? A cloud of doubt descended on her. Was this going to be her life from now on? There was a pile of post on the kitchen table, one of the envelopes had fallen to the floor and as she bent down to retrieve it, she noticed a scrunched-up piece of paper. Picking it up she saw it was a letter from Mark's Spanish bank. It was written in Spanish and English, and though she knew she shouldn't, she straightened out the paper and read it. At first, she thought it was a standard letter about amendments to the terms and conditions of his account – it was no longer possible to make purchases using a credit card at physical gambling businesses – but as she continued reading, she could see this was being brought to Mark's attention because he had been using his card at a casino in Brighton. His last attempt to do so had been declined. She gripped the letter. Mark was using a credit card in a casino. Who gambles on credit? This was her proof.

Chapter Six

Claire sat in her favourite armchair next to the window, staring out. For Mark to be in so much debt and for her to be ignorant of it, frightened her. How much more was there that she didn't know about the man she shared her life with? She reflected on the past few months, trying to identify times Mark might have been gambling; how could she have been so blind? The streetlights lit as day moved to evening; she waited. Finally, she heard the whoosh of Mark's bicycle and the clink of it being locked up. Her hand, which held the damning piece of paper, trembled. Squaring her shoulders and inhaling deeply, she remained seated. He came through the door, and she said, 'Hello, Mark.'

'Jesus, Claire! You almost gave me a heart attack. What are you doing sitting here in the dark?' He switched on a lamp. She looked up at him, her eyes glistening.

'Not to wear out a cliché, but we need to talk.'

'Okay. What about?'

She held up the letter. 'This.'

Recognising it, Mark said, 'You've been reading my mail?'

'That I cannot deny, but in my defence, it was lying on the floor. Had you forgotten you'd left it there? Where did you have to rush off to in such a hurry that you didn't remember to hide it? Just like you've been hiding a whole lot more from me.' She held up some papers, his credit card bills. 'You owe twenty thousand pounds? Not to mention maxing out your Spanish credit card. And you've been applying for other cards. Did you think I wouldn't find out? How were you going to pay all this back without me knowing?'

'You've been going through my private affairs. What gives you the right?' Mark's face contorted as he ripped the papers from her.

'And what gives *you* the right to treat me this way? Lie to me? How are we supposed to build a life together when there's a whole part of yours that I don't know about? You have this huge problem that you've kept hidden. Do you have any idea how that makes me feel? I thought we had something special. Is that all a lie?'

'No. No. No.' He sank down onto the sofa and put his head in his hands. 'I don't know what to do, Claire. I've never got in this deep before. It's out of control.'

'What do you mean, "before"?' She sat next to him. Forcing him to look at her, she repeated, 'What do you mean by "before"? Are you telling me you've had a gambling problem in the past?'

'Yes. In Madrid. When I was married. It's why we split up. She couldn't take it and left me. For a while I fell apart and things got really bad, but eventually I came to my senses, and I quit. Then I moved to Almería and started afresh. I never told anyone the reason for my marriage breakup, I blanked it all out of my mind, that's why I didn't say anything to you. I wanted to believe it never happened and I swear I haven't gambled for years.' He clutched her hand. 'You must believe me. You do, don't you? Claire?'

Oh my God, she thought. She hadn't been sure how this confrontation would pan out but to learn Mark had this secret shocked her. In her heart she hadn't expected him to be honest with her this soon and she'd been prepared for a drawn-out discussion of accusation and denial. That he had confessed so soon, surprised her and his distress was disarming. She felt it left her with little option but to try and be understanding. 'I believe you. I still can't quite take this all in, but I do believe you. Now, what happens next?'

⁂

Hours later, Claire stood and stretched, her shoulders and back stiff with tension. After Mark's admission, they had both cried and hugged, then cried some more. Mark had promised her his gambling days were over. He swore he wouldn't let her down and would never lie again. They had held each other until Mark had had to leave her and go to work. He promised he would come straight back as soon as his shift ended. Left alone in the house with their conversation whirling around her head Claire felt she would go mad. She longed to talk it over with Alison but couldn't until she had a sense of what she was dealing with. Ever the analyst, she went online to find out all she could about addictions, and what could be done to help. There was a wealth of information, which she found comforting and overwhelming in equal measures. What was clear to her at least, was that this was not something they could tackle alone. They both needed the help of experts. Claire was resolute though; unlike his ex-wife, she would not abandon Mark. She'd see this through, whatever the cost. This relationship, this man, were worth fighting for, and fight she would.

Chapter Seven

Claire drummed her fingers on the table and debated whether to open the bottle of wine she had bought especially for tonight's meal. She'd cooked a curry, Mark's favourite. He was making a real effort to beat his addiction and she wanted to acknowledge it. This evening he was going to his first Gamblers' Anonymous meeting. It had taken some persuasion on Claire's part, but in the end, he'd agreed, but only by attending a meeting that wasn't local. He'd been worried that a patient might recognise him, and despite the anonymous nature of the organisation, it was a situation he wanted to avoid. Claire could understand that – she was just happy he was actively seeking help. However, it was getting late now, and she wondered what was keeping him. When she eventually heard him come back, she resisted the temptation to quiz him about how it had been, and instead smiled and said, 'Was the traffic bad?'

'Aye, the A27 was a nightmare. The rain didn't help. I'd forgotten how bloody awful the weather was in England. All those years of living in Spain I suppose. Something smells good' – he lifted the lid of a saucepan on the stove – 'ah, your famous chicken curry. And all the trimmings,' he said spying the table set with side dishes of chutneys and poppadums, naan ready to be heated. 'Are we celebrating or something?'

'I just thought it would be nice to do something special. And, in a way it is a bit of a celebration, you know. The first step towards recovery.'

'Don't talk to me about steps. I've heard enough of the twelve steps to recovery to last me, thanks.' He grabbed a bottle opener and poured himself a large glass, not offering one to Claire. 'Listen love, I don't think these meetings are going to be for me. There's a bit too much referral to a "higher power". I had enough of that growing up. It's fine for some, but you know I don't believe in anything like that. Here, take a look for yourself.' He thrust a booklet at her.

She glanced at the first step. 'Well, this is relevant, admitting you are powerless, and your life has become unmanageable.'

'Has it though? I wouldn't say it has. Not like some of them. You should hear what one bloke owed, makes my debt look like a drop in the ocean. Nah, I'm not like them.'

'Couldn't you give it a go though? Perhaps you need to go to a few to get into the mindset.'

'I don't think so. Besides, it's a huge chunk of my day to travel all that way and back. I've got better things to do with my time.'

'Such as?' Claire asked.

'Like doing some more overtime to clear my debt.

I don't want that hanging over me. Over us.' He took Claire's hands. 'I can do this. I did it before, on my own, without support. You'll see.'

Claire wanted to believe him, and this time he'd have her help; it was doable, wasn't it? 'If you're sure, Mark. And as long as you are serious about quitting, you'll always have my support.'

Mark wrapped his arms around her, and they kissed. It felt so good. It had been a while since he had shown her this level of affection. She really felt they'd turned a corner. 'Let's eat then, shall we? Then after, if you like, we could work out a plan for repaying the money you owe. What do you think?'

'I think that's a great idea.' He kissed her again.

The meal finished, Claire retrieved her laptop, and was busy showing Mark a spreadsheet she'd drawn up detailing possible repayment proposals to clear what he owed.

'This is all very slick,' Mark said.

'Numbers are my job,' she reminded him. Taking a deep breath, she continued, 'I'm going to pay off the balance of your credit cards, the main one with the bigger amount, and the newer card you've just got. I'll do that and you can make monthly repayments to my account.'

'Oh, I don't know about that. It's one thing for me to be in debt to a credit card company. I don't know how I feel about you doing this, it's such a lot of money.'

'Yes, it is, but I have this in savings, and it's not as if it's a gift. I do expect you to pay me back. It doesn't make financial sense to have such a large amount on a credit card. Look at the interest rates, especially the second one, just paying the minimum amount per month is costly. Much better to consolidate all the debts and pay me back without interest. You can set up a standing order over a period of time. I've outlined different amounts and timescales. You tell me which one is the most practical for you.'

'Claire, I don't know what to say. This is so generous of you.'

'There is a caveat. You might not like what I'm about to propose, but I am only doing so to try and make this easier for you.'

'You're making me nervous now,' Mark said.

'You have your salary paid directly to my account, and I give you a monthly allowance to cover your general outgoings.'

'So, you'd have complete control over my money?' He shook his head. 'I don't think so, Claire. I'm a grown man, not some kind of kid who gets pocket money from his mum. I'd feel…emasculated.'

Claire had been concerned this might be the way he'd react, and she'd gone back and forth with the idea before suggesting it. Had she gone too far? It didn't exactly say she trusted Mark, did it? 'You hate the idea then?'

'Just a bit. Look, you taking this on, it's going above and beyond. I accept that. But I have to be my own man.

If you're willing to do this, then you have to trust me to pay you back. And I will, you'll see. I've already signed up to do extra shifts at work. I'll have this cleared in no time.'

Claire waivered, not wanting to create more friction. Was it asking too much of Mark to surrender his financial independence? 'All right then, if that's the way you feel. But I'd still like to help. I can't bear the idea of your hard-earned income being used to pay interest, not when I've got the money sitting in the bank. Give me your credit card details and I'll make a transfer. Just one thing though. I'd like you to cut up the cards.'

'Fine, I'll do that now, and thank you. You're an amazing woman. I'm so lucky to have found you. Now, let's have a look at these spreadsheets of yours.'

Chapter Eight

The next few weeks passed in a blur for Claire. She was busy with a prestigious client who demanded a lot of her time and attention. This meant she had to spend most of her days at the office rather than working from home. Her usual part-time status had been revoked, as the client had requested she head up the project. Mark, too, was constantly working all hours of the day and night. Often, they'd only see each other at breakfast time, grabbing a hot drink and joking they were like passing ships in the night. Despite this, they remained good-humoured. Claire was pleased Mark was keeping his promise to clear his debt, and she had already received his first repayment, plus a little extra from the income he'd made from overtime. He, too, seemed more relaxed and as far as Claire was concerned, things were on the up. With all that had been going on, her swimming had been neglected, so after a particularly busy day she decided it was time to remedy this and headed to the Aquarium to put in some lengths.

She was luxuriating in a hot shower after her swim when she heard, 'Hi there.' It was Alison. 'I thought that was you getting out of the pool. I didn't notice you in the water.'

Claire beamed, pleased at this nice surprise. 'I didn't see you either, but then you know how I get when I'm in the water. I drift off, no pun intended.'

'What have you been up to that you missed swim club? I was going to call you and make sure you were all right.'

'I'm fine. Work's been bonkers and I haven't had time for much else. It shouldn't go on for too much longer though, and then I can go back to my regular hours. I've barely seen Mark.'

'But everything's fine between you?'

'Yes, fine, just work, nothing else.' Claire hadn't broached the subject of Mark's situation since they'd first spoken about it. She hadn't deliberately kept Alison in the dark, there just hadn't been the time. She'd tell her soon, although she wasn't sure if she'd go for full disclosure. She knew there was the danger that Alison would disapprove, or worry that she'd cleared Mark's debt, especially if she knew how much it was.

'We must get together soon,' Alison said. 'There's an idea I want to run by you.'

'About your job? Have you changed your mind about going for the deputy head post?'

'Oh no, nothing to do with work. This is about having some fun!'

'I like the sound of that. I could do with a laugh.

Look, I'd better go now. Sorry to rush off. Duty calls. Message me at the weekend, come over and we'll have a catch up.'

It was midday on Saturday. Alison had not long arrived at Claire's house. Mark was at work, and they had the place to themselves. Claire was slicing cucumber to go into a giant salad she was preparing. Seated at the table, Alison debated bringing up the topic of conversation she wanted to discuss, but in the end decided to wait until lunch was ready. In the meantime, they chatted idly about a TV series they were both following.

Claire brought the laden salad bowl to the table, adding accompaniments and condiments. 'Would you like some wine with your meal?' she asked.

'No, I'll stick with water, thanks. If I drink alcohol in the day, it makes me nod off, and I've some things to do once I get back.'

'Well, I'm going to have one. I haven't touched a drop all week, and it wouldn't do me any harm if I have a little snooze later,' Claire said, filling a glass and returning the bottle to the fridge. 'What was it you were going to talk to me about? Something fun, you said.'

'I don't know about you, but I've been rushed off my feet lately, then all that business with the school governor, I thought it was long overdue you and I spent some time together. It was you and Mark going away that inspired me, so I looked into short-break swimming holidays in the UK.' She picked up her phone, searched for something and handed it to Claire. 'How about three days away in the Lake District? It's a very reputable company. The lake swims and scenery are amazing. Plus, the accommodation is cosy, and the nearby village looks lovely. We could drive up over the May Day bank holiday.'

'I've been meaning to go up to the lakes and do some swimming for a long time. This looks very nice,' Claire said, as she scrolled through the images and itinerary. 'Yeah, I think it would be great to go. It can be my reward for all the hard work I've been putting in.' She didn't add that it would be good to be free of the need to watch over Mark, which despite her best efforts, she'd found herself doing. 'Let's go for it. I'll run it by Mark. I think he might have a free weekend coming up and I wouldn't want to upset him if he has anything planned for us, then I go away on a girly weekend. I'll speak to him later, then get back to you so you can book it. I take it we'd drive?'

'Yes, it ends up being more practical and we can share the driving.'

The prospect of a weekend swimming filled Claire with delight, and as much as she enjoyed Mark's company, she'd missed spending time with Alison. It would be nice to have something to look forward to. She didn't think Mark would have a problem with her going and besides, it might be good for them to have some time apart.

The women had spent the rest of the afternoon together, sprawled in front of the telly to watch a romcom. When Alison left Claire had dozed; the past few weeks had taken their toll and tired her. She would be glad to get back to her normal routine. She was just rousing herself when Mark returned. His face was set in a grimace, and her heart sank as the atmosphere in the room changed. Trying to turn it around, she plastered on a smile. 'Hi love. Busy day? You look done in.'

Mark said nothing, standing in the doorway. He kept glancing down at his phone.

'Mark? Hello there,' Claire said, waving her hand at him. 'Anybody home? I asked if work was busy.'

'Work?'

'You know, that big building called a hospital where you spend your time.'

'Work. Yes. It was fine. The usual.'

'Alison was here. She came for lunch, remember I told you.' Mark was still hovering by the door, making no attempt to come in and chat with her. She was getting a bit irritated now. 'She's suggested we go away for a weekend swimming in the Lake District. I'd love to go, but I thought I'd ask you first.'

'Right.'

'I thought I'd make sure the dates would be okay with you.'

'Yes, fine with me,' Mark mumbled.

'But you don't even know when they would be.' Claire

was getting annoyed now.

Rather than answer her question he said, 'Think I'll go to the gym, get a session in.' He turned and opened the front door.

'Mark.'

'What?'

'Don't you think you'd better take your gym bag with you before you go?'

Chapter Nine

It transpired that the dates Claire was going away with Alison fell on one of the rare free weekends Mark had. Though she didn't bring up the subject, she somehow felt that he had engineered this, and it made her cross. Sod him, she'd thought. She'd go away and have fun with her friend, then address it when she returned. Meanwhile she occupied her thoughts with planning for the trip, and tried to ignore Mark's numerous absences and his general air of distance when he was physically present. She reasoned he was struggling not being able to gamble, and she didn't want to nag. At least, that's what she told herself.

This evening, however, Mark was about and in a good mood. This was just as well because Alison was joining them for a takeaway, and they were going to go over their plans for travelling to the Lake District. The doorbell rang, Claire assumed it was Alison and was a bit taken aback when she saw her window cleaner instead. 'Oh, hello there, Rob,' she said. 'Bit dark to be cleaning the windows, isn't it?'

He laughed. 'I'm good, but not that good! No, you owe for the past couple of months cleaning. I missed you last time.'

'Oh yes, of course,' Claire said. She went into the kitchen to get the envelope stuffed with cash that she'd put on the windowsill. It wasn't there. She delved into a couple of drawers, the draught from the open front door hastening her search. Where the bloody hell is it? She was certain she'd left it out. After a few more minutes she gave up and went to the door. 'I'm sorry, Rob. I seem to have misplaced the cash I'd set aside for you. Would you take a cheque?' she said, wondering where the book was.

Rob looked grim. 'No. I don't take cheques. I've had too many of them bounce, it's a right pain sorting it out with the bank when they do.' He stood there and didn't show any signs of moving. Claire thought of asking Mark, but she knew he wouldn't have that sort of cash on him. This was embarrassing.

'Tell you what,' Claire said, 'give me a couple of hours, I'll go to a cashpoint, then drop it off at your house. I know where you live. I'd do it now, but I'm expecting a guest for dinner. Would that be all right?'

'It'll have to be, won't it? But I won't be cleaning your windows until you've paid. I let it slide for a month. I've got bills myself, you know.'

'I completely understand. I'm so sorry about all this. It's an oversight, I can assure you.'

Rob grunted something and walked away. Claire shut the door; the confrontation had made her uneasy. She'd barely closed it, when the bell rang again. Fearing it was Rob, she opened it and was relieved to see Alison.

'Who was that man that just left?' she asked. 'He was muttering away to himself. He didn't look very happy.'

'My window cleaner, bit of a mix up about paying him. I'll have to pop out later and sort that out. But don't worry about it, come in and make yourself comfortable. Mark's watching the match in the living room.'

Mark turned down the TV volume and hugged Alison. 'Good to see you, it's been a while.'

'Hasn't it? You two have been a pair of busy bees lately. You've been hard to pin down.'

'Yes, I'm doing a lot of overtime, and Claire's been working her socks off, that's why I'm glad she has the chance to go away. It'll do her the power of good. If I was any better at swimming, I'd be going with you. Claire showed me some of the photos and they looked amazing, mind you I don't much fancy the idea of plunging into all that cold water!'

'That's the beauty of a wetsuit, it does help, and of course we're no novices when it comes to swimming in cold lakes,' Alison said, referring to the training they had done in the past for an organised swim. 'The best bit about getting so cold, is warming up afterwards.'

'Like the relief you feel when you stop hitting yourself over the head with a mallet?' Mark joked.

Alison laughed along. 'Something like that!'

Claire said, 'What do we all want to have as a takeaway? I fancy pizza.'

'Sounds good to me,' Mark said.

'Me too,' Alison said. 'Make sure you order lots of garlic bread as well, I haven't eaten since lunchtime, and I'm starving.'

Menus perused and choices made, Claire waited for Mark to telephone the restaurant and place the order, but he made no move to do so. In the end she got out her phone; clearly, she would be paying for tonight's meal – again. 'It'll be 20 minutes. Anyone want a drink while we wait?'

Alison's phone beeped. She looked at it. 'It's Mum, she wants me to give her a call. Do you mind? I won't be long.' There followed a brief conversation in which it was apparent something unfortunate had happened. Finishing the call Alison said, 'Mum's found out today that she's going to have her cataract operation.'

'That's good news, isn't it?' Claire said, 'She's been waiting a while for it.'

'Yes and no. It clashes with the time we're away and she won't be able to look after Jamie. I suppose I could try and ask some of his friends' parents if it's okay he stays with them. Only trouble is, they'll expect me to return the favour, and I know from experience what a nightmare it can be when Jamie's friends come to stay. It takes me a week to recover!'

'I can do it,' Mark said.

'Really? It wouldn't be too much bother? You'd have to take him to his football match on the Saturday,' Alison said.

'That'd be fine. Be good to see him play, especially if he's as good as you say he is. He can bring over his computer games, that should keep us entertained.'

Claire said, 'Are you sure, Mark? I mean, it's the first free weekend you've had in a while.' She looked him in the eye, and wondered if he knew what he'd be letting himself in for.

'Honestly, you two. I work in an A&E department. I think I can handle a seventeen-year-old for 48 hours! It'll be fun.'

'You have a point there,' Claire said. 'And you'd be helping us both out. Thanks love. I'll make sure I'll leave you some food goodies so you don't have to cook.'

'Thanks so much, Mark,' Alison said.

'That's settled then' – there was a knock at the door – 'pizza's here. Come ladies, let's eat, then you can get planning.'

Chapter Ten

Claire was working from home. She'd been up early to try and get as much done as she could. It was a swim club evening, and she didn't want to have to rush there. Now it was lunchtime and as she'd worked straight through the morning, she decided to have a proper break rather than a rushed sandwich. Going to the fridge to get leftovers to heat she saw Mark had left his food there. Normally he'd take something substantial to keep him going on a long shift. *He'll be pissed off about that,* thought Claire. Nothing new there. He'd left in a foul mood that morning.

Eating her lunch she was disturbed by her next door neighbour's dog. It was barking and growling furiously. She tutted and waited for the noise to subside, but it didn't. Getting up she looked out of the window and was alarmed to see a man in the garden. Unsure as to what to do, and with her heart thumping, she kept out of sight. He came towards the back door. Inching the window open she called, 'What the hell do you think you're doing in my garden?'

He looked to the direction of her voice. 'I'm looking

for Mark.'

Pushing the window open further Claire said, 'He's not here. Why didn't you ring the doorbell?'

'No answer, and the side gate was open,' he replied.

Claire knew this was a lie, he hadn't knocked on the door, she'd have heard him, and she never left the gate unlocked.

'What do you want?'

'I told you. Mark.' He grinned to reveal a missing tooth. Reaching into his pocket he pulled out a packet of cigarettes. His fingers were tattooed, the nails ragged and dirty. He lit a cigarette and slowly blew out smoke. It was obvious he was in no way feeling awkward at the situation. On the contrary, if the smirk on his face was any indication, he was revelling in it.

'I told you. He's not here. Does he have your number? Should I ask him to call you?' Claire was desperate to get rid of him. She wondered where her phone was. Upstairs? Was the back door locked or unlocked? Sweat was starting to bead on her upper lip.

'Tell him Eddie was here. He needs to call me. Oh, and let him know how much I enjoyed meeting his missus.' He moved his hand to his crotch and touched himself, while at the same time running his tongue slowly along his lower lip. Sauntering away, he flicked the lit cigarette onto the lawn.

Claire slammed the window shut and ran to the back door, checking the handle; it was locked. Nausea engulfed her and she only just made it to the sink before bringing up her lunch. Wiping her mouth with a shaky hand, she didn't think she'd ever felt so scared.

<hr>

After that there was no way she could carry on with her work. She'd tried several times to reach Mark, but his phone went to voicemail immediately. She thought of contacting Alison, then dismissed the idea; she'd be in class. What would she say anyway? Alison would tell her to contact the police, but Claire didn't want to involve them, at least not until she had a chance to discuss it with Mark. How stupid would she feel if this Eddie bloke was a friend and she was overreacting? She was scared to stay in the house, but also to leave. She checked every door and window then repeated the process, and kept looking out of the window to see if the man had returned. In order to steady her nerves she had a glass of wine, then another, until finally the bottle was gone. It hadn't helped; instead, she was headachy and woozy.

Deciding to lie down she climbed the stairs, mindful to take her phone with her and a large kitchen knife, though what she thought she'd do with that, she didn't know. The effects of the alcohol meant she passed out once on the bed and hours later she was awoken by a sound downstairs. She grabbed the knife and hid behind the door, frightened to move. Hearing the tread of someone on the stairs, she gripped the knife harder. The light in the bedroom came on and she saw it was Mark. Feeling her presence he swung round, his mouth gaping at the sight of her.

'Claire, what on earth are you doing?'

Dropping the knife, she flung herself at him, he wrapped his arms around her automatically, and she all but screamed into his chest. The fear of the day resurfacing, and the relief that he was here.

Eventually the hysteria diminished enough for her to speak. 'Where have you been? I've been trying to reach you for hours!'

'Work. You know I switch my phone off for that, then the—'

'The gym?' Claire kicked his gym bag, which had been lying on the floor before he arrived. 'I've had enough of your lies. While you've been doing whatever it is that occupies all your time these days, someone came to see you.'

Mark arched his eyebrows. 'What do you mean?'

'A man called Eddie was here looking for you.'

'Did he touch you?' Mark sounded afraid.

Mark's response confirmed that she'd been right to fear the visitor. 'No. But there was a…veiled threat. I was terrified. He just appeared in the garden. What does he want with you? What have you gotten into?'

Mark sank onto the bed, his shoulders slumped. 'Money. He wants money.'

'You owe him money? How much?'

'A couple of thousand.' He looked at her, his eyes bloodshot.

'And this is a gambling debt?'

Mark said nothing, only nodding his head.

'But you told me you would never gamble again.

I believed you, although I've been having my doubts. The way you are behaving these days. I don't know you anymore.'

'I have stopped. It was a lapse. I swear. I'd had a bad day. I needed a lift, that's all. It got a bit out of hand.'

'I don't understand. How did this happen?'

'It would have been all right if I'd had one of my credit cards,' Mark said. 'If you hadn't insisted I get rid of all of them, I could have used them to get a cash advance and never needed to go to someone like him.'

'So this is my fault then?' Now her fear turned to anger. 'Is he a loan shark?'

'Not exactly. He hangs around the King's Arms. Some of the blokes I play poker with introduced me to him.'

Claire frowned. She knew the pub he was speaking of, but only by reputation. There were often reports of fights and skirmishes with the police there. 'Oh Mark. This is what it's come to? These are the people you're associating with? How could you?'

Mark said, 'Could you…I hate to ask but if you give me the money, I can pay him back. Make sure he never bothers you again.'

'How can I trust this will be the last time, Mark?'

'Please, Claire. I'm begging you. I don't mind what happens to me. But I couldn't bear it if, if…' He didn't need to continue, the implication was clear.

'Perhaps we should go to the police. If he's threatened you.'

'NO! You can't go to the police. You don't know

what these people are like. Please. Give me the money and we can move on. I promise. I'll never go near that place again. You must trust me. You have to.'

Chapter Eleven

Alison yawned as she filled the kettle. Her cat weaved around her, purring. She took a moment to enjoy the sensation of the velvety fur on her bare legs. 'Breakfast in a minute, Muffin. I must have my tea first,' she said. She loved Sunday mornings, the one day of the week when there was no schedule, no timetable to adhere to. Weekdays had always been busy, but now that Jamie was into his football, Saturdays were fully occupied with the pre-match panic of gathering all the accoutrements required of a budding professional. No matter how much she tried to instil in Jamie a sense of responsibility, the state of his kit left a lot to be desired, and getting himself out of bed on time, nigh on impossible. There would be shrieks of 'Mum!' ten minutes before he was due to leave, and she'd get dragged into the search for a missing sock or pair of shorts.

Tea drunk and cat fed, Alison slung on a pair of leggings and a sweatshirt so she could get the Sunday papers. No matter the technology, for Alison there was no substitute to wrestling with the arm-width-defying of a broadsheet.

After she trawled through the papers and had breakfast, she thought it was time to wake Jamie up. Until recently he'd been a surprisingly early riser, but nowadays getting him out of bed was like trying to rouse a patient from a coma. She supposed it was down to hormones; Jamie's worsening acne seemed to suggest so. Weren't most teenagers sleepyheads in the mornings anyway? Knocking on his bedroom door she said, 'Jamie, time to get up.' No response. She listened at the door, she didn't want to burst in and find him engaged in something she'd rather not see. Knocking again. 'Can I come in?' A mumble that might have been a 'yes'. Opening the door, she was met with a mixture of the musty smell of stale male, and the Lynx deodorant that Jamie was fond of liberally applying. Walking to the curtains and pulling them open, Alison said, 'I know it's a Sunday but it's nearly midday. You don't want to spend the whole day in bed.'

'I'm tired,' he said, pulling the duvet closer around him. 'Why do I have to get up?'

'For one thing, you need to get your chores done. You said you'd mow the lawn in return for all the ferrying around I've been doing for you. And secondly, you have homework.'

'I'll do it later. There's plenty of time.'

'Get up now and I'll make you a cooked breakfast.'

The bribery did the trick and Jamie emerged from beneath the covers. As he stood before her, Alison couldn't help but be surprised at how broad his chest and shoulders were. 'Goodness me, your weight-training is definitely working. Get much bigger pecs and you'll need a bra,' she said, poking at Jamie's bare chest. He went bright red and too late she realised she'd been insensitive. It was seeing his altered body that had shocked her. 'I'm only jealous, I wish I could make my boobs bigger!' Jamie's face and neck went puce, and Alison could tell her humour wasn't helping matters. Best to retreat. 'I'll get started on breakfast.'

'Extra eggs for me. I need the protein,' Jamie said, recovered enough now to make the request.

Jamie was all about protein now, he couldn't get enough of the stuff. His appetite was ferocious too, Alison couldn't keep him fed. When her eldest son, Callum, had gone to university she'd been pleasantly surprised at the reduction of her food bill. Now it was higher than ever. 'You can have two eggs, no more. I'll cook you an extra sausage,' she said as she left.

Once he'd eaten his fill, Jamie set about mowing the grass. Alison watched him remove Muffin from the centre of the lawn; gathering the cat, he planted a kiss on the top of her head and she responded by rubbing her jaw against his cheek. Alison smiled at the affectionate exchange. She was happy her son was a sensitive type, and he was an old softie where any creatures were concerned. Before football had swamped his ambitions, she had thought he'd become a veterinary nurse, or some other job connected to animals.

She returned to getting lunch ready. These days it seemed as if all she did was go from one meal preparation to another, such were the dietary demands of Jamie's training.

After lunch they settled down in front of the TV. Alison had urged Jamie to do his homework, but he pleaded tiredness. 'You've only been up a few hours. You can't be tired already.'

'My legs and arms ache,' he complained.

'Maybe you're coming down with something.' She held the back of her hand against his forehead. 'You don't feel hot. Do you have a sore throat?'

'No, just tired and achy.'

'It's probably all the training you've been doing. How long were you at the gym on Friday?'

'A couple of hours.'

'Plus the match yesterday. It's no wonder your muscles are complaining. You shouldn't be overdoing it, you know. You're still growing. Your body's already doing a lot of work.'

'Ryan says I have to push myself if I want to get into an academy. Ryan says—'

'Ryan. That's all I ever hear about these days, Jamie. There is more to life than football, and I'm not happy about all the hours you're spending weight-training. We might have to rethink this.'

'But you promised! You said you'd support me.'

'I said I would, up to a point. Your schoolwork must be your priority.' Jamie uttered something unintelligible and stood up. 'Where are you off to now?' Alison asked him.

'To go and do my homework. Happy now?'

Like most households, Monday mornings were always a bit manic, but today was particularly fraught. Alison had managed to put her shirt sleeve into some butter, and it had taken her ages to find a suitable replacement. Ever since the incident with the school governor, she was careful to look as smart as possible at work. In between hastily ironing a top and trying to wake Jamie, she'd discovered the cat had thrown up on the landing. 'Jamie! Out. Of. Bed. Now!' The steam from the iron hissing in her hand making her feel hot and sweaty.

Jamie's bedroom door opened and he stumbled out, putting his foot straight into a pile of cat vomit.

'What the...?' Muffin was at the top of the stairs. Oblivious to the commotion, she went over to Jamie and began to rub her head against his leg. 'Get away from me you disgusting thing!' He pushed the cat aside and she tumbled halfway down the stairs before righting herself.

'Jamie! What on earth do you think you're doing?' Alison was shocked by what she had just witnessed and went running after the cat. She was relieved to find Muffin none the worse for wear. As Jamie joined her, she expected him to be full of remorse, only to hear him say, 'It's only a cat, for God's sake.' He pushed past her leaving her open-mouthed.

Chapter Twelve

Claire was at Alison's house, after having been summoned there to plan for their trip to the Lake District. Alison excitedly unveiled a multitude of papers and maps for Claire to look at.

'Here are the trip notes,' she said.

Claire picked them up. 'There's certainly enough of them. You have been busy.' She scanned through the pages. 'It's very comprehensive. There's quite a lot of hiking involved, more than actual swimming. I'll have to dig out my walking boots.'

'Yeah, I think it might be a good idea to go for a couple of walks on the Downs beforehand, just to get in practice,' Alison said. 'I could do with the fresh air and exercise, blow the cobwebs away. A few hours out of the house would be good too. Jamie's a right grump at the moment.'

'That's not like him. He's usually very cheerful.'

'Not anymore. He's like a bear with a sore head these days, plus I've grounded him for a week. He got into a fight at school, can you believe it? I've never had any trouble with him for bad behaviour, now all of a sudden, he's turned into a ball of rage.'

'I can't imagine him fighting,' Claire said, 'he's such a gentle soul.'

'I dunno, maybe the football is bringing out a competitive streak that's not very positive. I wouldn't let him go training this week, so now I'm public enemy number one.'

'That's too bad. The last thing you need at home is a bad atmosphere,' Claire said, thinking of how things were for her with Mark. After the incident with Eddie, it had been strained between them. Against her better judgement, she'd given Mark the money to pay off his debt. She was scared of the repercussions if she hadn't. Mark's gratitude had lasted a few days before he returned to his now-constant dour mood. She was at her wits' end as to how to rectify things between them. She hadn't said anything about Mark's lapse; as far as Alison was concerned, he was attending regular Gamblers' Anonymous meetings and was doing well. She wasn't sure why she was being secretive. Shame? Embarrassment? Any time Alison brought up the subject Claire would steer the conversation back to work, or Jamie, though she was genuinely interested in what was going on with his life. She'd always been fond of him.

'Talking of Jamie. We've decided it would be better if Mark stays at your house for the weekend you and I are away, rather than the other way around. All his gaming stuff would be a lot to lug over to ours, plus his football paraphernalia.'

'Yes, he does seem to need a lot of stuff to get him

through the day,' Alison agreed. 'It would be easier. Trying to get Jamie to organise himself can be difficult. Are you sure Mark doesn't mind?'

'Not at all, he can throw a few things in a bag, and he'll be good to go,' Claire said. She thought back to the conversation she'd had with Mark, where she'd voiced her concerns that Eddie might return. There was no way she wanted Jamie exposed to any sort of harm. Mark had told her she was being overly cautious, but had agreed nonetheless. It was a concession Claire had thought was the least he could make.

'So, how are things at work? Have they found a replacement for the deputy head yet?'

'No, but they've been interviewing candidates all week. There was this one man, seemed very young, and really posh. I said "hello" to him and he looked down his nose at me. Turned on the charm when Mary called him into her office though. I hope they don't hire him, that's the last type of person I want to deal with.'

'I'm surprised someone like that would want the job. Isn't it unusual for a man to apply? I thought schools could only attract women.'

'Normally, yes. I must admit, I was taken aback to see him. I hope that doesn't sway the decision. At least I'm not in competition with him for the job.'

'I still think you would have been a good deputy head,' Claire said.

'That's what a couple of the other teachers have said. I did wonder if I'd done the right thing by not going for it. Maybe in a couple of years' time. It might be better to work somewhere you haven't been known as a teacher. Anyway, enough of that, let's think about our weekend. Have you seen the list of clothes that are recommended? As I've been doing more cold-water swimming, I've accumulated pretty much everything on the list.'

'Hmm. I think aqua shoes would be a good idea. Getting in at a lake is bound to be stony and wearing them will help keep my feet from getting too cold.'

'Yes, get a pair. You might want to consider a changing robe too. Once out of the water, you'll need to warm up as quickly as possible.'

'There are different things to consider, aren't there? It's not like swimming in the Med. Perhaps, as well as the walking, you and I should also do some of this type of swimming before we go away. I think I'll need to practise getting undressed by the side of a lake when I'm cold, for one thing.'

'Yeah, let's work it into a walk. I'll check out places we can go locally.'

The time spent with Alison had lifted Claire's spirits, and when she let herself into the house the television was on. Mark was home. A football match was finishing; he muted the volume.

'Hello there. How'd it go at Alison's?'

'Good. It was fun planning the trip. It'll be interesting to do this type of swimming. This company really do seem to know what they're doing. You should see all the information they provide.'

'Bit different to Sophie and Oliver's organisational skills then?' Mark said, referring to a previous holiday to Spain, which had had disastrous consequences.

'Just a tad. I wish we'd have used this company instead of them, and not have gone through everything we did.'

'But then, we wouldn't have met, would we? Or are you regretting that now?' Mark asked as he drew Claire to him on the sofa and put his arm around her.

The question was perplexing. *Was* she glad Mark was in her life? It had all been so wonderful when he'd first moved in with her. He'd seemed like the perfect man. Now with the gambling and the mood swings, today being case in point, she never knew where she stood and how Mark would behave on a day-to-day basis.

Seeing her hesitate, Mark moved his arm away. Not wanting another argument, Claire quelled her anxiety and said, 'Of course I'm glad I met you. I love you.'

'I know it's been difficult lately. I've been hell to live with and you've been so good, standing by me. It's made the world of difference. I know I can beat this addiction. I *am* beating it. And it's because of you.'

Claire snuggled into the crook of his arm. These were the words she wanted to hear. Suddenly, she knew everything was going to be all right.

Chapter Thirteen

It was a long drive from Worthing, on the south coast, to the Lake District. When Alison had first suggested the break, Claire had thought the journey too arduous to make for a three-day trip. But Alison's enthusiasm had been infectious. Her excitement at being able to drive Claire's Audi TT, such a contrast to her ancient and battered Fiesta, had meant she'd done most of the driving. In fact, Claire had had to insist they switch and Alison take a rest. The stops they'd made to break up the journey, and the singing along to old tunes on the radio, had all helped add to a holiday feel. Claire was glad she had agreed to the getaway, and with Mark seemingly back to his old self, it was looking as if things were on the up. She stretched in her seat and said, 'Be looking out for signs for the guest house. It should be somewhere along this road.'

'There!' Alison pointed to a sign. 'The next on the left.'

'We've made good time. It was worth the early start.' The guest house appeared. 'Great setting, isn't it?' The women had spent the latter part of the journey oohing and ahhing at the scenery. The dramatic mountains, swathed in varying shades of greens and dotted with the dark of elm and spruce trees, provided an impressive backdrop. From a distance it gave the illusion of a moss-like covering that was downy and soft to the touch.

Claire stood for a few moments, taking it all in. 'Oh my God. How amazing is this? No wonder Wordsworth said it was the "most loveliest spot". Can you imagine what it looks like in spring covered in daffodils? Makes *me* want to write poetry!'

'It really is stunning, isn't it?' Alison agreed.

Dragging her eyes away from the view, Claire said, 'Let's get checked in, then we can do a little exploring before we meet everyone.'

༺༻

A group of eight swimmers and two guides were seated in the lounge of the guest house. Formal introductions were made, and people had given their reasons for coming away. There was a shy-looking woman in her fifties called Tracey. She'd surprised Claire when she let them know she had been in the top ten in her age group for the last competitive open water swim she'd done. A boisterous trio of men in their thirties, all friends, had cited triathlon training and a couple, Jackie and Ian, in their sixties were keen competitors for open water swimming competitions. A serious bunch of swimmers, thought Claire. She looked around and wondered which group she'd be put with. As a proficient swimmer she was used to being the fastest person in the pool, but with these levels she was pretty sure she'd met her match. The two guides, Pete, in his fifties, and Jason, who looked to be in his twenties, were friendly and smiley. There had been a ripple of awkwardness when everyone had congregated, but they'd managed to put everyone at ease.

After a brief outline of the itinerary Pete said, 'It's great to meet you all. I'm sure you're going to have a great time and we want you to have fun, but safety is our priority. So I'd like you to pay attention to the next part of the talk.' He looked pointedly at one of the younger men, who was scrolling on his phone. Under Pete's scrutiny he hastily put it away.

Claire whispered to Alison, 'Wow, these people really know their stuff. We are in safe hands.'

'And no chance of jellyfish!'

Claire was glad Alison could make light of the topic of jellyfish, given the troubling history she'd had with them. And, it was true, the lack of creatures that could do you harm in the water was a definite plus. Of course, there was the cold to confront. She didn't relish those first minutes in the water while her body got used to the low temperature. When she and Alison had done a competitive swim in Suffolk a few years previously, she remembered suffering cold toes and fingers. This time, she'd come prepared, and those areas were covered – literally.

'Jellyfish aside,' Alison continued, 'I've really taken to cold water swimming. It's supposed to be very good for your health and I have to say, I can't remember the last time I got sick. That, coming from a woman who works with small children, is no mean feat!'

Pete looked at them and Claire nudged Alison with her elbow. 'Right, I think I've been through everything for now,' he said. 'All that remains is for us to get into the water for the acclimatisation swim and put you into groups.'

'How many groups will there be?' Claire asked.

'Normally three, but there aren't that many of you so it could be two, let's see what the levels are like,' Jason said, the first time he had spoken in a while.

※

The walk to the lake took them through a forest; the fresh smell of the trees carried to them on the breeze was calming. The quietness was only broken by birdsong and the crunch of twigs and earth underfoot. People did speak, but in reverent tones so the tranquillity of the place was not broken. The forest petered out and in front of them was the lake; its mirror-like surface reflected the verdant greenery of the trees surrounding it. Claire gasped as she gazed at it and felt an almost spiritual reaction. It didn't matter how cold it was going to be, she couldn't wait to submerge herself in this.

Claire was glad of her aqua shoes as she made her first steps into the lake because the bed was covered with small stones and pebbles. The cold nipped at her ankles, but the thrill of entering the water eclipsed any discomfort she felt. By her side Alison giggled with joy. A seasoned lake-swimmer, she felt no trepidation as she immersed her body and swam away. She made a V-shaped ripple as she moved with ease from the shore. Claire slipped into the water and followed her. It was different to being in the sea; she had to be more aware of her body position and make sure her hips were high. The water was clear, much clearer than she had imagined it would be, and it felt soft. No salt abrasion to worry about here. The group of swimmers spread out with Pete taking the lead. Jason brought up the rear in a kayak. Claire found herself toward the front of the pack; unsurprisingly the triathletes headed it, but she wasn't concerned about racing, she was savouring the moment. It had been a while since she had felt this free.

***

Claire made it back to shore and by the time Alison joined her, she had donned her swim robe and managed, in an ungainly fashion, to disrobe beneath it.

'What do you think?' Alison said. 'Could you be converted to this type of swimming?'

'With surroundings like this I could be. I think, with practice, I could get used to the temperature, about the only drawback is not being able to swim as long because of it. You know how I like to put in the kilometres.'

'How do you feel about swimming in a wetsuit?' Alison said, pulling on a woolly hat.

'I find it a bit restricting, and would prefer to wear

just a costume, but that wouldn't be sensible here.'

'Hot drink?' Jason had a couple of thermos flasks with him. 'Chocolate or coffee?'

'Chocolate!' the women called out in unison and laughed at themselves.

Pouring the drinks Jason said, 'Once you've finished, we'll head back to the guest house and discuss what groups you'll be in. Then dinner at seven.'

'Great,' Claire said. 'I'm famished.'

Alison rolled her eyes. 'Some things never change.'

Chapter Fourteen

'I think I might have overdone it a bit at breakfast,' Claire groaned, as she bent to lace up her walking boots.

'I told you not to eat that chocolate croissant on top of the English breakfast,' Alison said. 'I don't have any sympathy for you. You should have stuck to porridge.'

'Not everyone has the same levels of willpower as you. How was I supposed to resist those pastries tempting me? I feel as if I'll sink when I get into the lake, though we've got quite a hike up to the tarn, so I suppose I'll be all right.'

'Yes, I expect so. With yesterday's exertions we probably all need the extra calories anyway,' Alison said. The previous day's itinerary had been full on. They'd completed a morning and afternoon swim, plus the hiking between the two. 'I've enjoyed all the walking, haven't you? The scenery has been breath-taking and yesterday's swim in Rydal Water was fantastic. I couldn't believe how warm it felt.'

'Yeah, it was amazing how the shallower depth makes such a difference. And our bodies are getting used to the lower water temperatures as well, we'd probably find swimming in the Med too hot now. I've liked the walking too, and there aren't that many places as beautiful as this.' She stopped to look around her, trying to take it all in and capture the sensations she was experiencing. If only she could put how she was feeling into a box, which she could open up whenever she was feeling down. 'I'm glad we did a bit of hiking before we came away, raised our fitness levels, otherwise I wouldn't have been able to have enjoyed it as much.'

'Morning ladies.' It was Jackie. Despite being one of the oldest people there, she was always bursting with energy and yesterday seemed to have invigorated her. 'How are you feeling today? Any aches or pains?'

'No, we're fine,' Alison said. 'You seem perky.'

'Who wouldn't be? I live in the Peak District, and I didn't think it could be beaten for scenery, but here you've got the greenery, the mountains *and* the lakes. It's almost unfair,' she guffawed. 'I do love being out in God's creation like this.' She screwed up her face. 'You can keep your hot beaches and foreign countries. Now where's that husband of mine?' She turned back. 'Oh, he's talking to Tracey. Timid thing, that one. He's good with quiet people, helps bring them out of their shell. Think I'll go ahead and say "hello" to the boys.' She was referring to Matthew, Andrew and Dan, the triathlon friends. Jackie had taken rather a shine to them and liked chatting them up. They played along and flirted with her. It was fun to watch. Jackie's husband, obviously accustomed to his wife's gregarious nature, would smile and shake his head at her antics.

Pete came alongside Claire and Alison just as Jackie departed. 'She's quite a character, isn't she?'

'She sure is,' Claire said.

'Not shy either,' Pete said. 'Yesterday, she didn't bother with a changing robe and I got an eyeful as she bent down to pick up her towel.'

Both women laughed. 'Sounds like something she'd do,' Alison said. 'She's fun though, I like her.'

'Oh, me too. Don't know what my wife would think though, if she knew the clients were stripping off in front of me,' Pete said.

'Best not to tell her. What happens in the Lake District, stays in the Lake District,' Claire said, laughing.

※

When they made it to the tarn, the Norse word for pond or pool, the sun came out. They had been walking uphill for some time and parts of the trail had been tricky. At one point, Dan had slipped from a steppingstone to the bog underneath and got himself a muddy foot, much to the amusement of his friends. In contrast, Jackie had skipped across like a nimble-footed goat. Claire had had to concentrate not to meet the same fate as Dan. She wondered what it would be like in winter if it were this wet in June. The tarn itself was extraordinary. It looked like a caldera that had been filled with water, its sides sheer and lush. The surface shone darkly, though the water was crystalline. A buzz of excitement ran through the group at the prospect of swimming here, their own private pool provided by mother nature. After a few moments of hushed awe, there was a sudden scramble to disrobe and swim. Soon everyone was in the water.

Once in the tarn, there was no hurry to complete the planned kilometre, so they took their time and relished this, their last swim. Rather than freestyle, some used breaststroke so they could gaze up at the steep hillsides, or comment to a nearby swimmer. Even when they were finishing and getting out, they still had the place to themselves. They sat at the water's edge, bundled up in changing robes and woolly hats, blowing on hot drinks. The atmosphere was animated as they chatted and joked.

Claire said to Alison, 'You know, it never ceases to amaze me how swimming is such a cure-all for me. No matter how bad things are, it manages to lift my spirits.' She stared into the middle distance, her thoughts elsewhere.

'What's up, Claire?' Alison knew her friend was keeping something from her.

'I haven't been completely honest with you,' Claire said. 'There's something I should tell you, something about Mark. I wasn't going to mention it, but I don't like keeping things from you. A while back Mark had a…a lapse with his gambling.'

'Go on,' Alison prompted.

Claire proceeded to tell her about the latest debt she'd cleared for Mark, and why she'd done it. She'd been so scared that Eddie would darken their doorstep again and she was afraid for their safety.

'Is that why you didn't want Jamie staying at your

house this weekend?'

'Yes. I didn't want there to be any possibility at all of Jamie being put in harm's way. Mark thought I was worrying unnecessarily, but if you'd had seen this Eddie bloke,' – she shuddered – 'you would have reacted the same way. It's not what he said, it was the way he looked at me, and the implied threat. It scared the living daylights out of me. It's been good to get away, not feeling as though I have to keep looking over my shoulder every minute of the day. That or obsessing where Mark is all the time and trying to appear as if I'm not, so as to avoid another argument. It's exhausting and…'

'And what?' Alison prompted.

'It makes me fearful of the future, the unknown. What will be lurking? I believe I can be happy with Mark, but I can't be sure. What if it's all a terrible mistake?'

'Life is full of risk, Claire. There are no certainties, that's something I've learned to come to terms with as I've got older. When you're young, it all seems so simple, so straightforward. Look, at the moment you're having your doubts, but you'll know when it's right, it'll show itself to you.'

The group packed up their stuff and walked back to the guest house. As the weather was warm, they had an impromptu picnic in the pretty garden. There was much taking of photographs and swapping of details, with promises to keep in contact. It was with some regret that Claire placed her small suitcase in the boot of the car. The weekend had flown by, and it had been nice to be away. Until now, she hadn't realised just how tense she'd been. The past few months had been difficult, and there had been more than one occasion she'd wished for her days as a single woman.

Alison made a move to the driver's seat, but Claire stopped her. 'Hang on a minute, lady. I think I'd better do most of the driving. You have to get to work first thing tomorrow, I'm working from home so I can start a bit later in the day. Why don't you relax.'

'Are you sure?'

'Absolutely. If I get tired, I'll let you know and you can take over for a bit.'

The ride back was a quiet one, the women only speaking every so often. Once out of the Lake District, Alison nodded off, leaving Claire to her thoughts. It began raining, so she was forced to concentrate more on the driving and she was glad of the distraction. The journey back seemed to go quicker than the one there and Claire had to rouse Alison as she pulled into her driveway.

'Gosh, here already?' Alison said. 'I wasn't much of a driving companion, was I? I thought after the coffee at the last services I'd be wide awake, but I couldn't keep my eyes open. You must be tired.'

'I'm fine. Driving always soothes me,' Claire said.

Alison unbuckled her seat belt and said, 'It was a

great weekend. Back to reality now.'

'Yes. Back to reality.' Claire blinked as she watched the rain beat against the windscreen.

Chapter Fifteen

Claire hung back as Alison all but ran to her house, keen to see Jamie. Plodding up the pathway to the open door, Claire stepped over the threshold to find Mark in the hallway.

'Welcome back.' Mark pulled her into a bear hug. 'Did you have a good time?'

Feeling better enveloped in his embrace, Claire said, 'It was brilliant. A great break. Just over too soon. I feel knackered though, it was an energetic weekend and a long drive.'

'We'll get you home and you can have a nice bath. I'll rustle us up something for supper.'

'That would be nice.' The thought of a long, hot soak was appealing. 'I'll just say goodbye to Alison, and we can be off.' She went into the living room. 'We're going to' — she stopped as she took in Jamie's appearance – 'God Jamie, look at you. You're twice the size you were since last time I saw you.' She tried to mentally calculate when that was. She turned to Alison and said, 'What have you been feeding him on?'

Alison looked at Jamie. 'I suppose he has got quite

big, I see him every day so it doesn't seem as dramatic to me. I told you he's stepped up his training.'

'I want to go to a football academy,' Jamie chimed in, 'my coach says I stand a good chance, so I've been working hard on my fitness.'

Mark said, 'He's good. I watched him play on Saturday. I reckon he's got the makings of a professional.'

'You two had a nice time then?' Alison asked.

'Yeah, Mark's all right,' Jamie said, and then went all red.

Mark smiled and said, 'Right then, I think this one needs to get home.' He put his arm around Claire. 'She looks a bit done in.'

They said their goodbyes and left. In the car Claire asked Mark, 'Did you really have a good time with Jamie?'

'Aye. He's a good kid. Totally bonkers on his football though, it's all he ever talks about. His coach, Ryan, is enthusiastic about his prospects too. We had a talk after the match, he thinks he can make the big time, that's why he's pushing him so much.'

Slipping her shoulders under the warm, soapy water, Claire gave a sigh of contentment. There was a knock at the bathroom door. 'Are ye decent?'

She giggled and said, 'No, but don't let that stop you.'

Mark pushed open the door, he was holding a glass of red wine. 'Thought you might like some, it's your favourite.'

'Ooo, lovely,' Claire said wriggling up and reaching for the glass. Mark perched on the side of the bath and handed it to her. She took a sip. 'What a nice treat, and dinner being prepared too.'

'I wanted to do something nice for you. I know you've only been gone a few days, but I really missed you. And I haven't been the nicest person to live with lately. Having some time off work has enabled me to reflect on things and I've decided I will start going to the Gamblers' Anonymous meetings.'

'But I thought you said they weren't for you, too much emphasis on a "higher power".'

'I know, I had another look at the materials they gave me. I read them properly and I think I was being too hasty in rejecting their ideas. I'll give it a proper go this time, really stick at it. What do you think?'

'I think that's great. I'm pleased you've come to that decision.' Claire was relieved that Mark had finally acknowledged that beating this addiction wasn't something the two of them could do alone.

'Morning, darling,' Mark said, handing Claire a cup of tea.

Accepting the mug, she yawned. 'What time is it?'

'Gone eight. You were dead to the world, so I let you sleep. Some of us, though, have to go out to work. I'd best be off.' He leant down and dropped a kiss onto her forehead. 'Not sure what time I'll be finishing. I'll message you later.' He went to leave, then turned back to her. 'And last night. Was amazing.' He gave her a naughty smile and left.

Claire stretched out her legs and gave her toes a wiggle of satisfaction. Their love-making the previous night had been gratifying in many ways, not least because it had been a long time since they had been intimate. This and Mark's vow to face up to his problems meant she could begin to relax and look forward to the future once again. Hopping out of bed she was ready for her day. Once she'd put in a morning's work, she would check the times of the GA meetings. Suddenly there was purpose to their life together again.

❦

The morning passed quickly as Claire was busy pulling together loose ends of a project she'd been working on. Her company were pitching to a new client and she was heading up the team responsible. If she could pull this off, she'd be looking at a bonus, and a big pat on the back from the partners. Rather than being a distraction from work, her personal problems had actually helped. She'd found her job the perfect diversion and was able to immerse herself in it. That, and swimming, had been her salvation, these past few months.

While having a coffee she casually browsed the internet with the intention of finding out the times of the GA meetings. Now that Mark had committed to going to them, she wanted to make sure he followed up on his promise. She came across a page for Gam-Anon and thinking this was what she was looking for, clicked on the site. As she read, she soon realised that this wasn't for gamblers, but for partners, family or friends of those with an addiction. Paying more attention now she continued until she reached a survey entitled 'Are you living with a compulsive gambler?'. She hesitated. Did she really want to do this?

There were eighteen questions requiring a simple yes or no answer. She had checked eleven and looking at the results, it confirmed that she was living with a compulsive gambler. Biting at her thumbnail as she perused the questions again, she wondered what she was going to do. Was this relevant now that Mark seemed to have changed his behaviour? Certainly, things seemed to be more like they had been before the addiction had reared its ugly head. She needed to talk this over with someone, not Alison. It had been difficult enough admitting to Mark's lapse; besides, what if she was wrong? What if Mark's actions really were all in the past? How was Alison supposed to trust Mark if Claire was constantly voicing her doubts about him? Were these doubts valid?

Something occurred to her, the payments Mark was supposed to be making in order to repay his initial bail-out. After the first few had gone into her account, she hadn't paid much attention to checking them. The irony of an accountant being so complacent was not lost on her. If she were this sloppy with her clients' money she wouldn't be in a job for very long. She logged into her bank account; the monthly payments had been credited regularly, but the past two had not been made. Her stomach twisted. She found herself not wanting to believe that Mark could have lied to her; surely he couldn't be that devious? She needed to talk to someone, to hear from people who were going through the same thing. Scanning locations and times, she found a group in Brighton. There was a meeting this afternoon.

Chapter Sixteen

Claire's knuckles were white on the steering wheel as she raced back from the Gam-Anon meeting she had just attended. She hadn't known what to expect as she sat amongst a mixed group of people. They were welcoming and friendly, but she was still nervous, *she* shouldn't be here. She felt a growing resentment towards Mark because he had put her in such a position. What had she done to deserve this? At first, as she'd listened to people tell their stories, she was able to convince herself that she didn't belong here, that she was overreacting. But there was a woman whose story had started the same way as Claire's, the circumstances too similar to ignore.

Claire pressed her foot to the accelerator, her teeth clenched, the loud rock music she had chosen for the journey engulfing the space. Ahead, a red light loomed, and she jabbed at the brakes. The wheels of the car screeched to a halt, frightening an elderly pedestrian, who shook his fist at her and mouthed something she could not hear. The near miss had sent a jolt of adrenaline through her so with a pounding heart she pulled into the car park by Shoreham Old Fort and got out, her legs still shaking.

Taking a deep breath to calm down, she walked to the shore; the pebble beach underfoot meant she had to tread carefully. She stood, inhaling the salty air. The tide was out so beyond the stones was a large expanse of damp sand, on which a man held a kite. He bent to a small girl at his side and handed it to her, guiding her hands and speaking to her as the kite lifted into the air. Her eyes shone with delight and she gazed with wonder as it moved with the sea breeze. Claire felt a stab of envy at the simple pleasure and the joy it could bring. She looked at the father; the pride on his face was evident. Claire thought back to her own dad and the special times they had shared. Her heart still ached at his loss and she wished he were there to advise and console. She stood there a long time, the light faded and the air chilled. She was roused with a noise from her phone – a voicemail. She could see it was from Mark and as she listened to his breezy message, his tone upbeat and chirpy, a rage began to well up within her. Working late. Really? He sounded pretty happy for someone who had been asked to work hours after his scheduled finish time. The fact was, she didn't believe he was telling the truth, and she was going to expose his lie.

***

Claire was trying to find a space as she inched her way around the hospital car park. It had started to rain and people dashed from their cars holding umbrellas or coats over their heads. The place was crowded and finding a spot was proving elusive. On her second circuit she spied one; it was small, too small, and as she backed into it, she heard the screech of metal on metal. 'Shit!' She got out to inspect the damage; not too bad, the sound had been misleading. She contemplated making a swift exit but saw that the car she'd scratched was occupied. The next quarter of an hour was spent exchanging details and taking photos. The incident had served to heighten Claire's agitated mood as she marched to the hospital entrance.

She waited to be seen at reception. A&E was filled with people who'd been caught in the rain and the air was damp. Water dripped from umbrellas and the floor was smeared with dirty footprints. A baby cried and its tired-looking mother tried to hush it. The general atmosphere was a mix of dissatisfaction and boredom. *How can Mark bear to work here?* Claire thought, it was so oppressive. She'd only been here minutes and already she wanted to escape.

The wilted receptionist called her forward. 'Can I help you?'

'Yes, I'm looking for Mark Fraser. He's a senior doctor here.'

'Doctor Fraser, yes, I know him. Bear with me,' the receptionist said as she tapped onto her keyboard. 'You've missed him, I'm afraid. His shift finished two hours ago.'

Here was the confirmation Claire needed, Mark had lied to her. She thanked the receptionist and walked away, her shoes squeaking on the linoleum. Passing a small consulting room, its door ajar, she was stopped in her tracks by the voice she heard, its deep timbre unmistakable – Mark.

He escorted a patient out and she heard him say, 'You should be fine in a day or two. The antibiotics I've prescribed will do the trick.' As the patient thanked him, he saw Claire.

'Claire. What are you doing here?'

'I-I-' The wind taken out of her sails by his presence, Claire was momentarily at a loss for words. Then she remembered the litany of events that had sent her here. She was impatient to confront Mark and see what defence he had. This couldn't wait.

'Is there somewhere we could talk?'

'Now? You can see what it's like here. Didn't you get my message?'

'Yes. I didn't believe it.'

'You what? Why would I lie?'

'Why would you? You've been doing a lot of lying to me. You're quite the expert. I don't know what to believe anymore.'

'Jeez Claire, you're not making any sense. Yes. I had lied to you, but that's over. I told you, I've turned over a new leaf. I was even going to go to a bloody meeting this evening until I got stuck here. What more do you want me to say?'

'Why have you stopped making payments for the money you owe me?'

'I haven't stopped them, I set up a standing order.

You told me you'd been receiving them.'

'I had, but not for the past two months. There's nothing from you.'

Mark raked a hand through his hair. 'Look, I don't know what's gone wrong there…' He glanced past Claire. A nurse, clearly uncomfortable at inadvertently eavesdropping, was waiting to speak to Mark.

'Doctor, I'm sorry to interrupt, but we could use your assistance in cubicle 4,' she said.

'Yes of course. I'll be there in a second.' He put his mouth next to Claire's ear. 'Go home. We'll talk there, when I'm done.' He didn't wait for her reply and strode away.

Chapter Seventeen

When Mark got home, he was soaked through. He peeled off his sodden clothes and stood by the front door in his boxers and T-shirt, his feet bare.

'I think you're going to have to reassess cycling to work. Maybe it's time you got a car. You look like a drowned rat,' Claire said.

'That fits the bill then, doesn't it. Don't you see me as some kind of rat? How many times will I have to keep on proving myself to you before you trust me again?'

'I want to. It's just, I don't know, things keep happening that make me distrust you.'

'You're talking about the money? I told you; I don't know what happened there. I'm going to put on some dry clothes then we'll look at my account together, try and get to the bottom of this.'

Changed and with a hot drink and sandwich by his side, Mark opened his laptop and logged into his online bank account. Next to him Claire waited, anxious as to what would happen. Mark's attitude gave the impression of an innocent man. Surely he couldn't be this good a liar. She chewed the inside of her cheek and inched closer to Mark so she could see the screen better.

'There,' he said, pointing to an amount. 'That's my payment to you.'

'But that's months ago, have a look at this month,' Claire said.

'I don't understand.' Mark scrolled the cursor up and down several times. 'Where the bloody hell is it? I thought my balance was a bit higher than of late, but…' – he winced – 'I put it down to not throwing money away on gambling. I swear, Claire, there's nothing fishy going on. I don't know what's happened.'

'Go back to the standing orders you've set up. Let's see if we can figure out what's wrong.'

Mark did as she asked, and Claire peered closer at the screen. 'I see what you've done. You set the wrong date for the standing order to finish. You've put this March, instead of next year's.'

'What? No.' He looked; Claire was right. 'What an idiot. How could I have made a mistake like that?'

'It's easily done.' Claire was glad for the simple explanation. 'I'm sorry I jumped to conclusions; I think I was upset by a survey I'd just completed. It was on the Gam-Anon site. It seemed to confirm my worst fears and fuelled all my insecurities. That's when I knew I had to go to a support group to try and find answers. I was on my way back from one this evening. What people had said there, their stories, kept going around and around in my head. I had to speak to you.'

'You went to a meeting? Did it help?'

'Not really.' She told him about the story that had

freaked her out. How frightened she was that their situation was spiralling out of control and that she'd be recounting her tale in future meetings.

'I did a similar survey,' Mark said. 'Seeing the words "you are a compulsive gambler" on the screen. Knowing that it wasn't a person's opinion, but an objective analysis. It gave me a shock, I can tell you. Why do you think I gave going to the meetings a rethink? I want to be free of this addiction, and I swear to you, since that one lapse, I have not gambled. Trust is a hard thing to regain once it's lost. I get that, Claire, but turning up at my work raging, that's not going to help. Plus, this is not something that the hospital can ever know about. A doctor with an addiction. How will that look?'

'Yes, I know. I wasn't very discreet, was I? How much do you think that nurse heard?'

'Don't worry about her. She only caught the tail end of our conversation. Just enough to know we were arguing.'

'That's something at least.'

Mark finished the last of his sandwich then said, 'As we are online, why not look up the times of some meetings. I'll go to the next available one. You can come with me and see that I'm really attending.'

'That won't be necessary. I trust you to go. I can see you want to beat this. I know that judging by the way I acted today, it may not look it, but I really am here for you. We're a team and together we can do this.'

They hugged and Claire felt more optimistic that things were going to work out for the best.

'I've been thinking too,' Mark said. 'That perhaps it would be a good idea to plan a holiday. It would do us both good to have something to look forward to. I ruined our break away and I'd like to make that up to you.'

'A few weeks in the sunshine, a change of scenery. That's a great idea. We should do it sooner than later.'

'I'll see about the next available time off I can get. I think we should go back to Spain – recapture the magic it worked on us,' Mark said, his eyes twinkling as he remembered.

Rain beat against the windscreen, which was fogged with condensation. Claire had been in the car for over an hour and was beginning to wonder how long a GA meeting lasted. She hadn't wanted to, but Mark had insisted she accompany him to this, his first meeting since his false start. The meeting was being held in a community centre adjacent to a small church. As they were in Chichester, a cathedral city near to Worthing, Claire didn't know of any local cafés she could have gone to instead. She supposed she could have checked her phone to locate one, but she was struck with inertia and just stayed where she was, her eyes glued to the double doors of the centre where Mark had disappeared. He'd turned and offered her a limp wave as he opened the door. As he did this, a surge of love for him rushed through her. She couldn't remember ever feeling this all-consuming love before, certainly not for her ex-husband, for whom she had been filled first with lust, then fondness – not the depth and completeness she had for Mark. Some might call him her soulmate, but she disliked the term and believed it was bandied about far too much, and without any real sense of meaning. As she contemplated all these feelings she was scared by their significance and what it was to love someone with the disease of addiction. To love is to support, to accept that person unconditionally, but at what price? How far should the one you love be a priority over your own wellbeing? Didn't a person owe themselves a degree of self-love for their own preservation? Their relationship was still in its early stages; Claire had spent sufficient time as a single person to develop proficiency in self-reliance. She'd been disappointed enough in the past to become master at recognising those people who weren't good for her. She'd never had that sense about Mark, which was why she'd been so shocked that he'd been able to deceive her. Her self-defence mechanism was making it difficult to believe that Mark wasn't lying to her anymore, but she knew she'd have to take a leap of faith if what they had together had any hope of succeeding.

The doors opened and a stream of people spilled out; it looked like it had been a big group. She ran her eyes over the faces, then saw Mark, talking to a man. They shook hands and Mark walked away, looking at the ground, an intent expression on his face. Letting himself in he sat and leant against the headrest. Closing his eyes, he exhaled slowly.

Claire asked, 'Are you all right?' and picked up his hand, which was as cold as ice.

'No.' He opened his eyes to look at her. 'That was the hardest thing I've ever had to do. Admit out loud that I am a compulsive gambler, that I am an addict. Up until now, I've been kidding myself, not really admitting I have a problem. But, to say the worst thing about yourself in public, and then for those people not to condemn you. To understand, to tell you, you are strong enough to beat this.' He dragged his free hand down his face. 'It's one of the most humane experiences in my life. I thought being in the medical profession I'd seen all the acts of kindness I was ever likely to, but this, this was humbling.'

Chapter Eighteen

'Alison, I'm glad I caught you. There's someone I'd like you to meet.' Alison was on a step ladder and Mary Griffin spoke to the back of her legs.

Alison descended, holding a large collage of dubious-looking self-portraits done by her year 3 class. Blowing her fringe away from her face as she made the final step, she turned to find Mary was not alone. Standing next to her she recognised the young man who had been waiting to be interviewed, all those weeks ago.

'I'd like you to meet Owen Llewellyn. Owen is going to be our new deputy head. He's just accepted the position and as you were here, I thought it would be nice to introduce you.' Mary stood aside, beaming, and all but curtseyed as Owen stepped forward, his hand out-stretched.

'How do you do. So very nice to meet you. My, what dedication to be here on such a lovely summer's day,' he said, his crystal-cut English accent at odds with his Welsh name.

Alison hastily rubbed her dirty hand on her thigh before shaking his. 'Hello.' She took in the well-cut suit, the gleaming cufflinks, and a whiff of expensive cologne. She knew how she must have looked. It was the beginning of August and she'd come into the school to strip the walls of the posters and paintings in her classroom. She'd deliberately put on old clothes and knew the leggings she wore had a hole in them. She watched as Owen gave her an up and down and found her wanting. He managed to do this and keep a smile plastered on his face. She felt the stirrings of dislike but thought that uncharitable of her and tried to discard the emotion.

'It's fortuitous you are here, Alison, because I've told Owen that as one of our most experienced teachers, you will be able to offer your assistance helping him to settle in. You can be a type of mentor to him.'

'Of course, as your superior you can't really mentor me,' Owen said, 'but I will call on you from time to time to oil the wheels with the other teachers. You know, those types who don't like change or are resistant to new ideas. Mary tells me you are quite the hero amongst the staff.' He gave her a wide smile and she was treated to the sight of his perfect, white teeth, which did all but twinkle. 'I hope I can rely on you, Alison.'

As he said this, Alison couldn't help feeling his tone suggested more of a threat than an entreaty for help; perhaps her first instinct had been correct. 'I will do everything I can to ensure your start here goes as smoothly as possible.' She hoped she was putting forward a composed front. 'We're one big family here, you'll see.'

'Quite.' He arched an eyebrow, then to Mary, 'Come, Mary, let's see about that cream tea I promised you. It won't be the Ritz, but I'm sure the Ardington can manage something passable.'

As they left without giving her a backward glance, Alison muttered under her breath, 'Boy, I can hardly wait for the new term to begin.'

The house was hot as she opened the door. She'd forgotten to close the curtains in the south-facing living room. The day's sun had done a good job of raising the inside temperature to an uncomfortable high. Going into the kitchen, she found breakfast dishes and plates had been left by the sink, remnants of food now baked onto them. A jar of marmalade had been left open, its lid and the sticky knife next to it covered in a blanket of ants.

'Jamie!' she called. No reply. She stomped up the stairs. Jamie's bedroom door was open. The room was empty, his bed unmade, its covers trailing onto the floor. Just about every drawer was open. Clothes, clean and dirty, were strewn about the place. A typical teenage bedroom; Alison tried to placate herself with this thought, but she was tired, she had a headache and she'd been unnerved by her run-in with Owen Llewelyn. She really didn't need this. She wondered where Jamie was, then had a brief recollection of him talking about football training. Football, of course, that was all he had any time for, she was sick of it. She bent to pick up some of the dirty laundry, but stopped herself. She'd done enough work for today. Going downstairs and fishing out her phone she rang a number.

'Claire. You've got to rescue me. Fancy meeting me at the Aquarium and hiring a sun lounger by the outdoor pool?'

The women threw their towels onto the loungers. They'd been fortunate enough to find a couple together on the outer perimeter of the area surrounding the pool. As it was school holidays and the weather good, the place was busy with parents and children. The refreshment kiosk was doing a brisk trade, and was surrounded by those eager for a cool drink or ice cream.

'I'm glad I remembered to bring our own,' Claire said, passing a cold can to Alison. 'That's quite the scrum over there.'

'You're a lifesaver. Thanks. I rushed out of the house so quickly I didn't give a thought to take any drinks with me. Mind you, if you'd have seen the state of my kitchen, you would have run out of the place too!'

'That bad, huh? I thought you had Jamie well trained.'

'So did I. Up until recently he has always been very tidy, not like Callum. I wouldn't mind, but Jamie's become hyperactive, he has all this energy. It's just a pity he doesn't channel it into his household chores.'

'I thought you said he was listless and complaining

of aching muscles,' Claire said.

'He was, but that seems to have disappeared, now he's at the other side of the spectrum. There are times when I practically push him out the door to go football training or running; just looking at him bouncing off the walls is exhausting.' She sighed. 'I think the next few months are going to be difficult enough without having to manage his moods.'

'How come? You sounded ready to explode when you called. It isn't just about Jamie then?'

'No. Work. I was in school today, doing a bit of tidying up, better to get it done rather than leave it before term starts. I thought it would only be me and the caretaker in the place, so I didn't exactly dress up. It turns out Mary was there with the person they've recruited as deputy head, and there's me looking like a right scruff bag.'

'What's she like?'

'*He* is very different to the usual staff member. Very posh, lord knows what the children will make of him, he sounds like someone from *Downton Abbey*, and I don't mean one of the servants. Dressed in an expensive suit, Hollywood smile. I don't think I've ever seen a male teacher who looks like him. He's going to be very out of place, then there's his manner. It sounds a bit mean, as I only spoke to him for five minutes. Outwardly he appears to be friendly, but it seems false, patronising in fact. I've got an awful feeling he already sees me as his personal lackey. Mary has me ear-marked to give him special assistance, as if I won't already have enough to do at the start of the year.'

'Perhaps it's good you've already met him. Forewarned is forearmed,' Claire suggested.

'You might be right. I'll have to make sure I take extra care with my appearance on the first day. I might warn some of the other teachers too.' She leaned back and shut her eyes. 'This is nice. It's a wonder how a little sunshine can make you feel so much better. Fingers crossed the good weather will hold; a staycation is all I can manage at the moment. Not that I could pry Jamie away from his training anyway. What about you and Mark? You're not going away anywhere this summer, no last-minute deals?'

'Funny you should mention that,' Claire said.

Chapter Nineteen

It was coincidental Alison brought up the topic of holidays and getting a last-minute deal because that's exactly what Claire had done the previous day. Mark was keen to have a proper break; trying to handle his addiction and his demanding job at the same time was taking its toll. He'd told Claire he needed to recharge his batteries somewhere warm and sunny. He'd also admitted to missing Spain.

'I lived there a long time,' he reminded her. 'Not just Almería, but Madrid too – I had some good times there and made a lot of friends. Of course, that's also where I met Marta,' referring to his ex-wife. 'And until I screwed that up, we were the perfect couple.'

A twinge of jealousy reared up in Claire on hearing this, but then she remembered Mark telling her just how badly things had ended for his marriage. She reasoned too that there was added motivation for Mark to ensure gambling didn't ruin another important relationship. 'I've always liked Spain and if you're missing it, why not go for a couple of weeks' holiday there? Somewhere on the Costa del Sol, nearer to Málaga airport than where we stayed before, so there would be less travelling to do. All I need is a niceish hotel, a beach and the sea. What do you think?'

'Now you're talking, just thinking about it has me feeling more relaxed. I meant to mention to you earlier, I was looking at the holiday roster at work, and the first two weeks of September have become free. I pencilled my name in before someone else took them, I just need to know if you could get the time off.'

'I'm going into the office tomorrow, so I'll have a word with the powers that be,' Claire said. 'I don't think it will be a problem as the school holidays will have finished by then.'

Claire was right, getting holiday leave for that period had been problem-free. She and Mark spent a cheerful evening checking out destinations online before finally settling on the pretty resort of La Herradura, in the Granada province.

'I don't like the look of all those massive hotel complexes, a bit too impersonal for me.' Claire also thought that there were bound to be lots of families with pre-school children. Not exactly the calm and peaceful atmosphere she and Mark were striving for. 'How about this three-star? It says it's only 250 metres from the beach.'

'Three-star? I think we can do a bit better than that.' Mark tapped away on his laptop, continuing his search.

'If you let me pay half, we could go for something swankier. I don't know why you are insisting on footing the bill for all of this.'

'I told you. It's my treat, my way of thanking you and saying sorry. Here,' – he pointed and turned the laptop towards Claire – 'this won't break the bank. A boutique hotel on the beachfront. What do you think?'

Claire looked; it did seem to be ideal. 'It would be great to be so near the water. What's the availability like?'

'They only have two rooms left on the dates we want. Shall I book one then, before it gets taken?'

'Go for it.' The excitement of the getaway to a sunny climate with all the swimming they could do thrilled her and she was already looking forward to going.

As it was a warm evening, they ate dinner outside. By way of celebrating their forthcoming holiday, they'd cracked open a bottle of white wine, which was chilling in an ice bucket. No one else was in their gardens, and it was quiet, the only sound coming from a pair of cooing pigeons on a nearby roof. A neighbour's cat had climbed the fence and was sitting on the bench at the end of the garden, its eyes closed, soaking up the last of the day's sunshine.

'I see Smokey's here again. He spends more time in our garden than his own,' Mark said, eyeing the feline.

'So would you if you had to live in such a noisy household. I reckon he fears for his life half the time.

The other day, I saw the boys had dragged him onto the trampoline with them. Poor thing was trapped until Mandy rescued him.'

Mark laughed. 'Perhaps she should get them onto a football team. It seems to be a big enough distraction for Jamie, from what you say.'

At the mention of her friend's son, Claire said, 'I feel a bit guilty we'll be going away just as Alison is starting the new term. It sounds as if this new deputy head is going to be hard work. I would have liked to have been around to offer moral support. Why don't we have them around next weekend for something to eat? At least it will give her a night off from cooking and clearing up.'

'Fine by me. We could have a barbeque; you're always saying it's not worth all the bother for just the two of us. Why not let Jamie bring one of his friends? It'll keep him occupied, if he gets bored the two of them can do some gaming inside and leave Alison to relax.'

'That's very thoughtful of you. I'm sure she'd appreciate that. I'll speak to her about it.'

※

'I'll get it,' shouted Claire to Mark in the garden as she skipped downstairs. She opened the front door and was momentarily taken aback to see a young man there. 'Oh hello. I was expecting someone else.'

'I'm with Jamie and Alison, they're right behind me. Jamie's saying "hello" to a cat by the gate. Is it yours?'

'That'll be Smokey. I think he's making a bid for

adoption,' Claire said. She saw Alison appear. 'Hi there. I didn't hear your car.'

'No, we walked. It's a lovely day, and this way I can have a drink.' She saw Claire glance at the man with them. 'This is Ryan, Jamie's coach. You did say Jamie could bring a friend.'

'Sure, of course,' Claire said, opening the door wider. 'Come in. Mark's out in the garden.'

'Jamie! Leave the cat and come on inside,' Alison called out to her son.

'Hello Claire,' he said, kissing her on the cheek. 'We brought chocolates *and* wine!'

'Well, we'll have to invite you more often. Thank you. Go and say hello to Mark.' She said to Alison in a low whisper, 'I thought he'd be bringing a lad of his own age.'

'You don't mind, do you?' Alison looked anxious. 'I did suggest that, but it was Ryan or nobody.'

'No, not a problem. I would have got some more beers in, if I'd have known there was going to be another adult coming.'

'Don't worry about that. Ryan doesn't drink alcohol, "my body is a temple" and all that.' She rolled her eyes. 'But at least he's setting an example to Jamie. Anything that Ryan says is a golden rule never to be broken, and getting drunk is at least one teenage problem I don't have to worry about.'

'I hope you're going to partake,' Claire said. 'I don't drink as much as I used to, but I do indulge at the weekend.'

'Just give me a glass and fill it. We had an "informal" meeting today before the start of the school year so that Owen could introduce himself.'

Claire frowned. 'Didn't go well then?'

'Let's just say, I hope you have plenty of wine in!'

The women hung back in the kitchen to have a catch up, leaving Ryan to say hello to Mark. He eyed the steak Mark was cooking.

'You don't want to overdo that; you'll lose all the nutrients if you cook it too much.'

Mark replied, 'Don't you worry. I know what I'm doing. It's not the first steak I've barbequed.'

'Whatever.' Ryan stayed put, keeping watch. 'I had thought of going veggie, you know, for health reasons. In the end though the thought of not eating meat wasn't for me. And it's such a good source of protein. I have to think about that, you know, for muscle-building.'

'I'm sure a vegetarian could tell you there are plenty of other ways to get protein.' Mark clenched his teeth and looked over at Jamie, who was engrossed in his phone.

'Yeah, if you say so. But lentils and all that are not for me.' He rocked back on his heels, his hands stuck in his pockets. 'I was talking to a mate of mine the other day. He says he knows you and you might be able to do me a favour.'

'Really? Who's that then?' Mark said.

'Eddie.'

Chapter Twenty

'Phew! Put the air-con on, will you, Mark,' Claire asked as she flung herself onto the bed of their hotel room. She kicked off her sandals and stretched. 'I thought we'd never get checked in.'

'Yeah, the staff take laid back to a whole different level, don't they?' Mark said. He chuckled. 'I'd almost forgotten that about the Spanish, it's impolite not to chat and pass the time of day. It doesn't matter if you have customers waiting – they'll get their turn.'

'And boy did that old couple like a natter, going on about their 40th wedding anniversary and how they're going to celebrate.'

'I thought it was sweet,' Mark said as he lay next to her. He took her hand. 'I'd like to think one day, we'll be holding up a queue with tales of *our* anniversary.'

Claire stared at the ceiling. What did that mean? Deciding not to ask, she got up and slid open one of the double doors leading to the balcony. She was met with an impressive view of the sea, sparkling as if strewn with diamonds, under the afternoon sun. It was hot, and she lifted her face to bask in the sunshine. 'Mark, you should see the view, it's lovely.'

Mark stood behind her, encircling his arms around her waist and rested his chin on her shoulder. 'Now that was worth the journey here,' he whispered into her ear.

Claire leant back against him, and they stood silently. The knowledge of having two weeks here, stretching out in front of them, was a pleasant sensation. Nothing to do but swim, make love, relax and forget the realities of their lives in England.

Claire put aside the magazine she was reading and glanced across at Mark on the lounger next to her. He was engrossed in a thriller he'd bought at the airport. His nose was pink and the tops of his shoulders were peeling slightly. With his fair colouring he'd have to be more vigilant applying sun block. She fished around in her beach bag and found a tube.

'Here,' she said, tossing over the factor 50. 'I think you should put more of this on. Your lovely nose is getting burnt.'

'God, really? I put a load of the stuff on. I suppose there's no hope if you're a ginger!'

Claire laughed. 'Come on, I'll do your shoulders. You need to move into the shade more too.'

Together they manoeuvred the lounger underneath the sun umbrella then Claire coated Mark in a thick layer of cream. 'That should hold you for a while. I'm going to go for a quick swim, but I think you should stay out of the sun.'

'You go, I'm fine here.'

Claire grabbed her goggles and clipped her fringe away from her face. Her hair was short enough that she didn't need to wear a cap unless she was swimming some distance and needed to be visible in the water. 'See you later.'

Mark looked up from his book. 'Enjoy yourself.'

She strolled to the water's edge, which was inhabited by lots of children building sandcastles or clambering onto lilos. She smiled as she looked at a small girl who was encouraging her tiny friend to climb aboard the unicorn rubber ring she was perched on. Two boys were flinging sand at one another, and Claire had to dodge around them to avoid getting hit. The boys' mother apologised and shouted something to her sons in Spanish. At the water's edge she stood, the gentle wash of sea curling over her toes. It was pleasantly warm; no gritting her teeth to get into this water, she thought. She spat into her goggles to stop them steaming up and rinsed them in the sea. Wading out until she was waist deep, she put her face into the water and swam. Mindful of the multitude of floating bodies, she sighted frequently until she was some way out. She aimed at the buoy; it was surrounded by a party of teenagers who had paddled out there on stand-up boards. One of the group, a girl, acknowledged her with a wave.

'*Nadas muy bien*,' she said.

'Sorry, I don't speak Spanish,' Claire replied.

'You swim good. Very strong, is a long way.'

For Claire the swim to the buoy didn't represent much of a challenge, but it wasn't the first time a person had been impressed by her ability to do so. 'Thanks. It's just practice, that's all.' She waved and moved off parallel to the beach, toward the next buoy. This one was crowded too. Stand-up paddle boards have a lot to answer for, thought Claire. She swam two buoys along before she found one that was people-free, then she pushed back her goggles and floated, letting the current take her with it. She looked up at the sky, cloudless and so very blue. *I'm sure it's never that colour in England*, she mused. She drifted a while longer before swimming back.

At the loungers Mark had nodded off, his book propped open on his chest. Claire took a moment to observe him. She really did love this man. It was an overpowering sensation she had no control over and it unnerved her. In the run-up to the holiday Mark had demonstrated just how important Claire was to him. In a bid to beat his addiction he had read copious online articles and books. He attended GA meetings without fail. His determination and tenacity were impressive and she could not help but admire him for it. Leaning over him, she kissed him on the lips. He awoke with a start.

'Oh Claire, it's you.'

'Who else? Do you get many women coming up and kissing you?'

'Dozens, I have to fight them off.' Gathering up his book he said, 'How far did you go? I saw you swim to the buoy before I nodded off.'

'A few buoys along.'

'That's quite a way.'

'It took a while to find a buoy that wasn't mobbed with people. There was a time that if you swam out that far, you'd get a bit of solitude. That's all gone now, unfortunately, you don't have to be a good swimmer to get there. It's a shame.'

'Why don't you swim beyond the buoy if you want some peace and quiet?'

'Oh no, you never know what you might come across, jet-skis, boats. It could be dangerous, especially on your own.'

'I'd never taken you to be someone to scare easily.'

'It can be frightening. The unknown,' Claire said.

The days passed in a blur of sunbathing, sight-seeing and swimming. They had a lovely time looking around Frigiliana, one of the many white villages so emblematic of Andalusia. Nestled on the slopes of the Sierra Almijara, it afforded stunning views of the coast. The narrow streets were a cool relief from the heat as Claire and Mark traversed along them, admiring the ceramic mosaics which decorated the walkways. Clay pots filled with bright red and pink geraniums clung to every building, contrasting sharply with the whiteness of the walls. The place was awash with colour; the overall affect was spectacular and it was easy to see why it was such a draw for tourists.

As they walked hand-in-hand they came across a

small fountain, built into the wall. They stopped and Claire sat and trailed her hand in the cool water. She closed her eyes and smiled.

'Gottya! That's a lovely photo of you.' Mark said.

'Let me see.'

He sat next to her and showed her. 'Nice,' she said. 'Now let's get one of us together.' He stretched out his arm for the selfie and hugged Claire close, they giggled as the photo was taken.

On the way to the car Claire spotted a souvenir shop, its walls adorned with all manner of ceramics and ornaments. 'I'd like to buy a few postcards,' she said. They crossed the street and while Claire browsed, Mark went inside. He reappeared some minutes later.

'I got you a wee present,' he said. He held a leather bracelet with a name on it.

'Clara,' Claire said.

'That's your name in Spanish,' Mark said as he tied the bracelet around her wrist. 'There's a matching one for me. Will you do the honours?'

Claire looked at his bracelet, 'Marcus, makes you sound very exotic.'

'Ay, but with my red hair and pink skin, I don't think anyone's going to be taking me for a local, do you?'

She laughed. 'Probably not.' Holding her arm alongside his and examining the two bracelets together she said, 'Now we're a matching set.' It felt good.

Chapter Twenty-One

Claire rolled over in bed and found the other side empty. 'Mark?' No reply. Sitting up, she looked at the time, eight o'clock. Where was he? Getting up she opened the balcony doors to appreciate the view and the warmth of the morning. *Not much more of this*, she thought glumly. *Soon be back to England. What must it be like to live in a country where sunshine can be taken for granted?*

Turning back to the room she saw a slip of paper on the bedside cabinet.

Couldn't sleep, didn't want to wake you so I've gone for a walk. See you downstairs for breakfast. M xxx

She wondered what time he'd left, then shrugging it off, got dressed and made her way to the hotel restaurant. Breakfast was served in the outside courtyard. It had an arbour covered in lilac-coloured wisteria, which hung heavily and gave an enchanted look to the patio. Small, round metal tables and chairs were dotted about and the atmosphere was peaceful and private. Mark was sitting, a cup of coffee in front of him, its smell tempting. He didn't notice Claire because he was lost in reading his phone. His mouth was set in a hard line of concentration. Claire felt a twist in her stomach; she recognised that look.

'Morning!' she said with a false cheerfulness. *He's guilty about something*, she pushed the thought aside.

'Hello darling.' He shoved the phone into his pocket. 'What do you fancy doing today? I think I'd like to give the beach a miss, do something different.'

'Do you have anything in mind?' Claire said, helping herself to coffee from the pot on the buffet table.

'There's a nature reserve nearby, we could go there, it's only about a fifteen-minute drive, or so I'm told. Apparently, there's a nice cliff top walk, we could stop and have a picnic. I spoke to the receptionist and she told me the hotel do packed lunches we could take with us. What do you say?'

'Sounds like you have it all organised,' Claire said.

'You don't want to go?'

'I didn't say that.'

'Well, you're not exactly brimming with enthusiasm.'

Claire took a deep breath. 'When I came out I saw you looking at your phone.'

'So?'

'You looked… you looked stressed. The way you used to look when…'

'Oh, I see. You thought I was placing an online bet, did you?'

Claire paused. Is that what she really thought? 'No, I-I don't think that, no.'

'Who are you trying to convince, Claire? Yourself or

me? I thought we'd got over this, that I'd proved to you I wasn't gambling anymore. Everything I've done these past few months, isn't that enough?'

'Yes, yes, it is. Look I'm just being silly. I'm sorry. And a day out and about sounds great. We should make a move before it gets too hot. We don't want to be walking out in the afternoon sun.'

After a few hours of walking the cliff tops overlooking the sea, Claire and Mark were ready for a break. They found a shady spot and unpacked the picnic.

'The hotel did us proud, look at the food here. And I thought all we'd be getting was a sandwich and a piece of fruit,' Mark said. 'Here, try this.'

'What is it?' Claire said, looking at the pastry Mark was offering her.

'*Empanada*, it's sort of like a pasty, they come with different fillings, this is tuna.'

'Mmm, it's good and this cheese is amazing, I must ask what it is, see if I can get it in England.'

'That's goat's cheese, it's made locally. You might be able to get it back home, but I doubt it. Glad you came?' Mark asked.

'Yes, of course. It was a good idea and I'm sorry if I was acting a bit weird earlier. I've been so happy here with you, maybe I was scared it wouldn't last. I want you to know that I do trust you, sometimes I can't quite believe it when things are going well. I don't know, perhaps I'm just a natural pessimist.'

'I wouldn't say that. It's the past few years that have got to you, that's all. First, losing your dad, then Alison having to be hospitalised in Spain while you were there on holiday and just as you're getting yourself together, I go and blow it. I'd do anything to go back and change things. I don't know what got into me, but I'm pretty sure nipping it in the bud this early is a positive thing. It's been easier to quit the gambling this time around, probably because I have so much more to lose. Last time, things had already started to deteriorate between me and Marta. Instead of turning to her for help I just indulged myself more and more, then when she found out, she upped and left me. Went to live with her parents and told all her family what a waste of space I was. They were furious with me, especially her father, he'd never much liked me anyhow, didn't like the idea of his precious daughter marrying a foreigner. Do you know what he told me when Marta asked for a divorce? That he thanked God every day that we hadn't had children, that he didn't have grandchildren with tainted blood. He cursed me, he actually fucking cursed me. Can you believe that?' His eyes filled with tears.

Claire jumped up and gathered him in her arms. 'Oh Mark, I can't believe anyone could be so cruel. What an awful thing to do. Didn't he know that any type of addiction is an illness?'

'He didn't see it that way. He called me weak. The one positive of the divorce was that I never got to see or speak to him again.'

'And Marta? Do you know what happened to her?'

'She got back with an old boyfriend before the divorce was finalised. I believe they have a couple of kids now. She lives practically next door to her parents, so everyone's happy.'

'Sounds like you had a lucky escape.'

Mark put his hand up to Claire's face and said, 'It was terrible at the time, but if it hadn't happened, I would never have met you. And I am so glad, Claire Sadler, that I did. You make me happier than I've ever been.'

As they pulled into the hotel car park Claire said, 'I think I'll go for a quick swim before dinner, it's lovely being in the sea as the sun sets.'

'No time for that, missy.'

'What do you mean? I can be back and showered in no time. We only have to go next door to eat.'

'Not this evening. I have somewhere special I'm taking you. The taxi's booked for eight o'clock so we need to be in the lobby for then.'

'Where are we going?'

'It's a surprise,' Mark said, smirking. He knew she'd hate not knowing their plans.

'What should I wear then? At least tell me that.'

'Your poshest frock. We'll be eating outside, so you might want to bring a pashmina or something.'

'Okay. I'd better get started if I'm to look the part.'

At ten to eight both of them were in the lobby. Claire had chosen to wear a strappy, black maxi dress. She'd teamed it with red espadrilles and a red clutch. Inspecting herself in the mirror she'd been pleased with the results; the black showed off her holiday tan, though the faint white strap lines by her shoulders distracted from the aura of sophistication she was aiming for. She needn't have worried though; when Mark saw her, he visibly swallowed then told her she looked beautiful. He was looking good too, his blue shirt bringing out his eyes. The pink skin had subsided and was now a golden hue.

'We make a fine-looking couple,' Claire stated.

The minutes ticked by and Mark began pacing up and down. 'Where is that driver? The reservation is at eight thirty and it supposed to take nearly half an hour to get there.'

'Ah, so we are travelling some distance then?' Claire said, trying to work out where they were going. 'I shouldn't worry, it's only just turned eight, and the Spanish aren't exactly sticklers for punctuality. Even if we are a little late, I don't think it will matter.'

Mark mumbled something that Claire couldn't hear, then he said, 'Here he is!' Once in the taxi with the air conditioning on full blast he started to relax. Claire hoped that the venue wasn't going to be stuck up and stuffy, particularly if it was having a strange effect on Mark like this.

The taxi drew up to a modern-looking three-storey building. Claire peered out of the car window. 'A hotel,' she said.

'Actually, it's a *parador*. Normally, they're former castles or monasteries. This one was built in the sixties, so it's very new in comparison.'

They were greeted by an attentive and friendly waiter who seated them at a table close to the immaculate lawn, which was framed by tropical plants and trees. The sun had set and the mountain range behind them was now black against a deep orange sky. A flower from a frangipani tree had fallen to the ground. Mark picked it up and tucked it behind Claire's ear. The scent of it was intoxicating. 'There,' he said, 'even lovelier.'

Their waiter reappeared with an ice bucket and an expensive bottle of champagne. Claire didn't know when this had been ordered. 'This is all very extravagant, not that I'm complaining.'

'Nothing's too good for you. I want to make a toast.' He picked up his glass. 'To my Claire, whom I love very much.' They clinked glasses. Mark cleared his throat. 'Look, I was going to wait until we'd eaten, but I just can't. There's something I have to say. To ask.'

Claire swallowed, surely he wasn't going to—?

Taking her hand and looking into her eyes, 'Claire, you make me so very happy. The happiest I've ever been. I want to be with you forever and I hope you feel the same. Would you do me the very great honour of agreeing to be my wife. Will you marry me?'

Chapter Twenty-Two

'So, Ryan reckons this bloke is a scout.' Jamie shovelled another forkful of scrambled eggs into his mouth. Still chewing, he continued, 'Ryan says he's seen him filming us a couple of times and he's definitely not one of the parents. He arrives just before the game starts and sits on his own. Doesn't talk to anyone, just pays close attention to what's happening. Ryan says he's sure he's spotted me, 'cos he asked who I was the other week.'

Alison looked up from her marking, her face one of concern. 'So this man turns up every week to watch, what, just you or all the team?'

Between mouthfuls of food Jamie said, 'Ryan says it's difficult to tell, but he thinks it's me he watches the most. He films the game too.'

'Why would he be filming? I don't like the sound of this, Jamie. You know there are some dodgy people about. Has he ever approached you directly?'

'Nah, that's not their style. They film matches then send it to other scouts, you know, for their comments. Then, if they think you have talent, they invite you for a trial. He could be a scout from one of the big clubs.'

'Well, let's not get carried away now. You must remember how competitive this is. I don't want you to be disappointed.'

'Ryan says it's important to have a positive mental attitude. That part of being a professional sportsperson is the psychological as well as physical ability. That's the difference between success and failure.'

'Hmm. I think I'll go along to your next game and have a word with Ryan. And, if that man's there I want you to point him out to me.'

'Mum, you're not going to show me up, are you? I don't want everyone thinking I'm a little kid. I'm practically an adult.'

'Don't worry I won't, I am used to speaking with people, you know, it's my job. You're not an adult yet. And no matter what your age, you'll always be my little boy,' she said, ruffling his hair, knowing she could get away with it as they were alone.

Despite himself, Jamie smiled and allowed the caress. 'When I'm a top player, I'll be able to look after you. You won't have to work and be stressed all the time.' Getting up he said, 'Remember, I have practice tonight so I won't be back until late.'

Is that how he sees me? thought Alison, *stressed all the time?* Although lately it was probably a fair comment. The start of a new school year was always busy and chaotic until things settled down. This year seemed particularly difficult though. Owen Llewellyn was doing a good job of heaping extra tasks onto her, tasks that he should have been doing. She'd tried raising the matter with Mary, but in her eyes Owen could do no wrong and she had waved aside Alison's concerns, saying it was only natural he'd take some time to settle in. According to her, Alison should take it as a compliment of her knowledge and capabilities that the deputy head should seek her advice as much as he was. Alison didn't see it that way.

※

'Alison, you don't know where Owen is, do you?' Brian, one of the teaching assistants, asked her during the morning break.

'Isn't he in his office?'

'No, and his secretary doesn't know where he is either. She tried calling him, but his phone went straight to voicemail.'

That's fairly typical, thought Alison. In the few weeks since he'd started, she'd found it almost impossible to speak with Owen, that was unless he was asking her to do something for him. 'Is there a problem, perhaps I can help?'

'It's Zainab,' he said, referring to the teacher he worked with. 'I think she could do with a bit more support as she's fresh out of university. Don't get me wrong, she's doing a great job, especially as she's so new to this, but one of the children is being disruptive, talking back, not doing as she's told – you know the sort of thing, it's upsetting Zainab. I tried telling her it's par for the course, testing a new teacher, but she's taking it to heart.'

'It's not one of the Reynolds' clan, is it?' Alison said, referring to the family of four siblings at the school, all of whom were unruly.

'Yes, Courtney. She's very cheeky and is a bit of a bully. She needs someone to be strict with her and not let her get away with all she does.'

'I'll have a word with Zainab and let her know we've all been there. I can give her some tips on discipline that have worked for me. Once she's been observed and had some feedback for that she'll feel better too. If things don't improve, then Owen will have to step in. We don't want this to escalate.'

'I knew you'd have an answer. It's a shame you didn't get appointed as deputy head, you'd have made a good one. The others were only saying that the other day,' Brian said.

With the amount of unpaid deputy head work she was doing, Alison was beginning to regret not having gone for the job, but it was too late now. Her phone beeped and she glimpsed it was a message from Claire. *Probably wants to meet up and tell me about their time away.* She couldn't help but feel envious of the holiday Claire and Mark had just come back from. Staycations were all well and good, but not when you had to rely on the British weather. Despite the few weeks' holiday she'd recently had, the beginning of term, and Owen's demands, were making her feel frazzled already. Half-term seemed a long way away.

It wasn't only work that was proving stressful. Jamie's

school had been in touch, there were 'concerns' that needed to be addressed. She and Jamie were having a meeting with them later in the day. Jamie had always been a model student and Alison's only contact with his teachers had been on parents' evenings, where they had fallen over themselves to tell her what a lovely son she had. During her time as a teacher she'd had many conversations with parents of wayward offspring. She'd always found the encounters awkward and would only have them as a last resort. She'd joked with her colleagues that she was probably more nervous about them than the parents. Now that it was happening to her, she viewed it differently. It would be strange to be on the other side of the table.

'Sit up straight, Jamie.' Alison tugged at his arm as he slouched in his chair. They were waiting for the arrival of the headteacher at Jamie's school. The receptionist looked over and gave her a weak smile, which Alison returned in kind. Whilst Jamie seemed unbothered by the prospect of the meeting, Alison was very edgy. She knew how busy headteachers at a high school were, and this must be a serious matter if it wasn't being dealt with by a lesser member of the staff. The head, Ms McKenna, arrived and Alison sprang to her feet.

'Mrs Harris, I'm so sorry for keeping you waiting. Mini emergency, you know how it is.' Her smile was kind and she used both hands to shake Alison's. Looking down at the still seated Jamie she said, 'Shall we go into my office, then? Jamie?'

Jamie hesitated, then stood and followed the two women. He sat straighter in the head's office, Alison noted.

Ms McKenna shuffled some papers on her desk, made a note on one of them, then addressed herself to Alison. 'I'm very glad you were both able to come in today.' She made eye contact with Jamie, who quickly looked down, going red. 'I want to discuss some issues we've had related to Jamie's behaviour both in class and during breaks. Up until a few months ago he has always been an exemplary student, polite, popular, hard-working, with good grades in all his subjects. His teachers have told me they noticed a change in his personality toward the end of the summer term, but put it down to the extra stress of mock exams and studying. Given that he has always been such a good pupil, and a likeable young man, he was given the benefit of the doubt. However, this term Jamie's attitude seems to have worsened. Upon admonishment from his form tutor for not doing his homework,' – she looked down at her notes – 'Jamie told her to – "F--- off and die you old witch."'

Alison gasped; she'd never even heard Jamie swear and the thought of him being so insulting to a teacher appalled her. She jabbed at his arm. 'Did you say that?' Jamie hung his head and didn't reply. 'Jamie, I'm talking to you. Did you say that to your teacher?'

'Yes,' he mumbled.

Now it was Alison's turn to go red. Unexpected

tears welled up in her, and she bit her lip to stop them. Embarrassing enough to have to listen to this, without adding to the humiliation.

Ms McKenna continued, 'As bad as I can see you think this is, it's not what worries us most.'

Oh God, thought Alison, what is she going to tell me next? This was excruciating.

'It's his aggressiveness that troubles us. Scuffles in the playground are one thing, but punching another pupil is another. Fortunately, the boy in question, Noah, was not badly hurt and didn't want the matter to go any further.'

'But Noah is one of your friends. What were you thinking, Jamie?' Alison couldn't believe this.

Ms McKenna continued. 'But another incident occurred on the same day as the witch comment. Jamie got angry in class and threw a chair across the room.'

Alison was stunned; this was not like Jamie at all, he was such a gentle soul. Then she remembered the way he'd been with their cat, and she shivered. Why hadn't she taken more notice of that at the time? The rest of the meeting passed in a daze for Alison as she tried to process all she'd heard. A plan of action was drawn up which Jamie agreed to. He conceded he needed to change, which was at least something, and Alison made assurances that he would be back to his normal self. She tried to remember exactly when Jamie had started to change, but couldn't pinpoint it exactly. She needed time to think.

Chapter Twenty-Three

Claire and Mark had eaten at the restaurant at the end of Worthing Pier and were strolling hand-in-hand along the promenade. The sun was shining but a stiff breeze was blowing in from the sea. Overhead seagulls screeched, dipping and gliding on the air currents. A gust of wind whipped at the light scarf Claire was wearing and goose bumps flared on her arms.

'Cold?' Mark asked.

'A little,' she admitted. 'Shall we go and get a coffee or something? Warm up a bit.'

'Yeah, that would be nice. Shame to go home just yet. I wanted to go into the town centre anyway,' Mark said.

As they headed towards the café they frequented Mark stopped and pulled Claire to him. 'Why don't we have a look in here?' He indicated the jewellers nearby.

'Why?'

'I think it's about time we got you an engagement ring, don't you?'

Claire didn't say anything. With her first marriage there had been all the traditional trappings: a church wedding and big reception, then a Caribbean honeymoon, all costing an arm and a leg. Did she really want that the second time around? Was it appropriate? While she inwardly procrastinated Mark propelled her to the jewellers' window display.

'No, not these,' she said, looking at the array of diamond solitaires, too similar to her previous engagement ring. 'Let's look at something a bit different.'

'Anything you want,' Mark said, kissing her on the cheek.

Claire's eye was drawn to a square-cut sapphire, very simple, on a gold band. 'I like that.'

Mark bent to get a better look. 'Really? It's very plain. And second-hand.'

'I think you'll find they call that vintage. It's from the 1930s. I like it. It's different.' And this marriage will be different too, she thought. When Mark had proposed she had surprised herself by immediately accepting. When it came down to it, she couldn't imagine not being with this man for the rest of her life; the alternative didn't warrant consideration. She couldn't remember ever feeling like that about her first husband, that surety that she was going to love this person for ever.

⁂

Claire stretched out her hand and looked at the ring on her finger. With her other hand she held a cup of coffee. At the jewellers they'd asked to see the ring and try it on. When it fitted perfectly, everyone saw it as a positive sign.

'I don't often see that,' said the sales assistant. 'I think this ring wants to belong to you.'

'I do too,' Claire said. 'It's perfect.'

'I'd better get it for you then,' Mark said.

Claire had been so enamoured with it, she'd insisted on wearing it straight away, no bended knee and presentation required, she'd assured Mark. Now she sat, cuddled up to him, constantly looking at it and not quite believing it was there.

'I can't wait to show Alison,' she said. Although she wondered what her friend would say. Claire had never discussed the topic of marriage to Mark and this was going to come as a surprise.

'I thought you'd be glad for me,' Claire said. 'Don't you want me to be happy?' When she'd told Alison her news, the response hadn't been congratulatory; instead she'd asked if Claire was sure.

'Of course, I want you to be happy. I'm your oldest friend. I only want the best for you.'

'And you don't think that's Mark, is that what you're saying?'

'I'm only trying to look at it objectively. You haven't known each other that long and you're already having problems.'

'You mean Mark's gambling? I told you, he has that under control.'

'Does he? Does he really? How can you be sure?

Look, I really like Mark. I think basically he's a good guy and I've no doubt that he loves you. Why not wait a while before making a big commitment like marriage – just in case.'

'In case he can't control his addiction? You know addicts of any sort never see themselves as cured, just recovering. Exactly how long do you think is a suitable time to wait, hey? And, if there are problems, we can face them together. Every marriage has a few bumps in the road. It's not as if you and Gavin had the perfect marriage.'

Alison moved her chair and stood, looking down at Claire. 'What's that supposed to mean?'

'Don't you remember, after you'd had Jamie and had postpartum depression. Jamie got colic and wouldn't stop crying. What did Gavin do? Moved in with his mother. I don't exactly call that supportive.'

'He only did that for a month or so, just while he was studying for the last part of his masters. He was struggling with that and working full-time with hardly any sleep. You know how it was.'

'I thought it was terrible of him, but I kept my thoughts to myself because I didn't want to add to your burdens. If you really want to know, I thought Gavin could be selfish, you were always the one to compromise. I think you've forgotten about all the times you'd come crying to me about something he'd done or hadn't done. I've often wondered, if he'd lived, whether you'd still be together.' As soon as she'd said those words, Claire instantly regretted it and knew she'd overstepped the line. By being defensive, she'd gone on the attack. 'I'm sorry Alison. I didn't mean that.'

'I think you'd better go,' Alison was gripping the back of the chair. Her eyes filled and Claire could see she was trying not to cry.

'Alison, I' – Claire reached out to her, but she backed away and pointed her finger at the door.

'Leave. Now. Before either one of us says anything more we'll regret.'

Knowing it was useless to argue, Claire picked up her bag to leave. 'I'll call you later.' But her words were met by the slamming of the front door. She stood and could hear Alison sobbing on the other side. She couldn't bear the sound; her stomach twisted, knowing that she had caused her friend such anguish.

Chapter Twenty-Four

While Claire's life had taken a turn for the better, Alison felt as if hers was imploding. She was still furious with Claire for her comments about Gavin, although she couldn't pinpoint why. Because they were true? Had she built Gavin up to be some kind of saint and their life together one without complications? Or because she was genuinely offended and Claire was speaking out of turn? If she'd had more time, she might have been able to assess her feelings, but that was in short supply these days. Home and work problems filled her head to bursting point, until sometimes all she wanted to do was scream out loud 'Stop!' and allow herself the space to think. After the meeting at his school, Jamie had had privileges stripped away, pocket money, gaming, and no football.

'Please, Mum. You can't stop me going to training and matches. What if a scout is there and I'm not playing? I'll miss my chance.'

'It's only for two weeks, you're lucky it's not longer. I don't think you'll miss out. If you're the next Lionel Messi you'll get spotted no matter what. Just stop going on about it, you're driving me mad with all this incessant football talk. I've had it. Enough!'

'I fucking hate you!' Jamie screeched, his eyes bulging, his face red with rage.

'Do. Not. Speak to me like that. Do you hear me? Do you want a month-long football ban?'

Jamie said nothing. He left, slamming the door and running upstairs to his bedroom.

Alison exhaled and rested her head in her hands. Where did my sweet little boy go to? She looked at the pile of marking in front of her, better get to it, and reached for the first notebook. After this she had to look at Zainab's lesson plans. Owen was supposed to have been observing the new teacher but had somehow managed to delegate it to Alison – 'you have such a good rapport with her and she trusts you' – was his justification for side-stepping the job. Since Owen's appointment she'd found that many of her colleagues would come to her for advice and queries which would normally fall within the deputy head's realm. When she'd tried to point this out, they told her they found it difficult to talk to him, either because he simply was never to be found or he was ineffectual. When Owen did take the time to listen to a teacher, nine times out of ten, he would come to Alison anyway to ask what should be done, thus exacerbating the number of questions directed her way. She could see she would have to have a word with Mary about this, but was put off from doing so in case it looked like sour grapes on her part.

It was Friday morning in the school staff room. Alison was chugging her coffee, relieved the weekend was almost upon them, when Mary approached her, a worried look on her face.

Moving Alison to a corner, Mary said, 'I've just heard from Owen, he's called in sick.'

'I'm sorry to hear that,' Alison said as she wondered what was coming next. 'Do you know how long he will be away for?'

'The doctor has signed him off for two weeks.'

'Two weeks? What's wrong with him, though I don't suppose you can tell me.'

'Normally no, but this could be long-term sickness and would affect you directly. I'm afraid Owen is suffering from stress brought about by his workload. He told me he felt the school had let him down and not offered sufficient support. That the teachers did not respect him. He used the term "bullying".'

'What!' Alison said this so loudly that several of the teachers turned. She could see them trying to listen. Whispering now, she said, 'I'm sorry, Mary, but that's a complete load of rubbish. Everyone, particularly me, has bent over backwards to help Owen.'

'Yes. Quite.'

'Why are you telling me this?'

Looking sheepish Mary said, 'I was hoping you would be able to step into the breach, be acting deputy head while Owen is away.' Alison's eyes widened at this.

Mary coughed and continued, 'Of course, you would be offered deputisation money to reflect the position and we would have a substitute teacher to cover your class.'

'Would you now.' Alison's mind scrambled to take in this information. On the one hand, it would be good to see if she was up to the job, especially as she hoped one day to do it on a permanent basis. She was already doing so many of Owen's duties, she might as well get them officially recognised. On the other hand, there were her pupils. She was just getting to know them, some had been tough nuts to crack and it was only now they had begun to trust her. If a cover teacher were brought in, all that would be lost and she'd have to start over. Then again, the extra money would be useful, especially since she'd learned the costs involved if Jamie got into a football academy. He'd mentioned the possibility of going to a private one; the fees were exorbitant, though the figures had been bandied trivially in the way teenagers do when they expected their parents to pay for something.

'So, can I rely on you to step in?' Mary said.

'I don't know, Mary. It's a big ask. Can I have the weekend to think about it?'

'Yes. Yes of course.' Mary touched her arm and looked her in the eye. 'But please do give it serious consideration, won't you?'

'I will. I promise.'

Chapter Twenty-Five

Claire checked her phone; still no replies to the multiple messages she'd sent Alison, some of them hadn't even been read. She was beginning to worry; they wouldn't usually be out of touch with one another for more than a day or two. Replaying their last conversation, Claire could have kicked herself for being so insensitive. The truth of the matter was that Alison's comments had hit a nerve and she'd been lashing out. So stupid. She couldn't fall out with Alison, she just couldn't. Well, if Alison wasn't answering her messages or picking up then she would just have to see her face-to-face. Grabbing her keys she hurried out.

Pulling up outside Alison's house she saw a couple of wheelie bins abandoned in the drive. There were no others in the street. You'd think one of her neighbours would have done this, thought Claire as she pulled the bins back into their place at the side of the house. Ringing the doorbell, her heart thumped. She hadn't planned what she was going to say, but she wasn't leaving until things had been made right between them. Jamie answered the door.

'Hi there. Is your mum about?'

'Nah, at work.'

'On a Saturday?'

'She's at work all the time now. She's got a new job.'

'Really?' Claire wondered what this might be. 'Can I come in and wait for a bit?'

'Sure,' Jamie held the door open for her. 'She didn't say when she would be back, it could be a while.'

'That doesn't matter. You can keep me company. It's been ages since I've seen you.'

Jamie shrugged. 'If you like.'

Entering the house, Claire wrinkled her nose; there was a whiff of something bad coming from somewhere. She followed Jamie into the kitchen.

'Do you want a cup of tea?'

'That would be nice,' Claire said. She found the source of the smell. The bin was full, its contents overflowing, and a bag of rubbish was leaning against it. The sink was full of dirty dishes and old tea bags had been left scattered on the countertop.

Jamie opened a cupboard for a mug. Finding none, he retrieved one from the sink and gave it a cursory rinse.

As the kettle boiled Claire went to help herself to milk. She opened the fridge; its only contents were wrinkled fruit and a putrid cucumber, and she gagged slightly at the stink that emanated from them. Grabbing the milk, she opened the top and tentatively sniffed. 'Ouf! Milk's off.'

'Oh yeah, Mum did ask me to get some more. I forgot.'

'And I expect she asked you to clean up too,

didn't she?'

Jamie hung his head. 'Yes.'

'Shall we tidy up a bit, then? Before you go to your football match.'

'I don't have one.'

'I thought you had a match every Saturday?'

'Mum wouldn't let me go. I'm grounded.'

'Really, why's that, then?'

Jamie looked down at his feet and said nothing. Not wanting to push it Claire said, 'Tell you what, we'll get this place sorted out, then go to the supermarket for provisions. What do you think?'

'Can we get some decent food in? We've been eating a lot of frozen stuff and I should be eating properly. You know, as part of my training.'

'I don't see why not. Better get this done first. Why don't you put these plates and things into the dishwasher, and I'll put out the rubbish. Where are the bin bags?'

'That's the last of them,' Jamie said, he dumped two carrier bags onto the kitchen counter. Claire was loading up the fridge, having given it a clean beforehand.

'Great. Pass me the stuff for the fridge, then I'll make us something for lunch.'

'I'm going to clean the bathroom,' Jamie said.

'My, aren't you the great helper? I'm sure your mum will be very pleased with you for that.'

'I'm hoping, if I'm good, she might let me go to

football next week. I can't miss another match.'

Jamie looked distressed at the thought of this and Claire was concerned. First, finding Alison's home in the state it had been; she was always so houseproud. Then this communication breakdown with Jamie, the two were normally so close. There was something off with Jamie too. His acne was out of control and his former skinny frame had been transformed, his tee-shirt barely able to contain his chest, the sleeves straining against his biceps. She'd have a chat with him over lunch and see what she could discover.

<hr>

Alison was shattered. It was gone five and she was driving home from school. She hadn't expected to have to work as long as she had. When she'd accepted Mary's offer of acting deputy head, she didn't think it would be like this. The full scale of Owen's neglect had only come to light once she'd started probing. So much to be done and still a substitute teacher to be found. If Mary thought she could continue both roles she had another think coming. She'd give it another week tops, then she'd down tools.

She put those thoughts to the back of her head. At least the day had been productive and should have cleared things for the week ahead. Right now, all she wanted to do was slide into a warm bath. Too late she remembered the grocery shop still had to be done. Takeaway again, she thought. She didn't imagine Jamie would have done the chores she'd set either. She sighed; she really didn't want another slanging match with him. Since the meeting at the school and his subsequent football ban, he'd been hell to live with and they'd argued every day. Lord knows what the neighbours must be thinking.

As she let herself in, Muffin came to meet her, purring and demanding attention. Alison remembered they'd run out of cat food the day before. 'More tuna for you Muffin,' she said, picking up the cat and burying her head in its soft fur. 'That's if we have any.' Preparing herself for the worst, she walked into the kitchen and was met by a lemony scent, the surfaces clear of clutter and gleaming. The bin was not only empty but looked as if it had been cleaned. Flowers were arranged in a vase and left on the table. A card was propped up against them. Opening it she saw it was from Claire.

Dropped in to see you earlier, but you were at work. I wanted to apologise for what I said about Gavin. I'm really sorry. Please say you'll forgive me. I hate not being friends and I miss you!

Gave the place a bit of a clean and got some food in. Hope you don't mind. Jamie helped, he's a good lad.

Lots of love,

Claire xxxx

PS: I took the liberty of getting you a bottle of wine. It's in the fridge chilling.

Alison opened the fridge; it was filled with food, the wine was there, her favourite. She closed her eyes and leant on the door. Wiping at a stray tear she grabbed her phone to make a call. It was answered immediately.

'Thank you,' she whispered.

Chapter Twenty-Six

Jamie and Ryan were in Alison's kitchen. They had joined forces to try and persuade her to reverse her decision and let Jamie take up his training and play in the match the following Saturday. Alison had had another tumultuous day at work. At last a teacher had been found to cover her former class, though Alison had spent the best part of the day seeing that she was acquainted with the workings of the school. Mary had fluttered around them too, trying to be helpful but only managing to hinder proceedings. Owen's assertions of being bullied had turned Mary into a bundle of nerves, despite Alison's reassurances that his claims were completely unjustified and would come to nothing. So, when Alison returned home she felt blind-sided by their collaborative appeal to reinstate Jamie's privileges, and was unable to put up much resistance. It would be nice, she reasoned, not to be constantly doing battle with Jamie; hopefully he'd learned his lesson. Plus, she just didn't have the energy to firefight at home and work.

'It's the right thing to do, Mrs H,' Ryan said. 'I'm sure those incidents at school were just one-offs. I've had a word with Jamie and told him to channel any negativity and turn it into something positive. He knows that if he wants to be a professional, he'll have to have the right mindset.' He tapped the side of his head to emphasise the point. 'Jamie won't let you down. Not now I've had a word with him. Will you, Jamie?'

Jamie shook his head. 'I won't, you can count on me.'

'Good lad. Now, what way are we going?'

'All the way.'

'To where?' Ryan asked.

'To the top!' The two high-fived as Alison looked on, the seeds of intense dislike for Ryan growing. She was uneasy with his increasing influence on her son, and she didn't like the way he patronised her. For the moment she didn't know how she was going to deal with it. Once things settled down at work she'd have to address these issues, but for now it was good to see Jamie smiling again.

'So, match fit for Saturday, hey Jamie?' Ryan said.

'Yeah, I'm going for a run in a bit, then I'll be at the gym tomorrow.'

'I'll see you Saturday morning then,' Ryan said. 'I'll pick you up first thing.'

'Actually, I can give him a lift. Thank you all the same,' Alison said. 'I'd like to come along to the match. I haven't been for a while. Claire and Mark said they want to go too. The four of us can go out for something to eat afterwards. How about Chinese, Jamie, would you like that? Oh I know you have this special diet you're following, but one meal won't hurt, will it?' She looked at Ryan, daring him to challenge her. For a moment it looked as though he would, then he said, 'I suppose it would be okay, as a one-off.'

'That's settled, then. Thank you, Ryan. I'll see you out,' Alison said.

Mark stamped his feet and pulled his coat tighter. 'It's a bit nippy, isn't it?'

'Do you think so? I feel fine. You must be used to much colder, those Scottish winters are fierce,' Claire said.

'Aye, but you're forgetting I haven't had to endure one of those for a long time. All those years in Almería have turned me into a right softie where cold weather is concerned.'

'What about Madrid, it gets cold in the winter there.'

'But there's always sunshine and blue skies, not murky and damp.' He looked up at the grey clouds and shivered.

'We'll just have to think of ways to warm you up when you get home then,' Claire said, kissing him.

'I'll keep you to that.' Mark wrapped his arm around her and brought her close to him. 'Here's Alison.' He indicated with his head.

'Morning you two. How's it going?'

'Mark's complaining about the cold,' Claire said, giving him a squeeze.

'It *is* a bit chilly, and there's nothing like standing on

the side-lines of a football pitch for a couple of hours to freeze your toes off,' Alison said. She'd come prepared and was wearing a huge puffer coat. 'I'd normally only take this out in the depths of winter.' She pulled the zipper up to her chin.

Alison nodded to a few parents that she knew, her eyes searching the crowd. 'Are you looking for someone in particular?' Claire asked.

'What?' Alison dragged her gaze back to Claire. 'I'm trying to find the man Jamie's told me about. Apparently, he often comes to matches and films the whole thing. Jamie seems to think he could be a scout and of course is all excited at the prospect of that, particularly as he seems to be focusing his attention on Jamie. I just want to make sure that's all it is. If he's going to be showing images of my son to someone, he needs to speak to me first.'

'You're right, there could be a sinister motive for what he's doing so best to check him out. I would have thought if there was a scout then Ryan would know about it, especially if he comes here regularly.'

'You'd think that, wouldn't you? And of course, there may be, but Ryan's not exactly good at keeping me in the loop about things.' She gave a cursory look around. 'I'll keep my eyes peeled during the match. Let me know if you see anyone filming and I'll go and have a word.'

The teams filed out and there were shouts of encouragement from the crowd. Jamie saw them and waved; a grin spread wide on his face. Alison said, 'I haven't seen him this happy for a while, I'm glad I relented and let him play.'

~~~

The match started and it wasn't long before Jamie's team, Stormforce, scored a goal.

Mark shouted, 'Well played Jamie.'

'But he didn't get a goal,' Claire said, confused at Mark's praise.

'No, but he defended well, and passed the ball to a player who was in a position to score. That's good teamwork. I can see why Ryan is pushing him.'

Alison yawned and covered her mouth.

Claire had spotted it. 'Tired or bored?'

'Tired. Very. I was at the school this morning at the crack of dawn. As we're eating out after the match, I knew I wouldn't be able to go back later. I've been going in every Saturday for weeks now, sometimes even on a Sunday. I can get so much done without interruptions.'

'I hope the head appreciates your dedication. Any word from Owen?'

'No, not really. His doctor has now signed him off for a month, so it doesn't look as if he'll be coming back anytime soon. With mental health issues, as you know, you can't determine an end date. Though…'

'What?'

'I shouldn't say really, but…well I can't help but feel sceptical about Owen's health. I know you can never tell what a person is feeling inside, and that people can be good at hiding things. It's just, I saw Owen coming out of a supermarket not long ago. He was with a woman, laughing and joking. And, I could have sworn he had a suntan.'

'No! You don't think he's lying about his illness, do you?' Claire was aghast. Having battled stress and depression herself, the thought that someone might fake it appalled her. 'Have you said anything to the head?'

'No, I didn't want to, just in case I was wrong. Mary seems – well, seemed – very fond of Owen, and I wasn't sure how she would have reacted if I'd aired my suspicions. I'll keep my head down and just get on with things. I'm slowly getting on top of the workload now that I have a system in place. And you've been a godsend, doing the shopping for me then tidying up and keeping an eye on Jamie.'

'I'm more than happy to help,' Claire said. 'I know you have a lot on your plate, but I'd like a quiet word with you about Jamie.'

'Is something wrong?'

'Maybe. Now's not the time. Let's try and meet soon to chat about it.' Seeing Alison's face she added, 'It's nothing that can't wait.'

The match continued and Stormforce did well, scoring another two goals. When the final whistle went, they had won by 3–0. The winning team were ecstatic, jumping up and down, hugging each other.

'Good result, great match. I really enjoyed it,' Mark said. 'I think I'll congratulate the coach.' He wandered over to Ryan. The two men spoke for a while then Ryan moved closer to Mark. His body language seemed conspiratorial, and Mark jerked away from him, his expression angry. He said something and strode away.

'Come on, let's go,' Mark said. 'We'll see you by the car, Alison, okay?'

'Sure,' Alison didn't ask what had just transpired and said, 'I'll get Jamie and we can be off.'

As Claire and Mark walked towards the car, Claire asked. 'What was that all about with Ryan? It looked like you were arguing.'

'Let's just say, he asked for a favour that I wasn't willing to grant.'

Chapter Twenty-Seven

'You haven't seen Smokey, have you?' Mandy, Claire's next-door neighbour, asked. 'I know he likes to camp out at yours.'

Claire was unpinning washing in the garden when Mandy popped her head over the fence. 'Sorry, no. In fact, I haven't seen him for a few days.'

'Maybe he's got so fed up with my boys, he's packed his bags and left home.' Mandy chuckled. 'Some days I feel the same. Would you keep a look out for him?'

'Sure. Mark and I won't be here for a couple of days though. We're going to Scotland to see his parents.'

'Giving them the good news?'

'Yes. We thought it would be better to do it in person, plus I've only met them once so it will give me a chance to get to know them. I expect we'll have to go to Sheffield next and do the same with my brother.'

'Do you want me to water any plants while you're away?'

'Nah, don't worry. We'll be back before you know it.'

'Have a good time!' Mandy stepped back and could be heard calling for her cat.

Settled in their seats on the flight to Edinburgh Claire asked Mark, 'What do you think of Jamie?'

'I think he's a grand lad. I've grown to like him very much. Bit obsessed with his football, but there are worse things he could be doing.'

'I'm worried about him. Perhaps worried is a bit too strong a word. He's different somehow. I've tried to pin Alison down to talk about it, without success.'

'It's his age, that'll be all.'

'No, it's more than that. I've been spending a lot of time with him, you know, with Alison being so busy. And something's not right.'

'Like what?'

'For starters, his mood-swings are severe. Happy one minute, sad the next. And Alison's told me he's got very aggressive lately, that's a total personality change. He's never been that sort of boy. I know he's a teenager, but even so. Then there's his physique. You probably haven't noticed because you haven't known him that long. He used to be skinny, now he's so muscle-bound.' She laughed. 'But then again he does pretty much live at the gym these days! It might be all the protein powder he's consuming. He was showing me his selection the other day. He's got tons of the stuff. When I asked how he could afford it all, he said that Ryan gives it to him. Has a friend who gets it cheap. I just worry he's overdoing it and might be damaging his body by training too much.'

Mark sat very still, his jaw clenched. Then said, 'Have

you noticed any other changes in him? His acne is bad. Has it always been like that?'

'Now that you mention it, it has got worse recently.'

'This gym he goes to. Is it membership only?'

'No idea. It's the one Ryan uses. They train together.'

'Do they? That's very interesting. Maybe I'll take a look at it when we get back. See what it's like, if it's a suitable place for a young lad to be. Normally, there would be an age limit. I'm surprised they allow a seventeen-year-old in.'

'That'll be Ryan's influence,' Claire said.

'Oh, I've no doubt about that,' Mark said, picking up a newspaper and bringing the conversation to a close.

Claire had been tense about telling Mark's parents they were getting married, anxious they might think it was too soon. She needn't have been concerned; they were delighted.

'Will you be staying in England when you marry?' Gwen, Mark's mother, had asked as she poured Claire another glass of champagne. Mark was in the garden with his father, so out of earshot.

Claire thought it an odd thing to say. 'Yes, of course, though we might move house. Get something a little bigger but stay in the same area. We wouldn't want to move too far away from the hospital where Mark works.'

'Hmm. No, I suppose not,' Gwen said. 'I'll just go and top up David and Mark's glasses. Back in a jiffy.'

Mark came back a while later, his drink consumed. He looked happy, perhaps a little drunk, thought Claire. He stood next to her and gave her bum a pinch, giggling as he did so.

'Mark. Not in front of your parents. What will they think?'

'I'm sure they are worldly enough to know we're sleeping together. Besides, we're engaged. And they're very happy for us. See, I told you, you had nothing to be worried about.'

'Yes you did.' She gave him a peck on the cheek. 'Your mum asked me a strange question.'

'What was that then?'

'She asked if we'd be staying in England when we got married. I said "yes". Is there something you're not telling me?'

'Not at all. I was saying how much I missed the Spanish weather and lifestyle, that's all. She's just got hold of the wrong end of the stick.'

'Are you not happy in England then?'

'As I said, there are things I miss about Spain. I'm still readjusting to life in Britain, that's all. Now, let's get another bottle of bubbly opened.'

Claire and Mark were back from Scotland. The trip had been a success and the change of scenery welcome. They were parking in the drive. Mandy was out front, putting something into the recycling bin. She waved as they got out of the car.

'Hi there,' Mandy said. 'Did you have a nice time?'

'Very. It'll be good to be in my own bed though. Sleeping on a futon is not the most comfortable thing. Did Smokey turn up?'

'No. Still missing. I don't know where he could have got to. They do say cats have multiple owners. He'll be somewhere, getting spoilt. If you could check in your shed though, he might have wandered there when you weren't looking and got locked in.'

Mark appeared with the bags. 'All right, Mandy?'

'Mandy was just saying that her cat's still missing. Maybe we should check under our bed. I have found him there before now,' Claire said. They all laughed.

Inside Mark said, 'I'll just put these upstairs, then we can have a cuppa.'

'All right. I'm going to check the shed for Smokey.'

Mark dumped the overnight bags on the bed. He heard a scream from Claire and rushed downstairs. Claire was gasping, leaning against the closed back door.

'What is it? Claire, what's the matter?'

'Smokey. It's Smokey. Outside.' Stepping aside she let Mark open the door. It was a sorry sight that met him. The grey cat lay there, its innards splayed out on the decking. It had been completely eviscerated.

Chapter Twenty-Eight

Mark held a shaking Claire. They were both shocked by what had happened.

'How am I going to tell Mandy?' Claire said. 'Bad enough to lose your cat, but this. This is deliberate and vicious. Who would want to hurt her this badly, everyone loves Mandy. Even her ex is a friend.'

Mark said nothing and gripped her a little tighter. Claire raised her head from his chest and stepped away. 'Unless it's nothing to do with Mandy. Do you think someone thought Smokey was our cat and wanted to hurt us? Send *us* a message? We should contact the police. At the very least it must be a crime to kill an animal like this, then to leave it for us to find.'

'NO!' Mark said, then quieter, 'I don't think it would be a good idea to involve the police. Too many questions.'

'But once Mandy knows, she's going to want to inform them. It'll be out of our hands.'

'I'll move the cat. Wait until it's dark and put it by the side of the road. It'll look as if it's been run over.'

Claire pulled away from Mark. 'Sounds as if you have it all figured out. You'd better move him out of sight, if that's your plan.' She hugged herself. 'I'm going to put my stuff away.'

After she'd unpacked, she took a long, hot shower, the events of the day unsettling her. Although neither she nor Mark had mentioned his name, she couldn't help but think that Eddie was behind this in some way. But why? The debt to him had been repaid. She believed Mark when he said he wasn't gambling anymore. What purpose did it serve to leave a mutilated cat on their doorstep? Opening the window in the steamy bathroom, she could hear Mark's voice. He was in the garden, talking to someone on the phone. She strained to hear what he was saying.

'…you, the answer is no. Can ye not get that into your thick skull? If…' he'd turned away and she couldn't hear the rest of what he was saying. One thing was clear. Mark knew this incident was directly linked to them. And he knew who was behind it.

When she came downstairs sometime later Mark was in the living room on the phone. This time he was speaking to his mother.

'Yes, got home no bother. No, not until tomorrow evening. Yeah, a few nights on duty, then I have a couple of days off. Huh huh, will do. Speak to you soon. Bye.' He saw Claire, 'Mum sends her love. Still mithering on about setting a wedding date.'

Claire smiled, then shifted from foot to foot. 'Have

you…have you—'

'Yes, I've wrapped Smokey up in a blanket and put him in the shed. I'll leave from the back gate in a bit and find a spot for him. I'm going to the gym where Jamie works out. I'll take a look around, pretend I'm interested in becoming a member and get a feel for the place. On the way home I'll "find" Smokey and take him to Mandy's and tell her I discovered him by the side of the road.'

Claire let out a sigh; at least she wouldn't have to talk to Mandy just yet. She'd have the night to hone her shocked and sympathetic face for when she next met her neighbour. She hated lying, and she wasn't very good at it. 'Right, okay.' She looked at her feet.

'I might as well make a move now,' Mark said, then, 'Make sure you lock all the doors once I've gone.'

Claire did as he said her body trembling as she turned the front door key.

'Would someone get that phone, *please!*' Alison found herself speaking to an empty reception area. Her office was adjacent to it. Not ideal. The comings and goings of a busy school and the incessant ringing of the phone meant she was constantly interrupted. Concentrating for any length of time was nigh on impossible. Tina, the receptionist, sprang up from beneath the countertop.

'I'm here!' she squeaked, her voice high-pitched and childlike.

People are going to think it's one of the pupils; Alison giggled at the thought. If they had children working here, they would have done a better job than Owen. It was incredible how much havoc he'd wreaked in the short time he'd been in the job. What had Mary and the board been thinking when they'd hired him? A question she asked herself way too many times. She turned her attention back to her work.

Mary knocked gently on the door. 'May I come in?'

Alison put down her reading material and tried not to look irritated.

'Are you busy? Silly me, of course you are.'

'No, it's fine. How can I help you?'

She sat down and opened a notebook. Alison could see the pages were full, this wasn't going to be a five-minute chat. She resigned herself, smiled and leant forward.

<hr />

After 45 minutes, Alison had to interrupt Mary, who was in full flow. 'I'm sorry Mary. I will have to stop you. I'm observing a teacher in' – she looked at her watch – 'exactly five minutes.'

'Oh my dear, I'm so sorry to have kept you. Of course, you must go. Perhaps, once you've finished, we can pick up where we left off?'

Inwardly Alison groaned. She'd been hoping to make it out of school on time today, be back for Jamie and have a meal together. 'Sure, Mary. Maybe next time we can schedule a meeting if you have a lot to discuss. Now, if you'll excuse me, I really must go.'

Letting herself out of the classroom Alison smiled. The observation had gone well, Zainab had stuck to her plan and delivered the lesson's objectives. Even at this early stage of her career, Alison could tell she was going to be a terrific teacher. The tips she'd given her for dealing with difficult pupils had worked and there was a good rapport between her and the children. Thank goodness something was going right. The feedback for the lesson was going to be a delight to deliver. Perhaps there were some upsides to this job, she thought, and started to hum a tune that had been whirling around her head all day. She caught sight of Mary in the corridor all but running towards her.

'Oh Alison. Thank goodness I've found you!'

'What on earth's the matter? You look terrible,' she said observing Mary's ashen face.

'The timing. It couldn't be worse. Oh dear, oh dear.' She clasped a hand to her mouth.

'Calm down, Mary. Talk to me.'

'They're coming. In 48 hours.' She then uttered the words that every teacher, deputy head and head dreaded.

'We have an Ofsted inspection.'

Chapter Twenty-Nine

The sound of someone crying is never nice to hear, but when it is children weeping over the loss of their pet, it is hard to bear. To know that animal is dead because of something that is somehow your fault is gut-wrenching. Claire watched from the upstairs back bedroom as Mandy's two little boys placed flowers on Smokey's burial site. She could see them being comforted by their mother. Mandy wiped a tear from her face. The loss was poignant as Smokey had been presented as a fluffy kitten, on the night their father moved out of the family home. Both parents thought it might soften the blow of the separation for the boys, though a cat is little compensation for the gap left by a father. Claire wondered if Smokey would be replaced. She'd get them a hundred cats if she could ease their pain. The evening before, Mark had done what he'd said he would, knocking on Mandy's door with his fleece acting as a shroud. He must have played his part well, because the story of Smokey's demise was not questioned in any way and Mark was thanked profusely for his kindness in returning the creature.

'Claire. I felt terrible. The wee boys were heartbroken and Mandy was so grateful. She said I was a very kind person. Kind. I'm just a liar, that's what I am.' Mark choked back tears and Claire thought he might be talking about more than the business with the cat. She put her arm around him.

'What do you think we should do next?'

'What do you mean?'

'Well, if this was a message, a warning for us in some way. How do we know something else isn't going to happen?'

'It won't,' Mark said.

'How do we know that?'

'Trust me. It's sorted.'

'So you do know who's behind it?' Claire said. 'Is it Eddie?'

'Can we just leave it? Forget it ever happened. Please.'

Claire withdrew her arm. 'If you say so.'

'I do. Anyway, we've other matters to think about.'

'Such as?'

'The gym where Jamie trains.'

'God, I'd totally forgotten about that with everything else going on. How did it go? What's the place like?'

'For starters, I wouldn't really call it a gym. It's just a large room with weights and a few running machines. There isn't even a proper changing room, just some mouldy showers and a few hooks to hang towels. The clientele is all male from what I could see, all massive, body-builder types.'

'What are the staff like?'

'There aren't any as such, just one guy and an ancient computer behind what passes for reception. What there is a lot of is all those protein drinks and powders for sale. And you were right, they cost a lot, there's no way Jamie could afford them. When I asked about how I could join, what the prices were and so on, this guy kinda looks me up and down and says that I don't look the type to use a gym.'

'That's a bit cheeky.'

'Aye, well, then he asked if I was police, because I was asking a lot of questions and being nosey. I was "requested" to leave the premises.'

'Doesn't sound like the type of place Jamie should be hanging around.'

'Definitely not. Alison can't know what it's like, there's no way she'd let him go there if she did. I think you need to have a word with her pronto.'

'Right. I've been trying to speak to her.'

'You'd better do it soon. And, while you're at it, tell her she needs to see that Ryan has nothing more to do with Jamie. He's bad news.'

'Are you serious? Jamie worships him. I do know though, that Alison says he's a bit full of himself, a know-it-all, and that she doesn't like him very much.'

'Tell her to trust her mother's instincts, that Ryan needs to be cut from their lives. Seriously, Claire. Do it.'

'Okay, okay. I'll call her today and tell her I need to speak to her, that it's important.'

'Good.' Mark flopped back against the sofa, looking relieved.

Claire let out a groan as yet again her call to Alison went straight to voicemail. She knew Alison had another phone the school had given her, but she didn't have the number for that. It was no use, she was going to have to try via the school's main switchboard. The call was promptly answered, by what sounded like a child, and Claire thought she must have misdialled for a moment. Then realising it was an adult she said, 'Could I speak to Alison Harris please.'

'Can I take your name,' the voice chirped.

'Claire Sadler.'

'One moment please.'

After what seemed an age, the voice returned. 'I'm sorry, but Mrs Harris is not available. Can I take a message?'

Frustrated, Claire said, 'Yes, can you tell her to contact me as soon as possible. Tell her it's important.' Ending the call Claire thought about her next move. Why was it so difficult getting hold of Alison? Surely now that she'd been in the job a while, things must be under control. She knew Alison's organisational skills and her ability to prioritise were excellent. Claire couldn't imagine her not getting on top of things at this stage. The school day was over, so Jamie might be at home. Perhaps she could talk to him? Warn him that Ryan wasn't a very nice person and it might be better if he found another coach. Even as she imagined the conversation, she didn't believe Jamie would agree, but it was worth a go.

Claire was popping in so often that Alison had told her not to bother ringing the doorbell and just let herself into the house with the spare key she'd long since had. Claire opened the door, treading on some post left on the mat. Scooping down to retrieve it she heard a movement in the kitchen. She went in and saw Jamie gulping down some water. At the sound of Claire, he stuffed something into his pocket, his face pink with embarrassment – or guilt? She couldn't tell.

'Hello! Just dropping off a few provisions,' she said, holding up the bag she was carrying. 'I got you some fruit and some of those nuts you like.'

Relaxing now, Jamie said, 'did you get eggs? We've run out.'

'Yes, and milk, gallons of the stuff. I got you these too.' She passed him a bag of Haribos. 'I know they're your favourites and you're allowed to eat them pre-match for an energy boost.'

Jamie eyed the bag longingly.

'But if you have a few now, I won't tell anyone.' Claire winked and Jamie tore open the sweets, stuffing them into his mouth. He took the shopping bag from Claire and as he did so she caught a glimpse of his flexed bicep. Seeing this as an opening, she said, 'Blimey, Jamie! Are you training for Mr Universe?'

He beamed and held up both arms, bending and flexing to show them to their best advantage. 'My training is really working. Great, isn't it?'

'I thought you were fine as you were.'

'Nah. I was a right weed. Now nobody messes with me.' He shoved another sweet into his mouth. 'And,' he said, chewing and talking at the same time, 'I'm so much faster on the pitch now. It's only a matter of time before a scout spots me. At least, that's what Ryan says.'

'You spend a lot of time with Ryan.'

'He's my best friend. Plus he's a really good coach. He's helped me tons, with loads of things, not just the training and stuff.'

'Wouldn't you rather have a friend your own age?' Claire asked.

'Nah, all they want to do is game. They don't have any ambitions, no discipline. Not like me. I know what it takes to get to the top.'

This is going to be harder than I thought, Claire said to herself.

Chapter Thirty

News of the Ofsted inspection spread through the staffroom and with it the dread of what was to come. It was hard to tell who was most fearful: the old-timers who'd been through and survived or those fresh into teaching. The unknown can be terrible to tussle with and those with the least experience were feeding from the negative energy which abounded. Mary was anxious and this wasn't helping with the overall confidence levels of the team. Alison found herself propping up the morale of the staff, who, given the head's aura of despair, looked to her for leadership and support. She was surprised that rather than feel pressured and stressed by the atmosphere, she seemed to gather strength from it. In previous years she'd had to follow instructions; now she was the one giving them. It felt empowering and invigorating. She wondered if she should feel guilty about this, but reasoned a man wouldn't question himself in this way and dismissed the thought. Besides, at least at work she had a level of control and people listened to her. At home, Jamie's moods continued to yo-yo, and she never knew from one moment to the next how he would react to the simplest things. Last night he'd gone berserk because she'd eaten the last banana, telling her how selfish she was and that his dietary requirements were very specific. He accused her of not taking his football aspirations seriously and once again raised the matter of attending a private football academy.

'I know if I were to go to one, I'd definitely get spotted. Ryan says they have connections to all the big teams. What are the chances of a scout seeing me playing at our grounds? Zilch. You've got to let me go.'

'It isn't a question of *letting* you go. It's the money. The fees alone are bad enough, but then if you board as well, it's sky-high. I just can't afford those kinds of sums.'

'You could re-mortgage the house?' Jamie looked at her, his eyes wide open and innocent.

'Really? That simple, hey?' Alison knew exactly who had put this idea into his head. 'Get us into heavy debt?'

'It would be an investment. When I'm earning loads as a professional, I'll buy you a massive house.'

Alison smiled at the sentiment and naivety of the statement and felt touched. His next comment shook her.

'What about Dad's insurance money?'

'What?'

'When Dad died. You must have got a big payout from his life insurance. Where's that gone? Have you spent it all?'

Now she knew this wasn't Jamie speaking; there was only one person she knew who would be this callous.

Taking a deep breath, she said, 'That's for your future.'

'*This* is my future!'

'I mean university or a deposit on a flat. I'm not going to discuss this any further, Jamie. Now if you don't mind, I have work to do.' She was thinking of all the notes on the inspection she still had to read. She was already late home and had thought being away from the school's surroundings might make all the information easier to take in. It looked like she'd got that wrong.

'You're always working! You say you love me, that you want what's best, but all you ever think about is your precious school. I might as well not be alive!' He ran upstairs.

Alison's shoulders slumped; the rant was a familiar one. She pinched the bridge of her nose with her fingers. She could feel a headache coming on; she hoped it wasn't the beginning of a migraine. Did she have any of those special tablets, just in case? Better check. She went upstairs to see. Jamie's bedroom door was ajar, she peeped in. He was sitting at the end of his bed, his head hanging down onto his chest. She tapped on the door. 'Can I come in?'

'Suppose so.'

Sitting next to him she took his hand. 'You probably don't believe me, but I love you and your brother more than anything else in the world. I know I've been away at work a lot, but it's temporary. I've just got to get through the next few weeks and then things will be back to normal. I promise.'

He took his hand away to rub his eyes. Had he been

crying? 'Yeah right.'

'I mean it.' He didn't look convinced and she tried to think of a way to cheer him up. 'Why don't you see if Ryan wants to go for a run or to the gym?' She wasn't overly keen on pushing the two of them together, they already spent an unhealthy length of time in each other's company as it was, but she was desperate to put a smile back on her son's face. The suggestion did the trick.

'Do you mean it? I've done my homework and everything.' Suddenly he was all enthusiasm.

It was amazing how galvanizing her idea had been and Jamie was out the door within ten minutes, leaving Alison to the peace and tranquillity she had craved, but which now left her feeling bereft.

※

There had been no time to wallow as Alison had to get down to her reading. During the day she'd helped Mary log in to the Ofsted provider portal and upload some pre inspection documentation. The pupils' parents had also been sent an email informing them of the date of the inspection.

'We're very lucky they've given us as much notice as they have,' Mary had said. 'I've had times when we got one day and once, they gave us 15 minutes' warning. Of course, I was a lot younger then and things didn't seem as stressful. So much hinges on the outcome of an inspection these days. Parents don't want to send their children to a school that has less than a good grade. It's a lot of pressure. I'm so glad I have you here to help me, Alison. I have to admit, I'm not sure Owen would have been up to this.'

'Talking of Owen, I was looking through the list of things that the inspectors will want to see when they arrive. One is the current improvement plan, that sets out the longer-term vision for the school. Owen was working on this,' Alison said. She knew, because he always gave this as his reason for never being available; why when he was on the premises he was locked away, not able to answer questions or observe lessons.

'Isn't it on his desktop?'

'Not that I can see,' Alison said. She'd looked in all the obvious places but had so far come up with nothing.

'Oh dear. I'll have to call him.' Mary scribbled another note to herself.

The missing improvement plan wasn't the only issue related to Owen. His lack of teacher observations was going to cause problems. The inspectors would question why none had been done. Also, why, this late in the term, a teacher/parent evening hadn't even been planned let alone carried out. As a head with many years of experience, Mary had really dropped the ball by not ensuring Owen was carrying out his duties properly. This must be why she was so uneasy, thought Alison.

Mary said, 'I can gather together most of the details required by the inspectors, but could you help with a few?'

'What do you have in mind?'

'The school timetable and current staff list are

straightforward enough, if you could see to that? And can I ask you to deal with the open cases with children's services too?'

'Okay,' Alison said, thinking the latter would require a lot of work. It was this she was now doing at home. Later she would have to read through and work on the inspection checklist for deputy headteachers. It was going to be a long evening; she doubted if she'd be going to bed before midnight.

Jamie came back while she was still working. He was in a better mood and even asked if she wanted a cup of tea. He brought it to her before going upstairs. Alison would have loved to be able to go to bed, but there was still a lot of work to be done.

※

It was one thirty in the morning and Alison was exhausted. Despite her best efforts she hadn't been able to look at everything on the checklist. Reasoning she'd do a better job of it after some sleep she decided to call it a day and go to bed. She set her alarm early and would see what she could do in the morning. She yawned and stretched, wishing the inspection were over.

Chapter Thirty-One

Claire couldn't remember how many messages and voicemails she'd left Alison in the past week – too many. She called again, not really expecting a response, and was startled when Alison answered.

'Finally! I was beginning to think you'd dropped off the planet,' Claire said. 'Haven't you seen all the messages I've sent?'

'Yes. Sorry about that. You wouldn't believe what my life has been like. We've got Ofsted coming in on Friday and with Owen out of the picture I've been rushed off my feet.'

Claire heard her exhale, she sounded tired, fed-up. 'Oh God, poor you. How come it's so busy this time?' she said, not remembering previous inspections having this effect on Alison.

'I'm acting deputy head and Owen's done such a bad job, I've had to deal with his mess before I could start on the inspection paperwork. Then there's Mary. I don't know what's going on with her, she's all over the place. It's like she's never done this before and completely forgotten the ropes. I feel as if I'm doing her job as well. Plus, the teachers are constantly coming to me with their worries.'

'Couldn't they go to someone else?'

'There *is* no one else, that's the trouble and I don't want them to feel abandoned, particularly the younger ones. It's bad enough trying to retain staff as it is. So you see, I have a good excuse for not getting back to you. I only answered this time because I'd picked up my phone to make another call and saw it was you. I can't chat for long. What did you want to talk to me about?'

Claire thought for a moment. Clearly this was not a good time to raise the matter of Jamie; Alison wouldn't be in a position to do anything yet. Telling her she had concerns about him would only worry and distract her from the job at hand. Friday was only two days away. 'It can keep. We'll talk at the weekend.'

'Is everything all right? Is Mark okay?'

'We're fine. You don't have to worry about us. I'll let you go. Ring me when you can and we'll fix a time to meet up.'

Claire pondered what to do next. She'd really wanted Alison to hear what she had to say about Ryan. She felt useless not being able to do anything directly. The phone rang, she jumped, and it fell onto her lap. Seeing it was Mark, she answered.

'Hello love. How are things?'

'Not bad, it's quiet here for once. I'm on a break so I thought I'd call and see if you'd been able to get a hold of Alison?'

'Amazingly I did, though only for a few minutes,

she's—'

'Did you tell her about Ryan? Warn her?'

'No.'

'Why on earth not, Claire?'

'Because the school have an Ofsted inspection and all hell has broken loose. Alison's up to her eyes in it and in no position to read Ryan the riot act. Better she deals with one emergency at a time. Don't you think?'

'I guess. But I'm not comfortable about it. When will the inspection be over?'

'Alison says Friday.'

'I suppose a few days won't make much difference. In the meantime, we could keep an eye on Jamie. Tell you what. My shift ends in a couple of hours. Why don't I meet you at Alison's house? We'll spend some time with Jamie, try and keep him away from Ryan.'

'Okay. I'm sure there are some chores I could do around the house for Alison. At least she won't have to go home to an unemptied dishwasher.'

'I'll see you there then. Bye.'

Claire had just finished hanging up laundry at Alison's house when the doorbell rang. She'd cleaned the bathroom and tidied up the kitchen and it felt good to be able to help out.

'Is Jamie here?' Mark asked, as she opened the door.

Claire had been going in for a kiss hello but Mark hadn't noticed and walked past her. 'Hello Claire. How are you?' Claire mimicked Mark's accent.

'Sorry love.' He kissed her and gave her a quick hug. 'Is he about?'

'No, but he should be here soon. Would you like a cuppa while you wait?'

'No thanks.'

Mark was definitely on edge and it was making her feel uncomfortable. She had the distinct impression something else was going on. 'I can message him if you want?'

'Aye. Do that.'

Jamie replied quickly to Claire's text. 'He'll be five minutes.'

'Good. Good.' Mark was pacing about.

'Mark. Will you sit down please. You're making me nervous.'

They heard the key in the door and Jamie appeared. 'Hello. You're both here.'

'Yes. Mark thought he'd keep me company. How are you, Jamie?'

'I'm okay,' Jamie said, looking in the fridge. 'No food, *again*.'

'Silly me. I didn't think to get any,' Claire said.

Jamie blushed. 'I wasn't having a go at you. It's not *your* job to feed me. Mum knows how important it is that I eat properly. She just doesn't care. All she goes on about is work.'

'Your mum has an important job to do,' Claire said.

'Aren't I important? Obviously not.' Jamie slammed the fridge door shut and helped himself to an apple from the fruit bowl.

Mark and Claire looked at each other, then Mark said. 'As the larder needs replenishing why don't we go out and stock up? Come with us, Jamie, and tell us what you need. We can go to Holmbush, to the M&S food hall, get the best. What do you say?'

'Anything I want?' Jamie asked.

'Within reason. I'm not buying you alcohol,' Mark said.

Jamie laughed. 'Don't like the stuff anyway. I'll just go and change, I don't want to wear my school uniform.'

He left, pounding up the stairs. Mark smiled. 'I thought that inducement would work.' He moved to the countertop where Jamie had left his phone. Picking it up, Mark flicked the switch to silent and pocketed it.

'What are you doing?' Claire asked.

'Slowing down Jamie's communication with Ryan. I'll hold onto this until you've spoken to Alison.'

The thumping on the stairs alerted them to Jamie's presence. 'All ready to go?' Claire said.

Jamie patted his body. 'My phone. Hang on, I'll just get it.' Coming back down, he said. 'It's not upstairs.' He looked around the kitchen. 'Have you seen my phone?'

'No,' Claire made her voice light. 'Mark?'

'No. You won't need it anyway, lad, come on now. Let's get going.'

Chapter Thirty-Two

It was Friday – D-Day – and the inspectors arrived just before 10am. There were three of them in total, one of whom, Patricia Grundy, was the lead inspector. They seemed nice enough, thought Alison as they introduced themselves. Richard was older and like a kindly uncle. Sally was a lot younger and very earnest. Alison wondered how many inspections she had done. Patricia had a capable, no-nonsense attitude but was friendly, nonetheless. Now that they were here Alison was calm. She'd done all she could; the staff just had to keep their heads and see this through. As they were a primary school, it was just one day after all, though the ramifications of a bad result would last a lot longer. Alison had been asked to attend the initial meeting, so she showed the inspectors into Mary's office and sat them down. When Mary came in Alison could see the tremor in her hand as she reached out to greet them.

Patricia began, 'I had a look at the schedule you sent and that seems fine. Do you have a group of pupils for us to speak to?'

'Yes. Alison's arranged that,' Mary said, gulping as if

to catch her breath.

'Sally is going to speak to them. Richard and I will talk with the teachers. Are they all able to attend the meeting?'

'Yes, yes. Alison has told them they all have to be there. They know when and where.'

'You've had quite a bit of input then, Alison?' Patricia asked. 'And you're not officially the deputy head?'

'No. Owen. Owen Llewelyn is away on long-term sick leave so I'm covering.'

'Alison is very capable. She is one of our most senior teachers.' Mary stumbled over her words.

'I'm sure she is,' Patricia said, smiling at Alison. There were a few more comments before she said, 'That's all for the moment. I still have things to discuss with you now, Mary, but I'll be touching base throughout the day anyway, so if you forget to mention something it doesn't matter. Perhaps Alison can show Richard and Sally to the first classes to be observed?'

'Happy to.' Alison jumped up. Mary looked at her as if she were afraid of being alone with Patricia. 'I'll see you later.' Alison gave what she hoped was a 'you'll be fine' look, and left.

The day was full on. When Alison wasn't showing the inspectors about the school, she was plying them with cups of tea and fancy biscuits. Then there were the teachers to contend with. Zainab was in tears as her troublesome pupil had decided to play up while the lesson was being observed and she had convinced herself this was the end of her fledging career. Alison had had to reassure her that the inspectors would have seen it all and it was how the teacher had handled the situation that they would be focusing on. In any case, no one teacher would be assessed and reported on. It was more holistic than that. She left Zainab sniffing as she went to check on the lunch that was being served for the inspectors, her own stomach growling. No time for her to eat just yet.

<hr />

'Do you think they'll be much longer?' Jessica, one of the teachers, asked. 'It's just I have a Pilates class at seven and I wanted to get home and sort Jim something to eat before I go.'

'I'm sure they won't be much longer,' Alison said, trying to sound upbeat. She didn't remember previous final meetings taking so long. She hoped nothing was amiss.

Brian, one of the TAs, scuttled in. 'Look sharpish, they're coming down the corridor and Mary does *not* look happy.'

Brian had a habit of being overly dramatic, so Alison didn't take much notice of him until Mary and the inspectors walked in. Mary looked terrible, her gaze teary. Alison glanced at Patricia, who seemed relaxed, certainly not like someone who was on the point of giving bad news.

When everyone was seated Patricia spoke. 'Firstly, I'd like to thank you for coming and for all the cooperation given to Richard, Sally, and me during the day. I'd like to give a special thanks to Alison for keeping us fully fuelled.' There was nervous laughter from everyone. 'I also want to comment on the excellent teaching the three of us have seen today. We've been particularly impressed with the way difficult behaviour in class was handled, not easy when you're being observed. It is very apparent that all the teachers are fully dedicated and professional. The lesson plans we have seen reflect this and you are to be congratulated. I have no doubts that all the teachers have the best interests of their students at the heart of everything they do.' She made eye-contact with several teachers, some of whom returned it confidently, while others squirmed and looked away. 'However,' she continued, 'there have been issues concerning failures in training and checking on the welfare of staff. There is also the matter of record-keeping which has not been kept fully up to date. The absence of the appointed deputy head may account for this. Be that as it may, the preliminary recommendation is that the grade of the school be changed from Good, to' – she stopped speaking and everyone in the room held their breath – 'Requires Improvement.' There was an audible gasp at this and people started talking amongst themselves. Alison looked across at Mary; she was crying. Her heart went out to her. Poor Mary, she'd been hoping the school would attain an Outstanding grade. What a blow.

Patricia held up her hand for silence. 'As I have said, this is our preliminary judgement. The school will be sent a draft report for a factual accuracy check within the next eighteen working days. There will be the option to comment on this.' There was more murmuring from everyone.

'So, the grade could change?' Jessica said. 'It's not set in stone. It could change back to Good?'

'I'd rather not comment at this juncture,' Patricia said.

The meeting ended and they started filing out. Brian said in a loud whisper to the person next to him, 'This is Owen's fault. Bloody waste of space.'

Alison was next to Patricia and could see she'd heard this. Patricia looked at Alison and said, 'Could I have a quick word with you in private?' Ducking into an empty classroom she said, 'Is there anything you would like to say to me? Anything I might add to the report?'

Alison said, 'I'm not sure I follow you.'

'Discretion is a worthy attribute, Alison, and I can understand the desire to protect a colleague. But, if I am not fully versed with the facts, I cannot give the correct recommendations. I'm sure you understand?'

Alison nodded, saying nothing.

Patricia scrutinised Alison's face, then handed her a business card. 'This has my direct email address – should you think of something you may wish to add to our findings.'

Alison took the card.

What a day. It had taken Alison the best part of two hours to extricate herself from the teachers and the multiple questions they had. Mary had crumpled at the end of the meeting and locked herself in her office. It had taken all of Alison's powers of persuasion to get her to come out. She was inconsolable and talking about retirement and needing to look after her husband. It was difficult to follow what she was saying in between her crying and clutching at Alison's hand. Now, Alison was home. She flung herself onto the sofa and slumped. The conversation she'd had with Patricia played over in her mind. Just what exactly had she been getting at? She had a fair idea, but what if she were wrong? She went over the situation in her mind, then brought out Patricia's business card. She kept flipping it over and over, trying to make a decision. Finally, she opened her laptop and began typing an email.

Chapter Thirty-Three

Claire was walking back from the train station. She'd been in London for work, one of the two days a week she spent in the office. The train had been packed so she'd had to stand for half the journey. She was glad she didn't have to do it every day like she used to and was looking forward to getting home.

Letting herself in, her feet squelched as she stepped onto the doormat. It was sopping wet and a pungent aroma hit her nostrils – petrol. She stepped back and noticed a box of matches placed on the ground by the door. Horrified she stood, looking around to see if anyone was nearby. She could see no one. Picking up the corner of the mat with her finger and thumb, she flung it onto the path. She went to pick up the box of matches, but snatched her hand back, not wanting to touch it— the police would want to examine it surely? There was no doubt in her mind that this was a direct threat and this time they would have to report it. Stepping over the threshold, giving the wet space a wide berth, she closed the door behind her and got a bucket and mop. Once she'd cleaned up, she called Mark, praying he'd answer.

She was in luck.

'Mark. Someone's been at the house!'

'What do you mean?'

'Petrol. Someone's poured petrol through the letterbox. And…'

'What? Claire, talk to me.'

She was shaking now. 'There was a box of matches left on the doorstep. Mark, I'm scared. What are we going to do?'

'I can't leave work now. Look, pack a few things and get out of there. Go to Alison's until I sort this out.'

'What about the police? Aren't we going to call them?'

'They won't be any use. I'll deal with this. Just do as I say.'

Claire went to the bedroom and pulled out a small suitcase. Shoving clothes into it carelessly, she stopped at the drawer where she kept her passport. Should she take that? She shook her head; she wasn't a criminal on the run. Stop being ridiculous, she chided herself.

Putting her case in the boot of her car, she noticed a scratch along the side of it. The car had been keyed. When had that happened? Today? She couldn't be sure. Was this connected to the petrol? She looked around again. The street was empty, but she couldn't help but feel someone was watching her. She got into the car, locking the doors, and feeling safer, sped away.

⁂

Arriving at Alison's house she was relieved to see a light

on. She didn't want to be alone right now. As Alison wasn't expecting her, she pressed the doorbell. She shifted from one foot to the other while she waited.

'You're a sight for sore eyes,' Alison said. 'I was just going to open a bottle of wine before dinner. You can help ensure I don't drink the whole lot!'

Claire couldn't speak.

'What's wrong? Are you okay?'

Shaking her head then finding her voice, Claire said, 'No. Can I stay with you for a few days?'

'Of course. Come in.'

She probably thinks Mark and I have split up, thought Claire, then as if to confirm, Alison asked, 'Have you and Mark argued?'

'No, nothing like that. It's something else.' She wasn't sure how much she should divulge until she'd spoken to Mark. 'I can't really say right now. But I do need to talk to you about something else.'

'Oh yes, I remember. We've got a lot to catch up on. Why don't you go and sit down, I'll fetch the wine.'

Sitting on the sofa, fiddling with her hands, Claire tried to gather her thoughts. Now that she had Alison's attention, how was she going to broach the subject?

'Here you go,' Alison said, handing her a glass. 'So, what did you want to talk about?'

'How did the inspection go?' Claire said, playing for time.

'Bloody awful! The school's been downgraded to "requires improvement".'

'Is that bad?'

'It's not good, especially as we'd been aiming for outstanding. Mary had put in a lot of effort since the last inspection working for that. She's in a state of shock. I had to see her home after the meeting. I didn't trust her to drive safely. The teachers aren't best pleased either. I feel like I'm the only one holding it together.'

How long will she be holding it together once I've said what I have to? Claire thought, hating the fact that she was going to heap more misery onto Alison's shoulders. Reluctant to do so just yet, she asked, 'So, what happens next? Can you appeal it?'

'Not exactly,' – Alison took a sip of wine – 'the school will get a draft report and will have the opportunity to comment on it. There is something I can do, have done, actually, that might change things in our favour.'

'About Owen and how useless he's been?'

'That, and something else. I don't want to say, it's a bit sensitive. And, if I'm wrong, well…'

They sat saying nothing until Alison broke the silence. 'Now. What is it you wanted to talk about?'

Putting down her glass, Claire looked Alison in the eye. 'Mark and I are concerned about Jamie. We think Ryan is a bad influence on him and it would be a good idea if you stopped him having contact.'

'I see,' was all Alison said. Claire chose her next words carefully.

'I know you've been distracted lately, with all that's been happening with work. You're such a good mother, but—'

'But what? I've not being paying enough attention to

my son?'

'No. No, well, maybe a bit. But Mark and I have been watching out for Jamie. It's one of the reasons I've been spending time here. Teenage boys can be vulnerable, as you know, especially when there's someone to take advantage, and with no father around I think Jamie has used Ryan as a substitute. He's looked to him for guidance because he's here on his own a lot. The thing that had alarm bells ringing for me was when he told me Ryan was his best friend. That's not right, is it? A grown man hanging out with a boy of Jamie's age all the time. Haven't you thought it strange?'

Alison was sitting rigidly, her hands clasped tightly around the stem of the wine glass. 'Yes,' she said not making eye contact. 'I have, on more than one occasion, but this is all about bloody football. Ryan feeding Jamie all this nonsense about being a professional. It was annoying but I couldn't see any real harm in it. I was hoping it would be a phase he would grow out of. Sure, he would be disappointed when it all came to nothing, but no lasting damage.'

'Hopefully not,' Claire said. 'There's something else. Mark checked out the gym where Jamie trains. I take it you haven't been there?' Alison shook her head. 'I thought not. Because from what Mark tells me it's not the sort of place a young boy should be hanging around. He told me it was seedy and had an air of criminality about it. He thinks there may be dodgy things happening there.'

'Such as?'

'I don't know.' Claire decided to be more open with her friend. 'The reason I'm here, why I want to stay with you. It's nothing to do with Mark and me experiencing difficulties. We've had some threats and although he won't tell me, I'm pretty sure it's down to someone Mark has had dealings with.'

'I don't understand. What kind of dealings? How is Mark connected to criminals? And what has that got to do with Jamie, or Ryan for that matter?'

'I don't know. If I did, I would tell you. But whatever's going on it's serious and you need to make sure Jamie finds a new best friend.'

'You think Ryan is grooming Jamie? That he's a paedophile?'

'No, nothing like that, at least I don't think so. Maybe it's drugs. I really don't know.'

'How could all this be happening under my nose, and I haven't noticed? And of course you're right. I need to stop Jamie seeing Ryan. I've known that for some time, if I'm honest. I suppose I was just hoping my gut feeling was wrong. This can't have been easy for you. Thank you for telling me. The question now is how do I do this? If I ban Jamie from seeing Ryan, and playing football, he's going to want an explanation. Whatever I tell him, he's more likely to believe Ryan's version than mine. Then I run the risk of Ryan exerting even more influence over Jamie than he already does.'

'We've thought much the same,' Claire said, 'and we've come up with a plan.'

Chapter Thirty-Four

As it turned out, Claire didn't stay at Alison's house longer than a night. She'd been working at Alison's kitchen table when a message came through on her phone from Mark.

Everything sorted, you have nothing to be worried about anymore. Come home.
I love you. X

Brief and to the point. Claire dashed out a note for Alison and stuck it to the fridge. She packed up her few belongings and headed home. Once there, Mark was waiting and he kissed her hello. 'It's good to have you home,' he said.

Claire noted that in her absence he'd been busy. He'd cleaned, although his attempts to eradicate the petrol smell hadn't quite worked and an odour persisted. It was doing battle with the heavy perfume of lilies, a bouquet of which were on display in the living room.

'The place is looking nice,' she said. 'Your message said everything was sorted. What does that mean exactly?'

'It means the people, the person who killed Smokey and poured petrol through the letter box, are never going to trouble us again.'

'How can you be sure of that?'

'I'm sure. You don't have to worry.'

'You haven't done anything stupid, have you, Mark?' All sorts of thoughts ran through Claire's mind.

He came over to her, wrapping his arms around her. She heard him inhaling her scent and he spoke into her hair. 'I would do anything for you, Claire. Anything. You mean the world to me.'

This did not answer her question nor reassure her. She dreaded to think what Mark might be involved in. What had he done to ensure her safety?

※

Claire was working from home and Mark had the day off, which was just as well because he hadn't slept much during the night. She'd woken and he wasn't in bed. When she got up hours later, she found him downstairs staring into space, a cold, undrunk cup of coffee in front of him. He jumped when he saw her.

'Penny for your thoughts?' she'd asked him.

'What?'

'You were miles away? Do you have any plans today?'

'No. I'll stay home. Is there anything you want doing around the house?'

Claire said, 'Not really, you've done all the housework already. If you want something to do you could go to the supermarket.'

'I'd rather stay with you,' he said.

'Why?' Then it dawned on her. Mark was still worried about leaving her on her own. Would this never end? 'Don't you think I'm safe here on my own? Is that it? Because if it is, your solution, whatever that was, hasn't worked.'

'No, we shouldn't be bothered again. I'm just edgy, that's all. I need to get out of the house. Can I take your car? Think I'll go for a walk on the Downs, get some fresh air, clear my head.'

'Good idea and yes, take the car, I won't be needing it. I'll put a few hours' work in and maybe we could go out for lunch somewhere. What do you think?'

'Sounds good. It'll be nice to spend some time together, try and relax.'

※

With Mark gone Claire settled down to work. She had a few phone calls to make and a mid-morning Zoom meeting, so the time passed quickly. She was grateful to be busy. Ever since her encounter with Eddie she'd been on her guard, and it was mentally exhausting. She hoped now things would be better. At least, even with all that had been going on, Mark's treatment for his addiction was going well. He attended his meetings and had also opted to go for private counselling, which he said was helping him a lot. He spoke to her at length about what was said in these sessions and she felt she was getting to know a whole new side of him. While she waited for her meeting to start, she looked down at the ring on her left hand. Maybe now she could allow herself the luxury of planning the wedding and their lives together. Moving home was a big part of that and after the petrol incident she was keen to make it sooner than later. Her house, which she'd always loved, now felt tainted and she wanted nothing more than to leave and start afresh. She would raise the matter with Mark at lunchtime. Her computer bleeped; the meeting was starting.

Mark was back by midday. 'I'm home,' he hollered up the stairs. He took off his shoes and padded into the living room.

'Hiya. Did the walk help?' Claire asked as she kissed him.

'Yes, it did, although it's awful muddy up there. It'll be all that rain from last week. Are you still up for lunch out?'

'Absolutely, I've been looking forward to it. I thought we could go to the Perch on Lancing Green.'

'Really? It's always packed there, you can never get a seat.'

'That's because we've only been at the weekend. It should be fine at this time of day, midweek.'

Claire's assertion was wrong, however; just as they arrived the heavens opened and the multitudes descended, seeking shelter. The place was packed, the floor wet with footprints and soaked dogs, of which there were many. 'We should have booked ahead. I'll go and speak to a waitress and see if a table's available.'

Mark grunted a response, which Claire didn't catch.

She came back to him. 'We're in luck, some people are leaving.' Mark followed her and she heard him curse as he tripped over a dog lead. The route to the table was an assault course of buggies, small children and animals. It made Claire want to laugh, but she could tell Mark wasn't seeing the funny side of it. When they made it to their table he said, 'Jesus Christ, it's like a zoo in here. Is it half term or something?'

'No,' Claire said, looking about her. 'All the kids here are pre-school.'

'And why does everyone have a dog?'

'It's a dog-friendly restaurant. I think it's nice.'

'Hmm. The cockerpoo dog shop must be making loads of money,' Mark said, scowling at a nearby pooch who was straining to greet him, its tail wagging.

'Bit grumpy, are we? I thought you liked dogs?'

'I do. I dunno what's with me. Maybe it's this weather.' As if to emphasise his point a gust of wind buffeted the window next to them, bringing with it lashings of rain. 'I miss the sunshine, being able to plan a day out and not needing to take several changes of outfit with you. I'm fed up looking at grey skies all the time, it's depressing. Don't you think so?'

Claire shrugged. 'I suppose I'm used to it. If you want the sun, it's only a two-hour plane journey away.'

'But what if it was just outside your door? Wouldn't that be better?'

'What do you mean?'

'I mean leaving all this behind,' – he gestured to the sky – 'being somewhere warm and sunny.'

'You're talking about Spain? Moving to Spain?' When she had thought of moving, she hadn't considered going abroad. Then she remembered what Mark's mother had asked her and she wondered if he had expressed a desire to return to Spain. Why hadn't he brought it up before now?

'Why not? I could walk back into my old job. Only the other day one of my old colleagues emailed me and told me they were short-staffed. And with your Irish passport you'd have no problems applying for residency.'

'What about my job?'

'You spend most of your time working from home. You could do that in Spain. All you'd need would be an internet connection.'

'That's not quite true. I do have to go into the office a few times a week. It's not like I could commute from Spain.'

'I'm sure you could come to some arrangement with your boss. They love you there. I'd bet they'd bend over backwards to find a way of keeping you.' He grabbed her hand. 'Imagine it, love. We could get a lovely villa over there, have a pool, really live life instead of just existing.'

'Is that how you see your life here? I thought you were happy.'

'I'm happy with you, but…If I'm honest I haven't settled at my job. I don't get on with my boss. I don't particularly enjoy the work I do here and I don't like my colleagues much either. Maybe that's why I started gambling again.'

'I had no idea this was how you felt. Why haven't you said something before now?'

'I think it's only just dawned on me. I was so pleased to be with you full-time, it eclipsed everything else. During my therapy sessions things came to light that made me realise I just don't enjoy being away from Spain. I've spent the majority of my adult life there. I miss it, plain and simple.'

Chapter Thirty-Five

'Congratulations, I thought this was on the cards,' Stuart, Claire's brother, said. She had rung him to tell him that she and Mark were engaged.

'Yeah, I could tell by the way he looked at you. And you, I don't think I've ever seen you so dewy-eyed. I told Julia wedding bells were imminent.'

'Clever old you,' Claire laughed. It was good to speak with her brother like this. Their relationship hadn't always been easy but had taken a turn for the better in the recent past. 'We're not planning to marry for a while yet, we want to move house first,' – Claire didn't say that this plan now took on new connotations, – 'so we thought it might be nice to have an engagement party. Nothing too big, just a few friends and family round for drinks and something to eat. We were thinking of Saturday week. Would you all be free?' She heard Stuart whistle through his teeth.

'I don't know about all of us. It's a long way to come down for the weekend. The kids have all their schoolwork to think about, not to mention all their extra-curricular activities. I swear they have a better social life than me and Julia. She's swamped with work; I think it would be too much to organise.'

Claire's heart sank, 'That's a shame. We could reschedule?'

'No. Don't do that for us. I'll come on my own.'

'Really?' Claire's voice lifted.

'Of course! I'll get the train down. I'll probably only be able to stay the one night though.'

'That's fine. I'll be glad to see you. Perhaps we could do a Zoom meeting with Julia and the children while you're here too?'

'I don't see why not. Look I'd better go. Message me the details and we'll talk again nearer the time.'

Claire ticked off Stuart's name from her 'people to ring' list and called the next person on it – Alison.

'Hi there. How are you?'

'Surviving. As you can imagine, the fallout from the inspection is pretty bad. The atmosphere in the staffroom is subdued. Mary is guilt-ridden about the appointment of Owen, although it's good she's acknowledged his incompetence. I was getting sick of her thinking the light shone out of his you-know-what. And there's still a possibility of the grade being changed.'

'How's that then?'

'After the final meeting, the chief inspector spoke to me. She gave me the impression that she knew many of the issues could be traced back to Owen not carrying out his duties effectively. She pretty much asked me to dish the dirt on him and implied if I did so, it could help. I did just that. I sent her a long email, detailing his conduct; what he was and wasn't doing. I also told her of my suspicions that he was lying about his illness. I was wary of doing that, but in the end, I felt I should. There's something else, I didn't mention it in my email and I'm not sure if that was the right thing to do.'

'About Owen?' Claire wondered what else he could be accused of.

'No. Mary. After the inspection she kind of lost it. Remember? I had to see her home because I was so worried about her. I went into the house, the state of the place, it was awful, like no one had done any housework for a long time. It transpires her husband had been diagnosed with Alzheimer's some time ago but has recently deteriorated. She's been struggling to look after him and run the school. When Owen was hired, she thought he was this bright young thing who would be more than adept in his role. It would appear he was very good at portraying himself as this professional, capable person, qualified to the hilt and the answer to everyone's prayers. The posh accent and the expensive clothes helped with that image. He fooled more than one person. It's a pity Patricia Grundy never met him. He wouldn't have been able to pull the wool over her eyes.'

'He didn't deceive you either, did he? Nor the teachers, from what you've said.'

'I guess. It's just a shame no one in authority noticed before it got to this.'

'Let's hope your email helps.'

'Fingers crossed,' Alison said.

'How's Jamie?'

'He hates me at the moment. I've stopped him going to the gym to train.'

'Bet that went down well.'

'He was *not* happy. Added to that he's lost his phone and accused me of taking it. I've also stopped Ryan giving him a lift to and from football matches. I'm doing that now. Of course, Jamie didn't much like that, but I told him it was either that or no football at all. It's been slamming doors and the silent treatment ever since.'

'I don't suppose he took kindly to you taking him to football instead of Ryan.' Claire didn't mention Jamie's phone.

'No, he didn't. The trouble is, it takes a chunk out of my Saturdays when I could be doing other things, but I have to live with it.'

'Mark or I could take him if you like?'

'Really? Gosh, that would be great if you could do it now and again.'

'We've also got a plan to get you back into Jamie's good books.'

'I'd love to hear it,' Alison said.

Claire explained what she had in mind and asked if Alison was happy with the idea. She was delighted and couldn't wait to tell Jamie.

'Wait until Saturday when we pick him up. We'll tell him together.'

When Jamie came downstairs on Saturday morning, his mum, Mark and Claire were assembled in the living room.

'What's going on?' he said, eyeing them with suspicion.

'Claire and Mark have something they want to discuss with you.'

'But first, let me give you this back,' Mark said, holding out a phone.

'My phone!' Jamie grabbed it. 'Where did you find this? I've been looking for it for ages.'

'I took it,' Mark said.

'You took it?' Jamie looked at his mum.

Alison held her hands up. 'Nothing to do with me. I've only just found out. And, I have to say, it's been very nice not having you glued to it when you're in my presence – not that that's been happening lately.'

'But why?' Jamie looked at Mark.

'To stop you contacting Ryan.'

'You have no right to do that! Stealing my property. I'll tell the police.' Jamie was incandescent.

'I didn't steal it. You have it now, don't you? It was the only way I could think to try to break some contact with that man. I know you won't want to hear this, Jamie lad, but he's bad news. You need to stay clear away from him. You think he's your friend, but he's not. Take it from one who knows. If you don't want to listen to your mother, listen to me, to Claire.'

Claire nodded. 'He's right, Jamie. You should have friends your own age.' She saw the anguish on Jamie's face as he tried to process what they were saying. 'I know this is difficult for you, but we've come up with an idea that might make it easier for you to adjust. We recognise that as well as football training and matches, you want to go to the gym. So Mark has arranged for you to have membership at the one he goes to. It's pretty fancy, we think you'll like it, and they have a special under 18s membership. You'll be able to train with people your own age under proper supervision.'

Jamie started to look interested, then said, 'But Mum won't be able to afford that, she won't let me go.'

'We're all chipping in, the three of us. And your mother is more than happy for you to go,' Claire said.

'The only sticking point,' Mark said, 'aside from you agreeing, is that as a minor you have to have a guardian on the premises while you train.'

'Well that's not going to work. Mum will never have the time to go there.'

'You're right,' Alison said. 'That's why Mark will go with you.'

'We'll just have to work things out in advance, around my shifts and that.'

'And at a push,' Claire said, 'as the gym is affiliated to the Aquarium, I can always go when Mark can't.'

'So Jamie. What do you think?' Alison asked. 'Are you going to take us up on our offer?'

Jamie looked at them, and grinned.

Chapter Thirty-Six

'I've brought you some tea, Mary.' Alison placed the cup and saucer on the table next to her. She covered the older woman's liver-spotted hand with her own. 'Please try not to be so upset.' It was the third time Alison had had to comfort her boss in the past week. Now that Mary had told her a little of what was going on at home, Alison was able to understand why her mind hadn't been on the job. Mary and her husband didn't have children or relatives who lived nearby to support them. It horrified Alison to think of having to cope with a situation like this alone. Up to this point Mary believed that a carer coming in once a day to help out would be sufficient. It was evident this was not the case.

'Thank you my dear. So kind.' She wiped her eyes and stuffed her tissue up the arm of her sleeve. 'I'm a nuisance, no help to you at all. You're such an asset to the school. I don't know what I was thinking not insisting you be made deputy head. I was a fool to even entertain the notion of employing Owen, for being swayed by that posh accent – as if that somehow qualified him to be a leader! My father would be ashamed of me.'

'How so?'

'I come from humble roots. My father was a coal miner, a union leader. Such a good man. I was the first girl in the family to go to university. He was proud of that, but I know he worried.'

'In what way?' Alison was interested, she knew next to nothing about Mary. Her genteel manner didn't give away much.

'He was worried I'd be embarrassed by my roots, that mixing with "posh" people would make me forget where I'd come from. And I'm ashamed to say for a while it was true. It wasn't until I met Michael in my final year that it changed. He was from a similar background, but unlike me he would boast about being the first person in his family to go to university. He'd brag about his dad being heavily involved with the unions. He made me see things very differently.'

'You've been together a long time then.'

'Yes, and now there are days when he doesn't even know who I am. He gets so angry. In all the years we've been together he's never raised his voice to me, not once. Yesterday he…he' – she took a moment to compose herself – 'he threw his plate at me, his dinner went everywhere, and the language he used. I hope you never have to see someone you care about suffer from this terrible disease. Sometimes I wish he would die.' She looked at Alison, her eyes brimming. 'What kind of person am I, wishing for that?'

Mary's declaration had disturbed Alison and she found it hard to shake the immense sadness it had stirred within her. For now, however, there was little time for sentiment. For all intents and purposes, she had the roles of headteacher as well as deputy head and she needed to focus. The first thing on her agenda was to raise the morale of the teachers. Without them on board there was no way the school would be able to recover from this, in any shape or form. It was a week since the inspection, time to move forward. She was confident her initial email would at least bring into question the grading. She had procrastinated whether to make Mary's personal situation known, but in the end had written a private email to Patricia Grundy. She felt guilty about this; although Mary hadn't been explicit, the implication was that their conversation had been spoken in confidence. She hoped that if it all came to light, Mary wouldn't see this as a betrayal. Alison's faith that all was not lost, and the reasons why, could not be divulged to the staff, so she had something else planned to cheer them up.

The teachers and teaching assistants had been called to the school hall, a large room with a small, raised stage framed by curtains. Everyone had assumed it was going to be another dissection of the inspection and had dragged their heels, complaining it was a Friday and they wanted to go home. Chairs and tables were dotted around, and people sat. Alison stood at the lectern and the staff braced themselves for what looked like was going to be a serious talk.

She took a deep breath and smiled. 'Hello everyone. Thanks so much for coming.'

'How long's this going to take?' Brian asked. 'Do TAs have to get involved in meetings about inspections?'

'I don't know about the rest of you, but I'm a bit sick of all this talk. The past week has been worse than working in the bank,' Lydia said. She was a teacher in her 40s whose former life had been as a high-flying banker. She'd left so she could do something more meaningful.

'That's because you care,' Alison said to her. She looked at those gathered. 'You all care. That's why you feel so terrible. You are a tremendous group of teachers and TAs. Each and every one of you is dedicated and does their job wonderfully. I mean it, everyone in this school puts their heart and soul into their work.'

'Everyone but that sorry excuse they hired as deputy head,' shouted Brian. There was a babbling of 'here, here!'

It was all Alison could do not to agree and she waited until they had quietened. 'We're not here to apportion blame, or to grumble, or to talk about the inspection,' – she went to the side of the stage and opened the curtains to reveal several trestle tables laden with food and drink – 'we're here to party. Because we're bloody good educators and we deserve to have some fun! And I don't want you to hold back and worry about drinking and driving. I've pre-ordered a mini coach to come at a time of our choosing, to get everyone home safely.

Now, all we need is some music. Can anyone oblige?'

There was a moment of stunned silence before Zainab squealed, 'I can!'

'Well, come and hook it up to the sound system. And the rest of you. What are you waiting for?' Alison said, indicating the drinks.

'I don't need to be told twice,' Brian said in a considerably better mood. Others followed his lead. The music started; the party had begun.

⁂

Some hours later, things were in full swing and showed no signs of abating. The stress and strain of the past couple of weeks were not forgotten but held at bay. Several of the teachers had thanked Alison. More than one had said Owen should be sacked and Alison replace him. Alison had been reticent about this. Getting rid of Owen was going to be a long, drawn-out process which she didn't want to contemplate.

Mary hadn't been able to stay for very long but had told Alison she would pop back once her husband's carer arrived. She appeared now at Alison's side, whispering in her ear.

'I've had a telephone call from Owen. He's resigned.'

Chapter Thirty-Seven

'Stuart's just taking out the quiches from the oven. He's a dab hand in the kitchen, isn't he? He made those from scratch, you know. I'm dead impressed,' Mark said.

'Yes, he and Julia try not to buy any ready-made food. With Julia being a food nutritionist and Stuart a nurse, they're aware of the dangers of eating too much processed food. They want to lead by example for their children,' Claire said.

'Very commendable. I should be the same, but I do love a pizza and after a day's work the last thing I feel like doing is cooking.' He looked at the buffet laid out in the living room. 'Looks nice. What time do you think everyone will arrive?'

'I said from seven, a bit early I know, but I don't think people will want a particularly late night as some of them are travelling quite far. It's a gathering more than a party. Alison said she and Jamie will get here a bit earlier to help with setting up, but to be honest there's nothing really for them to do, not with super-cook Stuart here.'

'Do I hear my name being taken in vain?' Stuart appeared in the doorway, carrying a bottle.

'I was singing your praises actually.' Claire glanced at the bottle.

Stuart got the message. 'Thought we deserved a glass before the guests arrived.' Just as he said this the doorbell rang. 'Too late! I'll get that.'

They could hear him welcoming Alison, and she and Jamie came in. 'Hi there,' Alison said and kissed Claire then Mark. She'd brought with her the cold air of outside. December was making itself known in terms of the weather.

'God, your hands are freezing!' Claire said.

'Yes. We walked here, it seemed a good idea at the time but I'm not so sure now.'

'You'll be wanting a nice hot cup of tea then instead of champagne,' Mark said.

'Let's not be silly,' Alison said, 'no need for such extremes! I'll stand by the radiator and heat up while I drink.'

'How are you doing, Jamie?' Mark asked. 'Recovered from your training session today?' Jamie had confessed to him earlier, when they'd been at the gym, that the personal trainer had really put them through their paces.

'Yeah. It was tough, but I enjoyed it.'

'How are you finding the new gym?' Claire asked.

'I like the sessions; the trainer has given me loads of tips and shows me how to use all the equipment. You get paired with another person and help each other. It's good working out with someone my own age.'

'You're going to the cinema with one of them, aren't you? What's his name, Ishir?'

'Ishaan,' Jamie corrected.

'Sounds like it's all working out well,' Claire said to Alison when they'd moved to the kitchen.

'I can't tell you how relieved I am that I've got him away from the clutches of Ryan. It's good he's mixing with boys his own age. He really likes Mark too.'

'Mark's grown fond of him as well. I think he's relieved he's found someone he can talk about football to, I'm no use!' There was a knock at the door. 'I'd better get that.'

Guests arrived over the course of the next half hour. There was a mini reunion of the swimming holiday Claire and Alison had been on. Debbie and Alan came laden with flowers, then Nisha and her husband, who'd gifted them a vase. Ben was last, he'd brought with him a girl he was seeing. The swimmers reminisced about the positive elements of the holiday and by tacit agreement the darker aspects were omitted. There was a convivial atmosphere to the event and Claire was glad they had chosen to keep it intimate. She said as much to Mark.

'This is nice. I feel like I can relax and be myself, rather than flitting about attending to guests' needs.' She thought back to her previous engagement party and the hassle of keeping bickering relatives apart. No, this was much better. She put her arm around Mark's waist. 'I love you, Doctor Fraser.'

He leant down and kissed her. 'And I love you, Ms Sadler.'

'Get a room!' Stuart shouted, then tapped on the side of his glass. 'A bit of hush please. Man trying to make a toast here. I won't ramble on. I just wanted to say how happy I am for my sister and Mark. They make a great couple and it's obvious for anyone with eyes how much they love each other. When Claire told me she was going to marry a doctor I thought that's great, we were missing one of those in our family of health workers, although we all know that nurses know far more about their patients than the doctors,' – he winked at Mark, who shook his head in mock outrage – 'and Mark is the missing part of the puzzle in Claire's life and I'm so glad for her. So, let's toast them.' He lifted his glass and said, 'The missing part of the puzzle.'

People were seated, eating goodies from the table and there was much praise for Stuart's cooking. Nisha was very impressed.

'You must give me the recipe for this dip, it's delicious,' she said, scooping up a dollop with a breadstick.

'There's loads left,' Claire said. 'I'll put some in Tupperware and you can take it home. I'll do it now in case I forget.'

Nisha followed her into the kitchen. 'I need a glass of water,' she said. 'It's nice to meet up like this outside of swim club. We should do it more often. We'll have to have a pre-Christmas do at our place.'

'That would be nice. Maybe you could tempt Oliver and Sophie to that,' Claire said.

There was a thud on the front door.

'Who can that be?' Claire wondered if it was Mandy. She hadn't invited her because she still felt guilty about Smokey and didn't want to be reminded of it tonight.

'I'll get it!' ever-eager Ben shouted over the din of music and laughter coming from the living room.

Claire heard a man shouting, the hubbub of talking had stopped. Going to see what was happening, she found Mark nose to nose with Ryan.

'I told you. Get lost. You're not wanted here!'

Neither man was backing down and there was a nervous hush. Not knowing what was going on, the group stood by wordlessly. Only Alison moved forward. 'I think you should go, Ryan. Please.'

'You'd like that, wouldn't you? For me to just disappear, like I was nothing. You. You think you're so much better than me.' He looked at Jamie. 'Take my advice. Get away from her clutches as soon as you can. She's a control freak who will ruin your life. You should have stuck with me. I would have seen your dreams come true. It's never going to happen now.' He spat out the final words.

Visibly shaken, Alison shrunk away from him and clutched Jamie to her.

'Right. That's enough!' Mark grabbed Ryan and manhandled him outside into the cold night. Ryan said something to Mark which no one else could hear, but it was provocative enough to induce him to raise his fist at Ryan. The others, seeing what had happened, moved forward and Stuart held onto Mark's arm.

Mark tried to shrug off his grip, but Stuart wouldn't

let go and said, 'Don't. I don't know what's going on here, but don't.' He looked about him; a few neighbours were leaning out of windows or at their front doors to see what the commotion was about. 'You've got a street full of witnesses and whatever your history with this bloke is, all they're looking at is a fight about to happen. You would have too much to lose. You know that.'

This calmed Mark and he nodded.

'Yeah, you're right.' He straightened.

Mark retreated and Ryan walked away, looking backwards towards them. Pure contempt on his face. In the darkness he tripped and fell, hitting his face on the gravel path. Jumping up he clutched his nose, blood streaming from it. 'You bastard! I'll get you for this. You'll see. You all think so much of your precious Jamie. Well, I know him, I can get to him. I know people. You'll be sorry.' He stumbled away.

Claire heard Mark shouting, 'Yeah yeah. Get lost, you piece of filth.' He turned and saw her watching. She'd never seen this side of him. Just how well did she know the man she'd agreed to marry? She felt her face crumple; the evening was ruined. As she ran inside she heard her brother say, 'One hell of a party.'

Chapter Thirty-Eight

No matter how much she begged him, Mark would not disclose the nature of Ryan's comment to him on the night of the party. Whatever had incensed him to such rage remained a secret. He was also spending an increasing amount of time out of the house. When Claire asked him where he had been he would offer a vague explanation of 'out walking' or 'driving' and she worried that he might have started gambling again.

'Please, Mark. Talk to me. Whatever Ryan said to you must have been bad for you to react in the way you did. I dread to think what would have happened if Stuart hadn't held you back. As it is we're lucky Ryan didn't report you to the police.'

'He wouldn't dare. He's no innocent. The last thing he wants is the police sniffing around.' His phone bleeped with a message and he turned away from Claire to read it. She hurt him tutting. 'I've got to go out.'

'Where to? Let me guess, "a walk".' Claire said.

'No. The gym. A bloke I met there suggested we work out together last time I was there. I gave him my contact details, that was him just now.'

'But you have to go into work soon.'

'I've got time for a quick workout beforehand. I'll go to the hospital straight after.' His abrupt departure didn't allow for any more discussion and Claire was left alone. Biting her thumbnail, she fretted. Was Mark gambling again? He was certainly acting oddly. Pacing about the house until she could stand her own company no longer, she rang Alison.

'Can I come over? Maybe stay the night?'

'Of course you can. Is everything all right?'

'Not really. I'll talk about it when I get to yours.'

※

'I brought cake.' Claire held up the box of pastries she'd procured from the expensive bakery at the end of the street where Alison lived.

'Oh dear. Things must be bad if you're reverting to cake to make you feel better,' Alison said. 'Come in. I'll make us a coffee.'

Once inside, Claire sat at the table, her shoulders hunched. She fiddled with the lid of the cake box, but didn't open it.

Alison eyed her whilst she made the drinks. 'So, do you want to tell me about it?'

'It's Mark.'

'I thought it might be. Have you got to the bottom of what went on with Ryan?'

'No. He's clammed up and won't tell me a thing. Worse, he keeps going out at funny times and won't tell me where he's going or who he's meeting. Today for example, he gave me some cock-and-bull story about having arranged to train with some unknown bloke at the gym. It's so obviously untrue, yet he expects me to swallow it. I'm worried he's gambling again.'

'Do you have any evidence he is?'

'No, not really. Just constant messages that come through and skulking in corners whispering down the phone. I can't keep challenging him all the time, it's driving me nuts.'

'I'm off now, Mum,' Jamie's voice could be heard from the hallway.

'Where are you going?' Alison asked.

'I'm meeting Ishaan in town. We're going to the bubble tea bar to hang out.'

'Again with the bubble tea?'

'It's nice, you should try it.'

'Judging how much of it you consume it must be. Still, better than that Red Bull rubbish, I suppose. How are you feeling?'

'A bit better.'

'Well, don't be too late back.'

'Nah. See you later. Bye Claire.'

'What's the matter with Jamie then?' Claire asked.

'I don't really know. He's had this rash, only it's not really a rash. He's been complaining of his skin being itchy, like it's burning. He's been very low too, and sleepy. I think he might be coming down with something.'

'Has he been like that for long?'

'A while. I should have taken him to the doctor's

before now, but you know how it's been. I've got an appointment for him, but it's not until next week. I couldn't get one any sooner as it wasn't deemed an emergency.'

'But he's fine, other than that?'

'We're not arguing all the time, if that's what you mean. And I feel much better about his friendship choices now. I met this Ishaan, he's a nice boy. Very polite and quietly spoken. I think he's going to be a good influence on Jamie.'

'That's a relief. At least that's one thing you don't have to be worried about,' Claire said.

'Until the next problem rears its ugly head,' she sighed. 'When did life get so complicated?'

'Tell me about it. Just when you think you've got your life on track, something else happens. My head feels as if it's going to explode going over and over everything. I can't switch off. That's why I wanted to stay with you. I didn't want to be left alone with my thoughts any longer.'

'I understand. And you're welcome to stay as long as you like.'

'Just the one night will be fine, thanks. Do you fancy going to the Aquarium for a swim, then lolling about in the jacuzzi after? Swimming always helps me feel better.'

'Yes, why not. I'll grab my stuff and we'll go. When we get back we can binge watch a box set.'

⁓

The swimming and Alison's company helped. Claire

slept well, despite the rickety nature of the bed in the spare room. It was good to have a bolt hole and even better to have another woman to talk to. She couldn't contemplate not having her friend nearby.

'You're still here?' Claire was surprised to see Alison when she went downstairs.

'Yep. I decided I had to force myself into more regular hours as far as work was concerned. There's no way I could have carried on the way I was, I would have put myself into an early grave or had a breakdown. It's strange though, that throughout all that's happened, I haven't felt stressed. I was trying to pinpoint what exactly it was. Then it occurred to me that I am energised by the role I've had. I think it's because I've got more autonomy, that I can direct the nature of my work. And the strangest part of it all is that I don't miss the teaching side of things. It's been so much a part of me for so long, I could never have imagined not doing it. I find I like mentoring the teachers, giving them the benefit of my experience in an official capacity. I've been thinking about my future and I've come to a decision.'

'What's that, then?' Claire asked.

'I'm definitely going to apply for the deputy head role. Looking back, I don't know why I had the doubts I did. And I know I can do a far better job at it than Owen. Not only that. I have the backing of my teachers. One of my previous fears was that they would be resentful having a boss who was a former colleague. Now I know that wouldn't be an issue, it's emboldened me to go for it.'

Chapter Thirty-Nine

'Please Claire, I'm begging you. Come home.' The distress in Mark's voice was difficult to hear. Claire closed her eyes.

'I was on my way. I said in my note it was only for a night. I needed some space. Someone to talk to.'

'You can talk to me,' Mark said.

'No. I can't. You keep fobbing me off whenever I try to. And I know you're lying to me.'

'I'm—'

'Let's not get into this on the phone. I'll be home soon. When do you start work?'

'In a few hours.'

'Okay then. I'll see you in a bit.'

Claire spied more flowers about the house when she arrived. 'We're going to need some more vases if you keep on like this.' She meant it as a joke, but it came out sounding snarky.

'I wanted to do something nice for you, that's all.'

'They're lovely, but I'd much rather have an honest conversation than a bunch of flowers.'

'Fair enough. Let's do it.'

'All right then. Answer me honestly; are you gambling again?'

'Direct and to the point,' Mark said, his features drawn and tired. 'No.'

'Be honest with me. If you've had a relapse, I can cope with that. What I can't cope with is being lied to.'

'I'm not lying. I am not gambling. On my life, I'm not. I went to a meeting yesterday evening, if you must know.'

'Were you having a wobble?'

'Not exactly, I thought it would be a good use of my time. I was going mad thinking you'd left me. You weren't picking up your phone or answering my messages.'

'Alison and I went swimming. And my phone wasn't on. To be frank I wanted a break, to switch off and do something normal. Not think about gambling or dodgy people you're connected to. This is not who I am.'

'It's not me either. I could kick myself for getting mixed up with Eddie. It's the most stupid thing I've ever done in my life, and my biggest regret. If I could turn the clock back…'

'Well, you can't, so we have to make the best of it and move on. Will you do something for me?'

'Anything. I'd do anything for you, Claire. Seriously, give up my life, even kill someone to protect you.'

Claire shuddered, thinking it was an odd thing to say. 'Do I need protecting?'

'No. You're safe. I've seen to that. It's best you don't know more than you have to. But it's over. We can make a fresh start. What do you say?'

Claire considered what he had told her. His declarations seemed genuine and she wanted nothing more than to forget the incidents that had gone before. 'Okay then. A fresh start. I do have one condition though, well, two really.'

'Name them.'

'You have to. Have to. Tell me if you have any run-ins with Eddie, no matter how insignificant they may be. If he turns up in your life again then it's better I know. I don't want to be surprised with an unforeseen encounter.'

'Done. What else?'

'We get out of this house. Sell up. Now. I don't think I will ever feel truly safe here again, knowing that Eddie could appear at any time.'

'Fine.'

'I'm talking immediately, calling an estate agent today for a valuation and putting the house on the market as soon as possible. Even renting somewhere else if it doesn't sell soon.'

'I've no problem with that. I'll help in any way I can.'

'Good,' Claire said. The prospect of moving did make her feel better, safer. They'd have to decide just how far away they wanted to be.

'I've told the estate agent I don't want them to put a For Sale board up outside the house. The last thing we want is for certain people to get wind of the fact we're on the move,' Claire said.

'I agree. That's a smart idea. Was the agent okay about that?'

'Not really. Not until I told him I was willing to put the place up for considerably less than he'd recommended. He gets less commission, but he gets it quickly. It's all about turnover with these guys. Sell as quickly as possible then onto the next punter. He's already got a couple of viewings planned for the weekend. He suggested an open house, but I thought it would draw too much attention so I declined.'

'Sounds as if we'll be out of here soon.'

'Yes. Which means we need to discuss where we're going to move to. How far will we need to go to be outside of Eddie and his colleagues' orbit? Going inland to Surrey would be too expensive. Besides, I want to stay by the coast, so I was thinking Chichester or Portsmouth. In terms of you commuting to work, they would be practical enough although you'd definitely have to get a car. What do you reckon?'

'What about my suggestion to go to Spain? Have you given that any more consideration?'

Claire was afraid he was going to raise this. She *had* thought about it, but aside from what to do about her job, she had a number of other misgivings. It wasn't easy to settle in a foreign country; there was all the bureaucracy to contend with, not to mention the cultural aspects to consider. She'd have to put in an enormous effort to bring her basic Spanish up to scratch too and she wasn't sure she was up to the task. Practicalities aside, she really didn't like the idea of being so far away from Alison. She realised Mark was unlikely to grasp this as a reason for not wanting to relocate. How could Claire describe her bond with Alison? To say this to Mark was bound to hurt his feelings and he wouldn't understand – she wasn't sure she did fully. Mark was looking at her, waiting for her answer. 'I have given it a lot of thought, and I can't, Mark. I'm sorry. I like Spain – for holidays. And I can't pretend it wouldn't be great to live in a place where the weather was sunny and warm. For better or worse, England is my home.'

'I see.' Mark sighed. 'I always thought it was a long shot. We'd better start investigating those places you mentioned. See what's available.' He sounded so crushed that Claire almost relented, but she stopped herself from doing so, knowing that this was not something she could compromise on.

Chapter Forty

'Come on, Jamie!' Alison was on the side-lines of a football pitch at the gym where he trained; they were setting up a youth football team. It was an initiative devised by his trainer.

'There are a lot of parents here,' Claire said, looking around at the clusters of adults.

'Yes,' Alison said, 'apparently there have been multiple requests for this and it makes sense if they have special gym sessions for teens. The two go hand in hand if you think about it. And if the team can get into the local league or attract scouts, it's all good publicity for them, and the Aquarium. I just hope Jamie does well here today and makes the team. Stopping him from going to that other gym was one thing, getting him to leave the football team quite another.'

'He couldn't very well carry on with Ryan in charge, could he?'

'You try telling him that. It took all my powers of reason to talk him out of going. This will be a Godsend if it comes off.'

Claire turned her attention to Mark. 'How's he doing?'

In a whisper he said, 'Not very well, to be honest. I'm surprised. Whenever I've seen him play before he's been the best on the pitch. Now here, even the younger kids are running rings around him. His coordination is all over the place.'

'Oh dear,' Claire said, knowing Alison would have to pick up the pieces if this didn't pan out. 'Do you think we should all do something nice afterwards to cheer him up?'

'Maybe,' Mark said. 'He might not be up for it. Hey, Alison. Are the two of you up to anything after this?'

'Nothing planned. Why?'

'I thought we could do something. Jamie might need cheering up.'

'That bad, hey? I'm not an expert, but even I can tell this is not Jamie's best effort.'

Jamie's try-out ended, they could see the trainer talking to him and shaking his head. The teenager slouched away, his arms hanging by his side.

'Never mind, Jamie. You can try again. You were just having an off day,' Alison put her arm around his shoulders. 'We thought you might want to do something. Go to the cinema perhaps? We could call Ishaan, get him to come along.'

'I just want to get out of here and go home,' he mumbled.

'If that's what you want, love.'

All four travelled back to Alison's house and Jamie went straight to his room without a word. The adults sat in the living room, discussing what their next move should be.

'If we're to keep him out of Ryan's grasp he needs to be kept occupied,' Mark said. 'I doubt his dream of being a footballer has gone away.'

'No, it most certainly has not,' Alison said. 'Although he doesn't talk about it as much. He's been very quiet of late, secretive, actually. He's been spending a lot of time with his new friend, at least that's what he tells me.'

'You think he's lying?' Claire asked.

'Might be,' Alison said, her attention drawn to something outside. 'What's he up to?'

'What?' Mark said.

'Jamie's standing in the middle of the road,' Alison said. Curious as to what he was doing she left the house. As she drew nearer she could hear him talking. His face was lit up and animated. She looked around to see who he was speaking to; there was no one about. Close now, she was able to listen to what he was saying.

'Yeah, I know, I was having an off day, that's all. Now that you're back you can help me. We can go to the park like we used to when I was little.'

Alison scanned the road; who was here? 'Jamie love. Who are you talking to?'

Jamie turned to her, grinning. 'It's Dad.'

For a fraction of a second Alison felt joy surge up within her, then the plummeting realisation that her husband was dead. Even now, years later, there were times when she momentarily forgot. A funny anecdote she'd think of telling him later, then remembering he was gone; the grief fresh and raw as if it had only just happened.

'He's come back. I knew he would. He came to tell me I should have played better today,' Jamie said.

Alison swallowed. 'Dad's dead, Jamie. He died when you were a little boy. Don't you remember?'

'But he's here, can't you see? He's holding Muffin. Look.' He pointed at nothing.

'Darling, Dad's gone.' She gulped back the tears that were threatening.

'Why are you lying? He's in front of you! He's smiling. Yes, Dad, I'll tell her. He said he's glad to be home.'

If only, she thought; tears spilled now and she wished so much that what Jamie was saying was true. A car beeped at them, the driver holding up his hands in a gesture of irritation. Alison wiped away her tears and touched Jamie's arm, moving him out of the road. 'Why don't we go inside, hey? It's cold.'

'What about Dad?'

Momentarily perplexed at how to respond she said, 'He can come too. Come on.' As she coaxed her son along the pavement he chattered to his dad. She bit down on her bottom lip and manoeuvred him into the house.

'Go in love.' Alison ushered Jamie into the living room. 'Why don't you sit with Claire. Mark, can I talk to you?' She motioned for him to follow her. 'Something's wrong with Jamie. He says his dad is here, he's talking to him.' She began to cry again, finding it hard to hold it together. 'What's happening to him?'

From the living room they could hear Jamie shouting, 'He *is* here! Can't you see? Dad, tell her!'

'Mark, I think you'd better come in here,' Claire called out.

They found Jamie pacing around the room, raking his hand through his hair and muttering. 'Tell them, Dad. Tell them you've come back. Look he's here, look, Mum.' He pointed at the place next to Claire.

Alison looked at Claire and then her son. 'Mark, please. What should I do?' She felt sick.

She went over to Jamie and tried to put her arm around him. Mark stopped her and whispered, 'Best not to touch him right now.' Then in a louder voice. 'I'm thirsty. Alison, could you get me a glass of water. Jamie, would you like one? What about your dad? Claire, go with Alison and see if you can dig out any biscuits for us, will you? Now, Jamie, shall we all sit down, hey?'

'Dad says he wants a chocolate biscuit.' Jamie sat and Mark joined him, leaving a space between them on the sofa.

'Alison, give me a few minutes please.'

In the kitchen Alison grabbed hold of Claire. 'Oh my God! What the hell is wrong with him?'

'I don't know. Don't worry, Mark will handle it.'

'Yes, yes.' Alison had to believe this. She breathed deeply, her breath shuddering away from her.

They were at the hospital where Mark worked; he was greeted by colleagues who swung into action when he told them what had happened. Jamie was led away and Alison accompanied him, her outward composure giving nothing away as to how she must be really feeling.

'Very admirable,' Mark said as she walked away. 'It's good that she's been able to stay as calm as she is.'

'She's had a lot of practice keeping cool under pressure, although I thought she was going to lose it earlier on,' Claire said. 'Is Jamie going to be all right? It's scary seeing him like this. What's wrong with him?'

'It looks like he's experiencing psychosis. If that's the case, he'll be given antipsychotic medicine which will help relieve the symptoms.'

'What would cause this?'

'It can be a number of things, schizophrenia or a bipolar disorder. But it can also be triggered by a traumatic experience or stress. And' – he paused before continuing – 'drug misuse.'

'You don't think Jamie's taking drugs, do you? He's so into his health, all that obsession with diet and exercise.'

'I'm not talking about the type of drugs you're thinking of. It's obvious now to me. I've been a fool not to spot it.'

'What do you mean?'

'You've commented on how his body has changed, right?'

'I just thought it was all the time he was spending in the gym.'

'But the mood swings, his unusual aggressive

behaviour, even his acne. It all points to the same thing.'

Claire tried to get her head around what Mark was saying and reached a horrifying conclusion. She looked at him, scared to say out loud what she was thinking.

'Steroids. Anabolic steroids,' Mark said.

Chapter Forty-One

'I'm going to have a word with Jamie's doctor,' Mark said, 'tell her they need to test for steroids. He's probably been on them a while.' His hands were clenched as he strode away in search of the doctor. Claire's legs wobbled and she sat in the nearest chair. The wait was a short one and Mark returned.

'Did you tell her?' Claire asked.

'Yes. They're going to test his blood and urine. If he's taken anything recently it will show up in his urine, so we'll know quickly if that's the case. I hope to God I'm wrong.'

'How do you think he got a hold of them? Do you think it's Ryan?'

'Without a doubt. When I took a look around that gym it was evident something of that nature was going on. It was the main reason I didn't think it was a suitable place for Jamie to be. If I'd have thought for one moment Ryan would be dishing out steroids to a minor, I would have acted immediately. But, despite everything, I did think he had Jamie's best interests at heart. I find it hard to believe he would stoop this low. What a scumbag.'

'But you can't be sure?' Claire said.

'If Jamie's test results are positive for steroids, then they could have only come from Ryan.'

'Where would he have got them from? They're illegal, aren't they?'

Mark's jaw tightened and his mouth set in a grim line. He spoke through gritted teeth. 'Yes, a class C drug. You can't buy them.'

'Mark. What have you done?' Claire's eyes were wide, her mouth gaped open.

Looking down at her, he attempted to speak. 'I—'

'There you are!' Alison came walking towards them. 'I was worried you'd left.'

'We wouldn't leave you on your own at a time like this, would we, Mark?'

Mark, his attention elsewhere, took a moment to respond. 'No. Of course not. We're here for you.'

'How's Jamie?' Claire asked.

'Sleeping. The doctor said the medication they gave him should help. In the meantime, they're waiting for his test results. She asked a lot of questions about any sports he was doing. Of course, I told her about the football, the running and the gym. She even asked about his skin. What's that got to do with his mental state? Mark?'

'It might be connected. They have to check every avenue,' he said.

Next to him, Claire squirmed. Wasn't he going to say anything?

Alison said, 'I'm going to splash some water on my

face, then shall we go for a coffee? We have a wait ahead of us.'

'Sure. We'll wait for you,' Claire said. When Alison left, she asked Mark, 'Why didn't you say anything to her about your suspicions?'

'Because that's all they are at the moment. There's no point in upsetting her unnecessarily.'

The wait was a long one and Claire began to wonder if they'd ever be told anything. Jamie slept, oblivious to his mother's distress, though she did her best to remain upbeat. Eventually, a doctor arrived and asked to speak to Alison alone. Claire and Mark sat outside on the hard, plastic seats. It was late now and a semblance of quiet had settled on the hospital. Neither of them spoke; there didn't seem much to say to one another. The doctor who'd been speaking to Alison left the ward, acknowledging their presence with a nod of her head. Alison followed shortly after. She was pale and her face was streaked with tears. Claire rushed over and embraced her.

Alison began sobbing and could hardly be understood. Claire directed her to one of the chairs and waited for her crying to subside.

Wiping her hand across her face, Alison said, 'the test results show…they show Jamie's been using anabolic steroids. They think this episode was the result of him taking too many at once, but it's probable he's been on them for months. Months! And I didn't know, too wrapped up in the problems at work to notice.' She began to cry again and Claire held her close. 'The doctor also said that because Jamie is only a teenager, the drugs might cause learning problems. They could have interfered with his hormonal systems and brain development. He could suffer long-term damage as a result. My darling boy…' She collapsed into floods of tears and rocked in Claire's arms.

Claire looked at Mark. 'Mark—' She didn't finish the sentence. The look on his face was one of pure rage. His hands bunched into fists.

'That bastard. How could he have…?' He stopped speaking and took a deep breath. 'Claire. I have to go.'

'Where? What are you going to do?' Claire asked, frightened at Mark's anger.

'To teach someone a lesson. This is a long time coming. Stay with Alison.'

'Mark!' Claire called after him as he ran down the corridor. He didn't look back.

❧

One of the nurses treating Jamie found Claire and Alison still sitting outside the ward.

'Why don't you go home? Jamie's comfortable and we'll take good care of him. You look done in, the pair of you. Go and get some rest. You'll feel better able to cope if you can try and get some sleep.'

'I don't think I'll ever sleep again,' Alison said.

'You'll need your strength, you'll have to try,' Claire said. 'Let's get you home for a few hours. Jamie's in good hands. What do you say?'

Alison acquiesced and allowed herself to be led to the car. She said nothing on the journey and let them into the house without a word. She sat on the sofa in a daze, absent-mindedly stroking the cat, who nuzzled into her neck purring. Claire said to her, 'How about I run you a bath? You'll feel better after that.'

Alison followed her dumbly and later, despite what she had said, fell into a deep sleep. Claire watched her from a chair by the side of the bed. Sleep was not waiting for her. Instead, she agonised as to where Mark was and what he might be doing. She feared for his safety. If Ryan was willing to endanger the health of a boy he liked, how was he liable to treat Mark, whom he hated?

Chapter Forty-Two

Alison's life had crashed about her. The consequences of her son's condition were so numerous it was hard to know which to address first in her mind. Uppermost was treatment for the psychosis Jamie had suffered. Today he was being moved to the hospital's mental health facility. She had a meeting with one of the doctors there. From the information she had thus garnered the fact that as the episode had been triggered by Jamie's use of steroids this should be a one-time event. He would still need a consultation with a psychiatrist and then there was the issue of the steroids. She stopped herself thinking about this. She could only deal with one matter at a time, otherwise she wouldn't be able to cope.

She said as much to Claire when she called.

'We were fortunate this happened with Mark around. The doctors have told me the rapid assessment and treatment will make a big difference to Jamie. I've tried calling Mark to thank him, but his phone is switched off.'

'Yes.' Claire hesitated before continuing. 'He does that when he's working. What will happen next with

Jamie?'

'Detox has been mentioned. For the moment though, it's all about securing his mental health. I'm in the mental health ward now, they're getting Jamie settled in. Look, I'd better go, I can see Jamie's doctor,' Alison said, she ended the call without waiting for a reply. She scuttled up to the doctor.

'Hello doctor. Do you have any news for me?'

'Jamie is being treated with neuroleptics, which are antipsychotic medication. The psychosis he had has receded and he is responding well so far.'

'How long will he need to be on those?'

'It's hard to tell at this stage. He'll be assessed after about four weeks and we'll take it from there. He could be on medication for a year, it all depends. Avoiding a repetition of a psychotic episode will be a high priority because of the danger it may pose to the patient.'

Alison didn't want to dwell on the possibility of her son being on long-term medication. Ever pragmatic, she wanted to focus on Jamie's overall well-being and what could be done. 'And the steroids? What about those? Can he just stop taking them? Won't there be problems of withdrawal?'

'There are withdrawal symptoms with any type of substance abuse, so we will have to taper Jamie's dosage. The amount of steroids in his system will be evaluated in order to do this. Then he'll undergo a medically supervised detox to stabilise his condition.'

'You said something about a consultation with a psychiatrist?'

'Yes, Jamie will be seeing one today. You'll need to attend that meeting. It's not my field but I can say that there are lots of things to consider. Why he chose to use steroids; does he have body dysmorphia, for example? Does he want to stop using them? And because he's a minor the police will have to be informed. I believe a report is being drawn up for this.'

'So much to take in,' Alison said. 'I do know why he was using them, in all probability.'

'That's something to raise with the psychiatrist. At least you have a starting point. Often the patients won't cooperate with the medical team.'

'He'll cooperate. I'll make sure of that,' Alison said. She was confident that Jamie would talk to her. 'Can I see him now?'

'Yes. Go right in.'

Jamie was sitting up in bed reading a comic book. He gave his mother a smile. 'Hello Mum.'

'Hello love,' Alison said, kissing him on the cheek. 'How are you feeling?'

'Weird, my head feels kind of fuzzy.'

'I expect that's the medication you're on. And' – she hesitated not knowing how to frame her next question – 'can you still see Dad? Is he talking to you?'

Jamie went red and said, 'No. When the doctor told me what had happened I didn't believe her. I can't remember anything about that day. Just coming home from football and feeling funny. Was I really saying Dad was talking to me?'

'Yes, darling, you were.'

'That must have freaked you out.'

Alison smiled and brushed hair away from Jamie's forehead. 'Yes, it did a bit. Did the doctor explain why that happened? Did she talk to you about steroids?'

He nodded, looking at the comic and rolling it into a tube.

'Why did you take them, Jamie? Did Ryan give them to you?'

'I didn't know they were bad. Ryan said they were like vitamin pills. He said all top athletes took them; it was no big deal. And they worked.'

'What happened on the day of the football trials?'

'I'd been to see Ryan the day before. I felt bad I wasn't allowed to train with him or be in his football team and I wanted to say sorry. At first he was angry, saying how he'd wasted his time with me. He said I was ungrateful, that all he'd wanted to do was help me, 'cos he didn't have anyone helping him when he was young. I was a bit scared, he was shouting and throwing things around. Then he calmed down and asked what I was up to. I told him how Mark had got me into a new gym, he didn't like that. Then I told him about my football trial for the new team and how nervous I was. He got these tablets out. He said they would make sure I'd do well on the day. He told me how many to take and said if I wanted to, I could always go back to him for more, but it was to be a secret.'

'I see. Do you still have those tablets?'

'Yes. I put them under my mattress.'

'You hid them? Why did you do that, Jamie?'

'I dunno.'

'Because you knew if I found out I'd be angry and stop you taking them? You must have known they weren't just vitamin pills, or are you stupid?'

'I'm not stupid!'

'You're going to have to prove that to me.'

'How?'

'By getting better. By doing everything I and all the doctors tell you. By never letting someone take advantage of you like this again. Can you understand now why I didn't want you to have any more contact with Ryan? That I love you and only ever have your best interests at heart – you must never, ever doubt that again!'

'I won't, Mum. I'm sorry.' He held his lips together and she could see he was trying not to cry.

'Good. That's all I ask. Together we can do this. Come here, give your mum a hug.'

Chapter Forty-Three

It had been 48 hours since Mark had said goodbye to her at the hospital and aside from a brief text message saying he'd be away for a few days, Claire had heard nothing from him. She was frantic with worry and had no one to confide in. If only Mark had given her some clue as to what he was doing. She knew he must be looking for Ryan, but what was he going to do once he found him? She shuddered at the prospect of Mark making things even worse. She knew enough to understand that Mark was in all kinds of trouble. Twirling her engagement ring around on her finger, she wondered if she should call the police. Her phone rang. She grabbed at it; her heart sank when she saw it was only the estate agents.

'Hello. I'm sorry, I can't really talk right now,' she said, wanting to get rid of them in case Mark was trying to contact her.

'Won't keep you long, Ms Sadler. An offer has been made on your house.'

'Right.' At least this was something positive. 'That's good news.'

'Yes and no,' the estate agent said. 'It's well under the

asking price, but it's normal to put in a cheeky offer and then we ask them to put in a counter bid. A bit of back and forth, I'm sure you know the drill.'

She did indeed. She remembered the haggling that had gone on when she'd had to sell her father's house. 'What's the offer?' The estate agent was right, it *was* cheeky. 'What's their situation? Are they cash buyers? Are they in a chain?'

'Not cash buyers, but they have a firm mortgage offer. They have sold their house and the one they were going to buy fell through and they're living with the woman's parents. They'll be desperate to get your place. We can push for a higher price.'

'Tell them yes.'

'What?'

'Tell them I accept their offer and I want this to go through as soon as possible. Don't take the house off the market until contracts are exchanged, and tell them that, so they know I mean business.'

'Ms Sadler, I really do think you need to stop and—'

'I've made my decision. Please tell them.' The call ended and Claire let out a long breath; she'd just agreed to throw away an awful lot of money. She had the feeling though that she would be in need of ready cash – and soon.

Alison was at home, time to shower and catch her breath. It had been full on at the hospital. The initial meeting with the psychiatrist had gone well. He was a pleasant man and Jamie had seemed to bond with him quickly. From now on, meetings would be between the two of them. The doctor had told Alison that Jamie would be more open if his mother wasn't sitting next to him. After that meeting, there had been another to discuss Jamie's detox and what drugs he would be put on to avoid sudden withdrawal symptoms. It was all very draining and exposure to a world that Alison was unfamiliar with; there was so much to take in and she'd asked lots of questions. Jamie had been embarrassed by this but the staff had been happy to answer. Now she had a few hours, she'd called Mary and arranged to see her. Alison had made a decision she was sure would be unpopular. She'd hadn't heard back from Claire or Mark so gave her friend a call.

'Alison. Sorry, I meant to ring you. I don't know where the time has gone.'

'That's all right. I've had my phone switched off most of the time anyway. I thought you'd like an update on Jamie.'

'Yes, of course. How's he doing?'

'Not bad, all things considered. He's talking to me more now than he has done in the past few months. He had his first meeting with the psychiatrist today.'

'Was he nice?'

'Yes, he was. He's also very young and a total dish, it was quite distracting. I don't think I'd want any doctor of mine to be that good-looking. Anyway, Jamie and he hit it off straight away, that's the most important thing.

I suppose Jamie will be better able to relate to someone younger too.'

'You sound better, maybe it's the crush you have on the doctor.'

Although her friend was attempting to be light-hearted, Alison thought she sounded off, as if she wasn't fully concentrating and just going through the motions of the conversation. 'I still haven't been able to speak to Mark. Is he there?'

'No.'

'Where is he then?'

'He's at work. No. He's at the gym, yes, sorry, I got muddled.'

'Are you okay, Claire?'

'Yeah, fine.'

'If you say so. I have a favour to ask. I wondered if you would mind staying with me for a while? I'm going to be out of the house quite a bit and Muffin could do with some TLC. You could use my desk to work at if you wanted. And – to be honest, I could do with the company, it's been tough coming home to an empty house. What do you think?'

'Er, I…yes. Yes. If that's what you'd like.'

Claire's reluctance was evident. Alison said, 'It was only an idea. If you don't want to that's fine. I can get a neighbour to come in and see to the cat.'

'No, no. It's fine. I'll get some things together and come over.'

'Thanks, I appreciate it. I'll be going out in a bit. I have to speak to Mary. I'll tell you about it later.'

When Alison returned from her meeting with Mary, Claire was ensconced in the spare room. She was so engrossed reading something on her laptop that she didn't hear Alison come in and jumped when she did.

'Sorry, I didn't mean to startle you.' Without thinking she looked towards the computer and was surprised to see Claire snap it shut. 'Have you been here long?'

'About half an hour.'

'I'm starved. Do you fancy something to eat?'

'I'm not really that hungry,' Claire said. She had her hand on the laptop. Alison got the impression that whatever she had been reading, she wanted to get back to it.

'Do you want to join me for a drink?' Alison said. She was keen to chat about her conversation with Mary.

'Not for the moment. I just want to finish off something here, a work thing. I'll be down in a bit.'

'I'll leave you to it then,' Alison said. *So much for having company,* she thought.

When Claire did make an appearance Alison had finished eating and was watching TV. She switched it off as soon as Claire joined her.

'Did your meeting with Mary go well?'

'Not the choice of words I'd use. She was quite agitated, to be honest.'

'That's good,' Claire said.

'Is it?' Alison was getting a bit irritated now. What on earth was wrong. 'Hello? Earth to Claire. Did you hear what I said?'

Shaking herself, Claire said, 'I'm sorry. Tell me again.'

'Mary is not happy because I resigned.'

'You did what?'

'I told her I needed to be with Jamie, devote myself to him one hundred per cent. Perhaps if I'd been more present in his life this wouldn't have happened.'

'You can't be sure of that. And even if you weren't working, it's not as if you would have followed Jamie around twenty-four-seven.'

'That's the gist of what Mary said, that resigning was a knee-jerk reaction and she wouldn't accept it. She asked me to think about it and offered an alternative that I may consider.'

'What's that, then?' Alison had Claire's full attention now.

'She suggested I take a six-month sabbatical. That would take me to the end of the school year and I could review my options after that. She doesn't want to lose me.'

'I can understand that. She'll be at her wits' end coping without you and dealing with her personal problems at the same time.'

'Yes, I feel bad about heaping more on her, but I have to prioritise my son over work. It might be different if I had a partner or even Callum here,' she said referring to her eldest son. 'Which reminds me. I need to talk to him about Jamie at some point.'

'He doesn't know?'

'I didn't want to worry him and he would have insisted

on coming home. He's got a big paper he's working on. I don't want his studies to suffer, and there isn't much he can do here.'

'He could be moral support,' Claire said.

'I have you for that though, don't I?'

Claire looked away and didn't respond.

Chapter Forty-Four

It was late and Alison had gone to bed, leaving Claire alone. There was still no news from Mark and she was beside herself with worry. Worse was not being able to say anything to Alison. How could she tell her that Mark had gone in search of Ryan? Wouldn't she be bound to ask why he felt the need to, and then why not go to the police directly? This was a question that rattled around her head and she didn't like the answer that she always came back to. Mark must be involved directly in the steroids supplied to Ryan. It was too awful to contemplate, let alone voice out loud, and especially to Alison. She'd spent hours on the internet researching the law related to supplying drugs. It scared her when she read that a person in a position of trust or authority would be dealt with more harshly. Mark was a doctor, a person who should be beyond reproach. Not to mention he would be fully aware of the negative outcomes of steroid abuse. Why had he done it? Yes, there had been the incidents that had frightened her, but she still couldn't understand why Mark had been so set against reporting them. She was confused and wished she were able to speak to Mark and confront him.

With nothing else she could do, she began investigating solicitors who specialised in criminal law. It could be that if he were charged Mark would need a barrister. They cost a fortune, but with the sale of her house imminent and the savings she had it was doable. She was calculating the potential costs when her phone rang. At last! Mark. Who else would be calling at this hour?

She didn't recognise the number and gave a cautious 'hello'.

'Is that Claire Sadler?'

She swallowed. 'Yes, that's me.'

'Good evening, I'm Judy, the staff nurse at the Queen Alexander Hospital in Portsmouth.'

Claire knew this was going to be about Mark and she felt herself go dizzy.

'Your fiancé, Mark Fraser, was admitted earlier on this evening.'

She slid to the floor. 'Is he, is he okay?' She closed her eyes fearing the worst.

'He was found badly beaten and unconscious in a backstreet. He'd been left by one of the bins and was only discovered when the rubbish was collected.'

'And how is he? Is he seriously injured?' Claire asked, her heart racing.

'He regained consciousness when the paramedics arrived. He has several fractured ribs and a broken nose. It would appear he was kicked repeatedly but fortunately he hasn't suffered from any internal bleeding.'

'A broken nose?' Claire repeated, already knowing who was responsible for the attack.

'He's been asking for you. Would you like to come and see him now? It's outside of visiting hours, but I can make an exception. I gather he's one of our own.'

'What?'

'A doctor.'

'Yes, he is, and yes, I'd like to see him. I'm in Worthing so it will take me a while to get there.'

Claire had sped along the empty motorway and arrived in under an hour. She was shown to Mark's bed. He was asleep and this gave her the opportunity to examine his face, which was a mass of purple, his nose encased, his eyes black. He had a cut on his forehead that had been stitched. She could only imagine how bad the rest of him looked. The pain she felt at seeing him like this made her inwardly squirm and it was all she could do not to cry out. She reached to pull a chair closer to the bed; its legs scraped on the floor, making a loud noise, and she cringed. Mark opened his eyes and reached out his hand. Claire took it.

'Oh my love. What have you got yourself into?'

'You should see the other guy.' His attempt at humour made him wince and he touched the side of his body.

'Are you in a lot of pain?'

'A bit. The painkillers help, I feel more woozy than anything else.'

'Who did this to you? Was it Ryan?'

Mark closed his eyes momentarily then looked at her. 'Aye, it was Ryan, him and his mate.'

'What were you doing? What were you hoping to accomplish?'

'I don't really know, to be honest. I was so angry, I wanted him to confess to what he'd done. Own up to it.'

'And did he?'

'Oh yes. He couldn't wait to tell me. He'd given Jamie the steroids and deliberately told him the wrong amount to take. He *intended* to make him ill. He said he wanted to get back at me and Alison for stopping him from seeing Jamie. He kept going on about how Jamie would have been his meal ticket and we'd put a stop to that. He wasn't making much sense. I wouldn't have been surprised if he was high on something himself. Then he went berserk and started hitting me. I fought back at first but then his mate joined in and I don't remember much after that.'

'You could have been killed!'

'On reflection, it was a stupid thing to do. I should have let the police deal with it.'

'I know why you didn't want to involve them.'

'You do?'

'Yes, I've worked it out, but I'm going to stand by you. I know that you did it to protect me. And I've made some enquiries. We'll get you a barrister, you're going to need one when they charge you.'

'Charge me. A barrister? What do you think I've done, Claire?'

'Supplied Ryan with anabolic steroids. I know he or Eddie must have blackmailed you. You wouldn't have done it otherwise.'

'Claire, no. You've got it wrong. That's what they wanted me to do. What they kept pressuring me for, but I always said no.'

'I…I don't understand.' Relief and confusion washed over Claire.

'No, I don't suppose you do. Looking back, it doesn't make much sense to me now. I do – did – have my reasons. But one thing I do know. It's time to come clean, to tell the police, whatever the repercussions.'

Chapter Forty-Five

Claire and Mark were in the day room at the hospital. After it transpired Claire's fears had been unfounded, she wanted to get to the bottom of things. What did he have to hide? It had been late and both of them were exhausted so she'd agreed to postpone the conversation. She'd managed a few hours' sleep in a chair and woke in the early morning with a stiff neck. They sat now, each in varying degrees of discomfort. Mark looked a sorry state but was due to be discharged today. He'd been kept overnight for observation, but his injuries didn't warrant a hospital stay any longer than that.

'I'll be glad to get home,' Mark said as he fidgeted, trying to sit in the least painful way.

'Let me guess. You hate hospitals.'

'Don't make me laugh, it hurts too much.' Mark grimaced. 'I don't think you'll find any doctor appreciates being a patient.'

'The nurse told me the police will be sending someone to take a statement for your assault. It'll be GBH, that's serious, Mark. What are you going to say to them?'

'I told you. The whole truth.'

'Before they arrive, do you mind telling *me* the whole truth? I have a right to know.'

'You do. It's complicated.'

'Start at the beginning then. Your gambling, getting into debt and going to a loan shark, and all about Eddie.'

He hesitated. 'I lied to you about how I met him. I told you it was in a pub, but that's not what happened. Eddie came into A&E complaining of chronic back pain. He wanted these high dose painkillers. He said he'd been on them before but had run out and couldn't get an appointment with his GP for weeks. He said the pain was unbearable and he couldn't take any more time off or he'd lose his job. He was very convincing, I felt sorry for him so I gave him the prescription. It was bedlam that evening at the hospital and I wanted to move onto the next patient so the consult was rushed, and I forgot to include it in my paperwork. It was only when I saw Eddie again, this time it was in the pub, that I remembered.'

'So you did the paperwork.'

'Yes. But I had to lie about the dates. Falsifying paperwork is a big deal for a doctor. I don't think people realise. Anyway, I see Eddie in the pub. He's all friendly like and we get chatting. He invites me to a card game and I went to a few of those. I lost heavily, but Eddie was very relaxed about it and I thought I could recoup my losses on the next game. At the time I was also online betting and getting more and more into debt. Then one day at a game, Eddie offered to take the debt on more formally, charge interest and so on. I refused, I knew what a bad idea that would be, no matter how friendly he appeared.'

'You could have come to me before it got to that.'

'I know that now, and look, you did bail me out. At the time though I wasn't thinking straight and I wanted to keep it all a secret. I couldn't be open about my addiction at work. Then Eddie came into the department again, all smiles like. "Would you believe it, Mark, I've run out of pills again. You couldn't sort me out?" I shouldn't have, it goes against good medical practice to prescribe for a patient if you don't have adequate knowledge about them and in Eddie's case I didn't. I didn't follow up on his story, just believed him. Plus, I knew he was not best pleased I'd refused his offer of a loan and I wanted to keep him sweet until I had the means to repay him. But then he paid you a visit.'

'That time when he was in the garden?' Claire recalled how frightened she had been.

'Yes. When you told me, I knew then that he was going to get nasty unless I took the loan out. So I did. Things started to escalate when Eddie came into A&E a third time. I wasn't on shift and one of my colleagues saw him and got suspicious about his story and checked through my paperwork. She came to me to highlight the discrepancies she'd noticed.'

'That was a good thing though, going to you rather than your boss?'

'Normally I'd say yes, but Margaret Montague is all pally with Mr Beauchamp. I think he might be her godfather or something, and she's looked down her nose at me more than once. She wouldn't be one to have my back – quite the reverse. That's why I didn't want to go to the police about Smokey, then the petrol. I didn't want my association with Eddie to come to light. I thought I could deal with it myself, make it go away.'

'How does Ryan come into this?'

'He and Eddie are "colleagues" so to speak. Ryan told me he knew Eddie and that's when the requests for steroids started. Ryan found out about my visit to his gym and got nasty. I should have gone to the police about my suspicions. Being a doctor, you have responsibilities that other people don't. It's part of the oath you take – to serve humanity. I'm not doing that if I turn a blind eye to illegal drug use, am I? But I kept quiet to save my own skin, that's unforgiveable. And look what happened. Poor Jamie, he could be messed up for life over this.'

'Really?' Claire was shocked. 'Alison said he was doing well.'

'He probably looks as if he is, but it'll take time to know for sure. When this all comes out, how do you think Alison will react?'

Claire hadn't thought of that. If Mark had acted differently would this have altered the outcome? 'I don't know. We can't be sure if the drugs Jamie had taken were already doing damage. How long has he been on them? It's only recently you found out about the gym. I hate to say it, but it could be argued that Alison should have been more vigilant about her son's whereabouts and what he was doing.'

'God, please don't say that to her. I don't want to start throwing accusations like that around,' Mark said.

'No, I would never say this to her. Society dishes out enough blame and guilt to working mothers. I just wanted to give you another side to the argument, that's all.'

'Fine. Just tread carefully though, hey? I'd hate for you and Alison to fall out. I should be the one to tell her, it's spineless not to and I've been too much of a coward already.'

'I think the opposite,' Claire said, taking his hand. 'It's brave to own up to something bad and suffer the consequences.'

'I don't deserve you,' he said, his voice catching.

'Sure you do.' She gave his hand a squeeze.

One of the nurses came in. 'Mark. The police are here to take a statement. You can talk in one of the family rooms. I'll show you the way.'

Mark inched out of the chair and stood. He exhaled and said to Claire, 'Time to face the music.'

Chapter Forty-Six

Callum kicked the door shut behind him as he manhandled his case into the hall. 'Mum!' There was no reply. Dumping his baggage he went into the living room where he found his brother engrossed in a book. 'All right, Jamie?'

His younger brother ran up to him and they hugged. 'I didn't know you were coming home. Mum didn't say.'

'She doesn't know. When she called me to tell me what had happened to you I was under strict instructions not to worry and to stay put. But I couldn't not come and see my little brother, could I? How are you doing?'

Jamie stepped away and shrugged. 'Okay I suppose. Bored. I can't do my football and I'm not allowed to do any training.'

Picking up the book Jamie had been reading, Callum said, 'You must be bored if you're reading *The Hunger Games*. It's a good book though, better than the film.'

'I got it from your room. You don't mind me taking it?'

'Nah. Read any of my books. I'll give you some recommendations if you like.'

'Callum! I thought I heard voices.' It was Alison. Mother and son hugged. 'What are you doing here? Not that I'm not glad to see you, but I thought I told you there was no need for you to come down. That everything was under control.'

'I'm starving, Mum, are there any of those biscuits I like?' Callum guided Alison into the kitchen. 'I didn't want to say anything in front of Jamie. But what the fuck, Mum, what has happened to his body?'

'Language,' Alison said automatically. 'You mean he looks so muscular?'

'Er yeah, like Arnold Schwarzenegger.'

'He's not that big. Is he?'

'Maybe not that enormous, but he's not the skinny bloke I saw in the summer. He's at least double the size. I knew I should have come home for reading week. I would have seen the changes and said something.'

'Looking at him now, I don't know how I could have missed it. School was frantic, but that's not an excuse.'

'I guess if you see a person every day you don't notice things as much. My girlfriend's been on a bit of a diet and it was only when a friend of mine commented that I saw she'd lost weight.'

'Bet you were popular,' Alison said.

'I might be young, Mother, but I know enough that when a woman asks, "do I look fat in this?" your automatic response is "no". That seems to keep me out of trouble.'

'Wow, she's a lucky girl.' She laughed. 'Is it serious?'

'Maybe, don't go reading too much into that. Enough

about me. I'm here to help you. From what you've said you're going to need some support. You can't just rely on Claire. Family, that's who you need around you. Have you told Granma and Grandad?'

'No, not yet. I'm dreading it. How do I explain all this to them? I can barely get my head around it, let alone explaining it to a couple of septuagenarians.'

'Do you want me to do it?'

'Would you?' She knew it was her responsibility but having it taken away from her felt like a blessing.

'Yeah. It would be better coming from me anyway. They won't shout at me.'

'You've always been able to wind your granma around your finger,' Alison said.

'We should have a chat about a plan of action for Jamie, but I don't want him to think we're cooking up something. Any chance of getting him out of the house for a bit? He says he's not allowed to go training, but he must be missing his football, you know what a sports nut he is. Why don't you call Claire and see if she would take him for a swim? She works from home, right, so could sneak out for a bit.'

'She did say if there was anything…though she's got her own problems at the moment, Mark…' She stopped; there was no way she wanted to get into all of that now. She hadn't spoken much to Claire, only to be told that Mark had been mugged and was taking some time off work because he'd been injured. She'd seen neither of them and knew she had to rectify that. 'I'll call her now, see what she's up to.'

It turned out Claire was suffering from cabin fever and more than happy to get out of the house to go swimming with Jamie. He'd been packed off on his bicycle and told to enjoy himself. Claire had said she'd take him out for something to eat after and see he was back by evening.

'That was good of her,' Callum said.

'Yeah, although she was very cagey when I asked about Mark. She changed the subject and only wanted to talk about Jamie. She says "hello" by the way. Now we have the place to ourselves, what did you want to say about Jamie?'

'It's not him exactly. I'm also worried about you.'

'Me? I'm fine. Sure, work has been full on and I've been extremely busy, and tired, but—'

'Sounds enough to be getting on with,' Callum said. 'And the next few months are not going to be easy, for either of you.'

'That's why I had resigned, except Mary talked me into taking a sabbatical instead. She managed to persuade me it was best for everyone concerned.'

'Best for her and the school, you mean. I don't think she's considering your needs at all.'

'She has a lot on her plate. It's not just the school and all that business with Owen. He resigned; you know I told you. Turns out his uncle has got him some high-flying job in the city and he'll be earning loads. What a waste of space. Anyway, there's her husband, he's ill, Alzheimer's, and she's his main carer.'

'That's very sad, Mum, but that's not your problem, is it? Her domestic situation is not your responsibility. She can seek help if it's needed. For you, well, it's not the same. You'll be seeing professionals with regard to Jamie's treatment, yes, but the day-to-day care will still be down to you. You can't exactly put him into a care home; at least Mary has that option.'

'She really doesn't want to go down that route.'

'Forget about Mary and what she does and does not want to do. You and Jamie are my concerns. Jamie will have withdrawal symptoms once his detox kicks in, you and he will have to deal with those. You don't need to be concerned with someone else's problems, you have enough of your own.'

'I know, but you shouldn't have to worry about me. You're young, you have your own life to think about.'

'And that doesn't include my mum and brother? How can I think of abandoning either one of you? You are and always have been an amazing mum. You've given me your support, it's time to return the favour.'

'How did I bring up such a mature young man?' She took his hand and gave it a squeeze.

'Let me help, Mum. Please.'

Chapter Forty-Seven

Alison gripped the envelope in her hand. She was sitting outside Mary's office waiting for her to finish a phone call. Her secretary smiled at her and eyed the paper in Alison's hand.

She knows, thought Alison. And Mary will know, the minute I walk in, she'll know.

Mary appeared at the door to her office and said, 'Alison. Sorry to have kept you. Please come in.'

Alison took a deep breath and launched into her prepared speech. 'I have something to tell you, this is very difficult… This school means such a lot to me…' She couldn't continue, the lump in her throat constricting her. She placed the envelope on the desk. 'My resignation. I'm sorry, Mary. I know I agreed to just taking time off, but I can't have my return to work hanging over my head while I'm helping Jamie with his recovery. I have to be there for him totally, physically, mentally and emotionally. I can't do that knowing I will have responsibilities elsewhere. My duty, first and foremost, is to my son. For the past few months, I've lost sight of that and something terrible occurred. That's never going to happen again.' She exhaled.

'You'd better sit down,' Mary said.

'You're not going to talk me out of it.'

'I'm not even going to try. It was wrong of me to do that last time. I'm sorry. So, is this effective immediately?'

'I wanted to discuss that with you. Perhaps I could come in a few hours a day as part of a handover to whoever will be the acting deputy head?'

'That would be helpful, and generous of you. The position has now been advertised again. The school governors are going to approach some of the other candidates who applied last time, which might make the selection process a little quicker.'

'And Ofsted? Have you heard back from them at all?' Alison asked.

'Yes. One of the governors told me that there are exceptional circumstances in our case and that the results will remain pending for the time being. I imagine we will get another inspection soon. The governing board say it's highly unusual and wondered if the inspectors had been influenced by any other factors.' She paused as if expecting Alison to comment. When she didn't, Mary continued. 'Personally, I think recent bad publicity for Ofsted has made them reassess how they deal with failing schools.'

'But our school isn't failing.'

Mary waved her hand in the air. 'A matter of linguistics. Dropping a grade, especially when I'd hope we'd improve it, is failing in my book. Not the way I'd wish to exit the profession after nearly forty years of service, but it can't be helped.'

'You're not retiring, are you?'

'It's overdue. Time to make way for younger blood. And to face up to some unpleasant truths.'

'You mean your husband?'

'Yes. I've had to admit he needs full-time care. Care that I do not have the expertise for. I've already started looking into it. There are some nice private residential facilities out there. It will mean selling the house, but it will be too big for one person anyway.'

'It's sad that you'll have to sell your home,' Alison said.

'At least I have that option, my dear. Think of the poor souls that don't have any resources to fall back on. No, a little flat, near Michael, will suit me fine. You and I have both been guilty of putting the school before what's best for us and our families, and that needs to be rectified. So, Alison, I accept your resignation and I wish you all the best with your son. I'm sorry that things went awry. All we can do now is try to put it behind us and move forward.' Mary's eyes were glistening and Alison tried to speak but found she couldn't.

Claire was waiting outside the hospital. Mark had a meeting with his manager to discuss recent events and she'd said she'd be there when he finished. It wasn't going to be an easy encounter and when she saw him walking towards her, his gait a little uneven, she knew it wasn't good news.

'How'd it go?'

'Not here.' He coughed. 'Why don't we walk to the pier? I need some fresh air.'

The day was cold and when they reached the end of the pier it was deserted. A fierce wind was blowing that made Claire cling to the railings, the cold metal gluing her hands to it. Mark stared, unblinking, into the distance. His eyes were streaming; from the gale or with tears, she couldn't be sure. She wanted to suggest that they go inside the Pier café and warm up but kept quiet, waiting for him to speak first.

'It's not looking good. Mr Beauchamp called me in because a colleague had brought his attention to the matter of a patient being prescribed drugs they shouldn't have. No prizes for guessing who that was. They have other concerns too, presumably my paperwork, and I've been reported to the GMC. Beauchamp advised me to seek advice from my medical defence union.'

'What did you say to him?'

'I was very candid. Told him everything.'

'But confessing to them. Surely that will help your case?'

He continued staring out to sea. 'There's more. Ryan was called in for questioning by the police about the steroids and he's throwing around all sorts of accusations.'

'The police won't take them seriously. They'll take your word over his, surely?'

'He's made a complaint about me, he said I'd

threatened him and pushed him. He has photos of his bloody nose. The police are considering whether or not to charge me with assault.'

'But you didn't touch him! He tripped.'

'That's not the story he's telling. And raising my fist at him, being angry, is assault, even if I didn't touch him. The issue with falsifying my paperwork is bad enough, dishonesty in a doctor is taken extremely seriously, but violence or the threat of it? That's not going to help matters, is it?'

'What's the very worst outcome?' Claire prised her hand away from the railing and touched Mark's arm.

'The very worst? It doesn't bear thinking about. The worst scenario is that I am struck off the medical register and not able to practise medicine.'

Chapter Forty-Eight

Mark noted the shocked expression on Jamie's face as he answered the door to him, then he remembered what a state he must look. The bruising had started to fade but was still startling. Mark's broken ribs meant he moved like an old man. He'd walked to Alison's house because it was easier than trying to drive; reaching to put a seat belt on was agony, then painful to wear, each jolt of the car inflicting new pain.

'What happened to you?' Jamie asked, his eyes wide.

'I got mugged. Stupid me thought I could fight him off. I should have just given up my wallet.'

'Does it hurt?'

'It looks worse than it is,' Mark said, wanting to downplay how bad he felt. 'Can I have a word with your mother? Is she about?'

'Yeah, I'll get her.'

Mark perched on the edge of an armchair. He wiped his forehead; despite the cold day he was sweating.

'Oh my goodness, Mark! Claire told me you'd been mugged, but she didn't say you'd been badly beaten up. You poor thing.'

Her sympathy made him wince. Would she be as kind when he'd finished telling her his story? He could see Jamie hovering behind her. This was not for his ears, at least not yet. 'Do you have time to talk? There's something important I need to say.' He eyed Jamie. 'Can we speak privately?'

'Sure. Jamie, why don't you get lunch started.' She turned back to Mark. 'Can I get you something to drink? Tea? Coffee?'

'No thanks, I'm fine.' His stomach was churning and he wished he could fast forward the time. 'I came here today to put the record straight about a few things. When I've finished talking you might end up hating me, and I can't say I would blame you. First though I want you to know how much I like and admire you. How I think you're a great mum and the boys are lucky to have you. And Jamie. During the past few months I've got to know him, and he's a good lad. I've grown very fond of him and it makes recent events even harder to take.'

'Mark, you're starting to worry me. How could I hate you? None of what has happened to Jamie is down to you. In fact if you hadn't warned me against Ryan when you did, who knows how things could have gone.'

'That's the thing though. I could have, should have, warned you earlier. I knew Ryan was bad news long before I voiced my concerns. I knew, well, had strong suspicions, that he was dealing steroids, yet I did nothing.'

'I don't understand. Why wouldn't you say anything?'

'Because I was covering my own back. You know about my gambling problem. The thing about addiction, the thing is, you'd do anything, anything to continue. Reason and logic go out the window and I got mixed up with some terrible people, criminals. My work was suffering and I allowed myself to be compromised.'

'Why didn't you go to the police?'

'Because the people I'd got involved with told me if I even thought about it…what I'm about to tell you, Claire must *never* know.'

'Okay, I won't say anything.'

'No. I mean it. You must promise never to say anything about it to her.'

'I promise, you can trust me.'

Mark let out a long breath. 'They threatened to do things to her. Terrible things.' He hesitated before continuing. 'They knew her routines, when she went to London, when she was in the house alone. Everything. They said if I went to the police, she'd be missing by the time I got home. I believed them. I thought that if I held them off, stalled them, I could somehow resolve the matter. They kept pressuring me to supply them with drugs – anabolic steroids.'

'Did you…did you supply Ryan with the drugs he gave Jamie?' She'd gone pale and Mark thought she might faint. He leant forward, but she composed herself.

'No. I. Did. Not. I swear as God is my witness. I'll admit I was so frightened for Claire's safety I thought about it. At one point I had my prescription pad in my hand, but in the end I just couldn't. It goes against everything I stand for. Everything the profession stands for, so I refused point blank. I thought Claire and I could leave, sell up and go to Spain. Escape it all. I was thinking of any way out. But in the end, it wasn't Claire they chose to punish. It was Jamie.'

'You mean Ryan did this deliberately, to get back at you?'

'Yes. You saw how mad he was that night at the engagement party. Then the things I said only made matters worse. He was out for revenge.'

'So that's why he did it?'

'Did what?'

'Jamie told me the night before his football trials, he went to see Ryan. He wanted to apologise. Jamie apologise to Ryan, how ironic is that? My boy felt bad for that monster. He gave Jamie pills, told him to take them beforehand, that they'd make sure he performed well. And my boy, my lovely, innocent boy, believed him, thought he was being kind. And did just that, overdosed on steroids.' She shook herself then looked afresh at Mark. 'You weren't mugged, were you?'

'No. Ryan did this.'

'How much of this does Claire know?'

'Everything. Everything apart from the danger she was in. But she's only just found out. I told her when I was in hospital because I knew she wouldn't believe I'd been mugged. I'd left home a couple of days before, in search of Ryan. I paid someone at his gym for information and they gave me an address in Portsmouth he uses. I went there and waited for him to turn up. I don't know what I had in mind, to be honest. I was just so mad at him; I wanted him to pay. When he surfaced, he wasn't on his own and that's when I got attacked. I was lucky not to be killed, that's the kind of person we're dealing with. Lying in my hospital bed gave me time to think. I knew he had to be stopped, whatever the risks. I'd have to tell the police.'

'What happens now?'

'He's been arrested and charged. There was CCTV of the attack, he wasn't bright enough to think of that, plus my statement. From something he once said to me, I think he has a record, maybe even served time, so I'm hoping he won't be let out on bail. Just to be on the safe side we've moved out of the house and are staying in an airB&B in Brighton. Claire's there now. I think we're going to have to rent somewhere until this all goes to court, even then, well, I don't know.'

'This is awful. It's like something you see on TV. You can't imagine it happening in real life, to people you know.'

'It's a nightmare,' Mark said.

'But what about work? I mean, if you're concerned about where you are living, won't they know where you work?'

'I've something to tell you about that too.'

Chapter Forty-Nine

'It's nice enough, better than staying in a hotel, I guess,' Claire said. She was speaking to Alison on the phone from the flat she and Mark were renting. She turned and hit her arm. 'But it's tiny. You can't swing a cat in the place. And working from here is, well, let's just say it's challenging. I'll be glad to be in the London office for a bit of elbow room.'

'It must be bad,' Alison said. 'It sounds like being in witness protection.'

'I still think Mark is overreacting. Moving out of the house seems a bit dramatic to me.'

'Maybe he's right to be cautious. Try and think of it as a holiday. There's plenty to do in Brighton. You could try out the new swimming centre. I hear it's amazing. And there are loads of restaurants and bars.'

'We could be here for months though, plus it's going to cost a fortune.'

'Mark told me about being reported to the GMC. How long will it be before he'll know the outcome of the investigation?'

'He says it can take six months if they can't sort it out

at a lower level. Really bad cases take years to reach an outcome. We're hoping it won't be brought to trial. His defence are confident it won't come to that. There's not much more we can do other than wait. In the meantime, I'll check out the swim centre, out of curiosity, but it won't touch the Aquarium's facilities. I'll still be going there.'

'Make sure you vary your routine, won't you? Perhaps you should avoid going to the swim club every Thursday.'

'God, you sound just like Mark. Are you two in cahoots?'

'No. It makes sense, that's all. They've shown us how vile they can be, why take any chances?'

Claire didn't want to dwell on this so moved the conversation on. 'Talking of you and Mark. How are you feeling about him? About his involvement with Ryan.' This was the first time she and Alison had had a chance to speak about Mark's visit. Mark had told her it had gone better than he'd expected but didn't go into much detail. Claire wanted to hear Alison's side of things.

'It was tough to listen to. I can't deny that,' Alison said. 'And I think an outsider who didn't know him, or you, would say I should be really angry. I've had time to think it over and whilst he acted irresponsibly, I can't be mad at him, especially as he's having to deal with this complaint. There are a lot of factors to take into consideration. All that's happened, it's the result of many things, some connected to the way *I* behaved. I can even lay some of the blame at Owen's feet. But we'd all go mad if we did the "what if" game. What if Mark had admitted his problems sooner? What if Mary had been more on the ball, or me for that matter? What if Ryan had chosen to focus his warped attention on another boy instead of Jamie? A person could go mad if they chose to go down that route, and I choose not to. My head is already full enough with making sure Jamie gets better, that his future isn't ruined. That's what I need to focus on.'

'You don't know how glad I am to hear that you bear Mark no ill will. And even though Mark and I will have a lot to deal with in the coming months, we're still here for you and Jamie. Anything we can do to help.'

'Thank you. At the moment I have Callum. As the Christmas holidays are almost upon us, he'll be here until the New Year. He spoke to his tutors at uni and explained to them, they were very understanding and have said they are willing to give him tutorials on Zoom and that his lectures can be viewed online. It seems these days anyway, that you don't have to be physically present for a lot of university study. The pandemic and lockdown instigated that. Anyway, Callum is spending a lot of time with Jamie, they go running together and talk about books they've read. Books! I could never prise Jamie away from football long enough to even glance at one in the past. Callum's a good influence. Jamie has never been that academic, despite the good results he got in his GCSEs last year. Can you imagine if all of this had happened then? I don't know how he would have passed any exams. As it is he's struggling with his ASs.'

'It's bound to take time for him to adjust. How is he

doing? Physically?' Claire worried about what Mark had told her with regard to Jamie's long-term recovery.

'He gets tired easily and has muscle and joint pain. He's upset that his body is reverting to how it was before he was on steroids. That scares me and I hope it won't push him to start taking them again. You imagine it's only girls and women who have problems with body positivity, but it's boys too. There's so much pressure on everyone to look social media perfect these days.'

'You said he was having trouble at school too.'

'Yes. He has difficulty processing information the way he used to. I'm grateful he's turned to reading, that's something, oh and cooking.'

'Cooking?'

'Would you believe it? He certainly doesn't get that from me. It started with a cookery programme he saw and now he's worked his way through all his grandma's recipes and cookbooks.'

'Is he any good? He might have to come over and show me what marvels he can do in this kitchen,' Claire said, looking around the minute space.

'He's *really* good. He was very into his diet and nutrition because of his football regime and it's morphed into producing these fabulous dishes. Of course, it's costing me a bomb buying all the fancy ingredients he absolutely must have, but it's worth it. It's great therapy and his psychiatrist has encouraged him to do something that makes him feel good about himself. I'm all for it, and if it keeps me from having to cook, that's an added benefit.'

'And work? What's happening about that?'

'I had a long talk with Callum and he made me see things more clearly. I resigned.' She went on to tell Claire about her conversation with Mary.

'Seems as if a lot of people's lives are changing at the moment. How do you feel about leaving work? You love it and it's been such a big part of your life for so long.'

'Yes, it has, but the biggest emotion I have at the moment is one of relief. That I no longer have to be spinning so many plates at the same time. I expect in the end I'll go a little stir crazy not working, but for the moment, I'm enjoying being a stay-at-home mum. I've never had the opportunity to do so in the past so it's good to experience it. And with Jamie being chef and Callum doing all the cleaning, I'm getting the chance to research what to expect with Jamie's recovery.'

Chapter Fifty

Claire had imagined a host of scenarios of how she and Mark would spend their first Christmas together as an engaged couple. In not one of them were they in a rented apartment where the boiler had packed up and the landlord uncontactable because he was skiing in Switzerland. Presumably there was no mobile phone reception on the mountains. That or he didn't want the hassle of finding a plumber on Christmas Eve. Fortunately, they'd been able to book a table at a local pub for Christmas lunch. It had seemed an amazing stroke of luck until they attended. The portion sizes had been minuscule, the Brussel sprouts as hard as bullets and the Christmas pudding cold. The atmosphere had been jolly enough though, with one big extended family in particular, laughing and joking – enjoying each other's company. This had only served to make Claire and Mark glummer, as they poked at their food and tried not to complain. They hadn't been able to find much to talk about; instead, they consumed vast quantities of alcohol. Once the second bottle of wine had been emptied, they moved on to spirits and staggered back to the flat, collapsing into bed, too drunk to feel the cold. Needless to say, Boxing Day delivered almighty hangovers and did nothing to improve either of their moods.

※

'That's great news, Ray. So when can we expect him? Right, I'll make sure I'm in. I've been spending a lot of time in coffee shops to keep warm! Yes, right, okay. Thanks.' Claire finished her call.

'Good news?' Mark asked.

'A plumber is coming, around midday.'

'On New Year's Eve? He'll charge the earth.'

'Apparently, it's Ray's brother-in-law. Says he knows a thing or two about boilers and has fixed this one before.'

'I hope he's not some kind of cowboy. I've had enough of taking showers at the gym and I don't suppose it's been fun for you commuting to the office just to work somewhere warm.'

'It could have been worse. The limbo time between Christmas and the New Year is always quiet on the trains. I actually got a seat for the whole journey to and from London. But having the heating back on and a hot shower for tomorrow will be good. We'll need to warm up after our dip in the sea.'

'Oh God. Is that still on? I thought you'd forgotten about it,' Mark said. 'It's going to be freezing tomorrow.'

'You'll be fine. It's literally a run into and out of the sea. They'll be loads of people there, you'll enjoy it.'

'I'd enjoy a lie in under the duvet more.'

Claire ignored him. She'd made arrangements with Alison to meet the next day at the Perch in Lancing. Jamie and Callum had agreed to come along too. It would be good to see Alison, she hadn't had much of a chance to over the holidays as she'd spent the time at her parents' house in Surrey. Alison's mother was very much into Christmas. Her house was always adorned with lights and a huge Christmas tree would grace the lounge, under which an obscene amount of presents lay. On Christmas Eve she insisted they all go to Midnight Mass – 'it's what Christmas is about, after all' – then on the day itself lunch with all the trimmings and after the Queen's speech, as she still called it. Claire had only attended once, the first Christmas after her dad had died. Alison's mum had insisted Claire not be alone, but it had been a difficult day and Claire had vowed never to attend again. She'd rather be in a crappy pub eating subpar food.

※

'At least the sun's shining,' Mark said, peering up at the sky. 'And the sea is very calm.'

'Careful now. Anyone would think you're looking forward to this.' Claire smiled. It was good of him to agree to come. Swimming really wasn't his thing, and certainly not the chilly waters of England. 'Looks busy,' she said, turning into the entrance to the Lancing Green carpark. 'I told you a lot of people would be doing this.'

'More like they've come to take a look at the idiots

going into the sea in the middle of winter! Where did you say you'd meet Alison?'

'Over by the ticket machine. She's there already.'

Alison was standing with Jamie, she waved to Claire and Mark. 'Callum's just putting the ticket on the car, then we can get onto the beach. Nice day for it, isn't it?'

'Aye, nice enough,' Mark said. 'How was your Christmas?'

'Good. My mum always outdoes herself. It's her favourite time of year and her enthusiasm is infectious. What about you?' She looked concerned. 'It must have been tough.'

'Not as tough as being in A&E when all the drunks roll in. But it has been strange not working over Christmas. The staff always go the extra mile to make things special for the patients. Everyone rises to the occasion and even those sceptical about this time of year seem less so. I would miss that. I would miss it all.' His voice croaked a little as he kept his emotions in check.

'Have you heard anything yet? From the hospital about your…your future?' Alison said.

Mark shook his head, then looked at Jamie. 'How are you doing? The detox going well, is it?'

'All right. I haven't felt great, but the doctors told me that's normal and will go away. It's funny not going to football. I really miss it, but I've been running and that with Callum. That's been good but school's hard. Studying for A-levels is difficult.'

'Jamie's not enjoying it as much as before, are you love?' Alison said, brushing hair away from her son's forehead. 'I think we might have to reassess the plans we had, but all in good time, hey?'

Jamie didn't say anything, just looked at the ground. Then as if remembering something he reached into his backpack. 'I brought these for us to wear for the swim.'

'Oh dear God no,' Mark said when he saw the Santa hats Jamie was holding.

Claire nudged him. 'What a fantastic idea! Thanks Jamie.' She grabbed one and plonked it on Mark's head. 'There, that'll keep you nice and warm!'

'Suits you,' Callum said, as he joined them.

At the shore swimmers were stripping down to their swimsuits. There were plenty of spectators, phones in hands, recording the event.

Mark eyed them and said for Claire's ears only, 'I didn't think there'd be this many people here. I'm not comfortable with all this filming. They'll be putting that on social media. We're supposed to be keeping a low profile.'

'It'll be fine, don't worry,' Claire said as she put her Santa hat on. 'Ryan's in custody, and after what the police have told us about his track record, he's not going to be let out any time soon. And Eddie, we'll be long gone before this shows up on social media. I don't intend hanging about afterwards.'

'Even so. It makes me nervous being here.'

'Come on, let's get to the water. The boys have beaten us to it.'

Callum and Jamie were in the water. 'Mark! Come on!' Jamie shouted.

Alison had her phone out. 'Join the boys, Mark. I want a photo of the three of you.'

Mark had little choice but to join them and the brothers found his facial expression, and the expletives that followed, hilarious as the cold water hit his body.

Claire was still laughing when they exited a few minutes later.

Mark was grimacing as he snatched the towel Claire held for him. 'Laugh away. It's you next.'

'Here.' Alison gave him a plastic mug. 'Have some hot chocolate. Our turn now.' She undressed and inched into the water. Claire was by her side. The two women gasped as the first wave touched their feet.

'Bloody hell! We must be mad,' Claire said. She turned around to see Mark grinning.

'How are you liking the water darling?' he said. 'Are you going to swim to the buoy?'

'Yeah yeah, very funny.' The very thought of staying in the water longer than necessary was not a pleasant one. She was all for getting straight back out, but Alison had other ideas.

'Not until we have some photos taken. Callum, take some pics with my phone.'

'Where is it?' Callum said from the shore.

'It's lying on the blue bag.'

'Where's that? I can't see it.'

'Could we get a move on? I've lost feeling in my legs,' Claire said, her teeth chattering.

Alison put her arm around Claire's shoulders and pulled her close. She was smiling widely and it made

Claire feel so glad to see her friend this happy that she really did warm up.

'Say cheese.' Callum held the phone up.

'Cheese!'

Chapter Fifty-One

The beginning of the year was its characteristically depressing self. Claire and Mark had decided to give 'dry January' a go and both were regretting it, but neither one of them wanted to admit it. Now that the heating had been fixed Claire didn't have to go into London on a daily basis, but the tiny apartment wasn't an ideal place to work. Mark still hadn't heard about his case and was gloomy in the extreme.

'I just wish I knew what the outcome was going to be. Why prolong the agony? Let me get on with the rest of my life,' he said to Claire as she tried to focus on her laptop screen. She'd been attempting to read a report but Mark kept interrupting and she was getting nowhere. Giving up, she shut the lid.

'Now, about the future. Don't you think it's time we discussed that? The house is all but sold.' Back when she'd thought she'd need the cash for a barrister for Mark, she'd been in a hurry to sell. Now that the necessity for money wasn't so pressing, she had rejected the low offer made and the house had had another, more realistic one. 'When it's sold, we need to consider just where we'll be living. I was thinking we don't buy another place just yet, that we rent for a while and see how we feel about things in say a year.'

'Sounds sensible.' Mark said.

'You don't sound too enthusiastic.'

'It's hard to feel positive about the future. I'm sorry, love.'

'Would you feel more positive if I suggested we rent somewhere in Spain?'

Mark's head snapped upwards. 'Spain? But I thought you said you didn't want to leave England, that Spain was just for holidays. That you'd miss Alison too much?'

'Yes, I know all that but a lot has happened since then. And, if the worst comes to the worst, I think you are going to need a new focus. A fresh start, although for you Spain is hardly that, I suppose. But you have a network of friends there and I think that will be important for your recovery. You're still dealing with a lot and I worry that the pressure you're under, will make you—'

'Start gambling again?'

'I don't want to think that, but you've got to admit it's a possibility.'

'It's always going to be a possibility, Claire. You know that. I will always be a *recovering* addict. Can you live with that?'

'I lived with it before, albeit unknowingly, I can do it again. I want us to be together. We can make this work because the bottom line is, we love each other, and we have already proved that in more ways than couples who have been together a lifetime.'

'Your faith in me, in us. It's – you're amazing. I know I've said it before, but I want you to know…' He stopped and there were tears in his eyes.

Claire gathered him in her arms. 'I know, love. I know. Which leads to something else for us to talk about.'

Mark lifted his head and looked into her eyes. His face was red and blotchy, his nose snotty. Claire didn't think she'd loved him more. She held up her left hand and wiggled her fingers. Mark understood the message. 'You want us to…to—'

'Get married. Yes. What's the point of being engaged if there's no wedding? If we're to locate to Spain it makes more sense for us to be married anyway. You already have permanent residency so my being your wife will make my application easier. Don't get me wrong, I'm not just marrying you so I can go and live in a sunny climate. I'd do it if we had to go to the North Pole.'

Smiling, Mark asked, 'When were you thinking of?'

'I've done some checking and we need to give twenty-nine days' notice. We could do it on the first of March. What do you think?'

'I think that sounds marvellous. Have you decided the venue, by any chance?'

'Brighton Town Hall. I had a look around, it's an impressive space.'

'You have it all sorted, we just need to book it all,' Mark said.

Claire smirked. 'No need. I've done it already.'

'You have! What if I'd said no?'

'Let's just say, I had complete faith that you'd be in agreement. I know you better than you think, Mark Fraser.'

'We'd better let my parents know before they go booking one of their last-minute winter cruises.'

'You do think they'll be happy for us? That it's not too rushed?'

'Trust me. They'll be delighted. And a month should be just enough time for my mum to get herself a new outfit. Now I think we'd better celebrate. How about a night out in Brighton? A nice meal in a fancy restaurant and a club. I'm in the mood for some jazz!'

Their evening out had been a great success. Mark had told anyone and everyone the reason why they were celebrating. The last time they'd been this happy together, so care-free, was on their holiday in Spain. Despite it all, they had plenty to look forward to and be positive about. Mark had even talked about the type of job he might do, if the worst happened. 'With my level of Spanish, I'm sure I could find something in tourism, or maybe in real estate. There are still plenty of folks from the rest of Europe who are looking to retire somewhere warm. What we'll need to do, after finding somewhere nice to live, would be to get you enrolled in a Spanish school. I don't want us to be anywhere full of expats. You need to have the full Spain experience and that means being where the Spanish live, and only the

Spanish. Otherwise, what's the point?'

Claire was pleased her idea was being met with such keenness. 'If I'd have known how happy this would make you, I'd have suggested it ages ago.'

'The important thing is you have and we can go!'

Claire grabbed one of Mark's hands. 'I'm sorry.'

'What for?'

'For not realising how much you wanted to be back in Spain. When you mentioned it before, I didn't take it seriously enough. I was only thinking about what I wanted. To be honest, I had no idea how much this meant to you.'

'You're not to blame. Remember, I've been guilty of hiding a lot from you. And when I asked about going to Spain before, it was only really to escape from reality. This is different.' His phone rang. Looking at the caller ID his face creased. 'Hello. Yes, this is Mark Fraser.'

Claire looked on as he spoke; from what she could gather, it sounded as if he was speaking to someone on the police investigation. She bit her thumbnail, waiting for Mark to finish.

'That was the police.' Mark looked serious.

'Yes, and?'

'They've tracked down Eddie. They're charging him. They also wanted me to know that they won't be pursuing Ryan's accusations of assault. They believe the CPS would consider the case against me too fragile, so it's been dropped.' Mark's hands were shaking. 'God, what a relief. One less thing to worry about.'

Chapter Fifty-Two

'Jamie. Have you used every pot, pan and kitchen utensil I own?' Alison looked around her kitchen. There wasn't an inch of surface to be seen. Jamie hadn't heard her over the noise of the food blender. She waited.

'Oh, hi Mum.'

'What are you doing?' Alison peered into the mixer.

'Blending cashews. I'm making a vegan lime and raspberry cheesecake.'

'Very ambitious. But no one we know is vegan.'

'Yeah I know that, but it's becoming more popular and I thought it would be interesting to see what the dishes were like to make and eat.'

'And do we have a main meal or are we just eating dessert?'

He laughed and Alison liked hearing the sound. He was in a better mood these days. 'No, silly. I'm doing gnocchi with burnt butter and walnuts. I found the recipe on the internet. I was looking for something a bit different to do.'

Alison automatically started clearing away and stacking the dishwasher. 'And your homework? Is that done?'

'Not yet.' He turned and busied himself with mixing something in a bowl.

'Jamie. I thought we'd talked about this. Getting your homework done before you started cooking.' She dipped her finger into the mixing bowl and licked it. 'Hmm, that is good.' Jamie grinned. 'Don't think you're getting away doing it, by bribing me with yummy food.' She was trying to be stern but failing.

'I won't be much longer, then I'll get to it, I promise. I wanted to do something special as Claire's coming over.'

'She'll appreciate the cake, that's for sure.'

Claire pushed her plate away. 'That was lovely. Thank you so much, Jamie, for such a delicious meal, you must have worked hard today. You really are a dab hand at cooking, aren't you?'

Jamie blushed. 'It doesn't feel like hard work. I love doing it. It's not like washing up or mowing the lawn. I wish I could do it all the time instead of schoolwork, that's so boring!'

'Life is full of boring stuff you have to do, love. You'll find that out the older you get,' Alison said, clearing the dishes away. 'I'll tidy up, just this once. You keep our guest entertained.'

'If you like it so much why don't you consider it as a career option?' Claire said.

'Mum wants me to go to university. My A-levels are

all chosen for me to apply for a degree in sports science. It's what I thought I wanted to do.'

'And now? What do you want to do now? You're allowed to change your mind.'

Jamie leaned closer. 'I'd really like to be a chef.'

'Have you told your mum that?'

He shook his head. 'No. I don't want to cause any more trouble. I've done enough of that already. Sometimes I hear Mum crying in bed, I know it's about me. She doesn't think I can hear her, but I can.'

'Perhaps you could talk to her, ask her opinion, you know as an educator. Believe me, Jamie. It's no use doing something like a degree or a job, just because your mum or dad wants you to. It's your life at the end of the day. And your mum only wants you to be happy.'

'She's always talked about me, and Callum, going to university. It's all right for him, he's clever, you should see all the books he's read, just for fun.'

'If you're serious about this, why not do some research on what it takes to go into catering? In my day you'd go to technical college or catering school if you wanted any qualifications. City and Guilds it was called, if I remember rightly. Of course, back then, a lot fewer people went to university, now they go whether they really need to or not. University's not for everyone, and that's fine. We're all different and having a degree doesn't necessarily make you better suited to a job. Plus, nowadays, it's not exactly a cheap option, the fees and living expenses would mean you'd go out into the world with the kind of debt I'd only expected if I had a mortgage, but then I am *very* old and a lot's changed!'

Jamie giggled, 'You're younger than Mum.'

'Yes, but don't tell her that.'

Alison came back in. 'All done. Now we can relax. Shall we see if there are any good films to watch?'

The three spent the rest of the afternoon lazily watching TV. Claire worried that she might have overstepped the mark by planting seeds of rebellion in Jamie's head; time would tell, she supposed. If Jamie was serious then he would have to present a reasoned argument as to why not going to university was right for him. She knew he'd have a battle on his hands as it had been Alison's assumption that both her children would receive tertiary education.

'Are you excited?' Alison asked Claire.

'Not as much as you.' They were on a shopping expedition for a wedding dress or 'wedding outfit' as Claire had called it. 'I am not going to be getting a long, bridal dress. This is my second marriage and I'm too old for lace and veils.'

'Nonsense! No one cares if you've been married before, plenty of women wear traditional wedding dresses, second, third time around. Look at Jennifer Lopez, and you're younger than her!'

'It's a bit different if you're a glamorous mega-star. I don't think a quiet registry office wedding warrants a princess ballgown, do you?'

'It doesn't have to be like that, there are plenty of styles out there. I'm sure the assistant at the place we're going to will tell you that.'

'I don't know how I got you to talk me into going to a bridal shop. I feel such a fraud. All I want is something simple, nothing frilly and fancy. And I certainly don't want a white dress.'

'Just try a few on, that's all I'm suggesting. If you hate them all we'll go to Primark!'

Claire laughed at this. 'I might hold you to that.'

'We'll have a glass of bubbly and get you in the right frame of mind. You've been far too calm and low-key – this is your wedding!'

'There's plenty of other drama in my life at the moment, thank you. This is me marrying the man I love and declaring it in front of the people I care about, end of.'

'Here we are.' Alison was looking in the shop front window, her nose practically glued to the glass. 'Oh, look at that, isn't it gorgeous?'

'If you're about twenty-five. Come on, Miss Romance, let's get this over with,' Claire said, pushing the door, the tinkling bell as it opened sending a petite, dark-haired woman scurrying over to meet them.

'Good morning, ladies, right on time! My name's Wendy. Which one of you is the blushing bride?'

'That would be me.' Claire raised her hand. This was going to be challenging.

'So, you must be Alison?' She shook both their hands. 'Before we get started would you like a glass of champagne?'

'It's a bit early for me, maybe later,' Alison said.

'I'll have hers,' Claire said. She noticed Wendy wrinkling her nose. Oh dear, no sense of humour. She was going to need a drink.

Settled in cream leather armchairs, Wendy proceeded to wax lyrical about the range of dresses that Claire could carry off. 'You are tall and slender so just about anything is going to suit you. Alison has told me you want something understated so I'm thinking a column or mermaid style dress, perhaps A-line?'

'What's that?' Claire asked and when Wendy indicated one of the nearby displays she said, 'Oh no, not for me.'

Not put off by Claire's attitude, Wendy ploughed on. 'I have set aside some gowns I think would be suitable. Would you like to follow me please.'

'This is *so* exciting!' Alison clapped her hands together in glee.

For the next two hours Claire tried on, and rejected, dress after dress. 'Too tight and I can't walk in it,' to the mermaid style. 'Too clingy, you can see my knickers,' to the column dress. 'Strapless, God no! I'll be freezing.' On and on it went, until even Wendy's enthusiasm started to wane. Claire was on her third glass of champagne by then. Alison was thinking this had all been a huge mistake, perhaps they would be buying something from Primark after all.

'I think we should call it a day,' Claire said.

'Perhaps come back at another time?' Wendy suggested. 'Choosing the right dress can't be rushed, often it takes several visits to find it.'

Claire had changed back into her clothes and was making an exit, when her eye was caught by a rack of dresses by the door that she hadn't noticed. 'You have short dresses?'

'Yes. Do you see anything you like?' Wendy's eyes glinted.

Scouring them Claire picked out one. 'This looks okay. Nice and plain.'

'Simple yet elegant,' Wendy said. 'Would you like to try it on?'

'Yeah, why not?'

In the changing room Wendy helped Claire on with the dress. 'I like the half sleeves,' she said. 'It'll be chilly in March and I don't want to be cold on the day. This material is nice.'

'It's Duchess Satin,' Wendy said as she zipped the dress up. 'The ivory suits your skin tone.'

Claire looked back at herself in the mirror. The dress flared gently and fell to her calves. It fitted to her waist, making it look tiny and the neckline dipped into a small v. Claire smoothed the fabric, the soft material under her fingers luxuriant.

'I look…' Embarrassed, she found herself on the verge of tears.

'Like a bride!' Alison had crept in and was actually crying.

Wendy beamed. 'I'll just get some tissues.' She'd made a sale.

Chapter Fifty-Three

'I don't believe it! Not charged? What about the things he did?'

'Aside from his visit to you, there's no proof that he was responsible for the business with Smokey, or the petrol. No witnesses and no specific timeframe. Eddie doesn't even need to provide an alibi.'

'Can't he be done for trespass? He was in my garden, uninvited.' Claire shuddered at the memory.

'He maintains the side gate was unlocked and he told you he was looking for me. He wasn't lying about that, we did know each other, so it has an air of legitimacy about it. The officer couldn't give much away but he sounded just as pissed off as we are that they couldn't charge him with anything. He mentioned the lawyer being very good, Eddie's probably at the station all the time and knows the ropes better than the cops. He'll be a slippery bugger, no doubt about that.'

'Do you think we are in any danger? If he's walking around free?'

'The police don't seem to think so. He'll want to keep a low profile and not draw attention to himself for a while too. I reckon for now we can relax.' Mark didn't talk about the specific threats Eddie had made against Claire. When he'd brought them up with the police, they told him without a third party hearing them it would be a case of hearsay and unlikely to stand up in court. *Especially as my reputation is blackened at the moment,* thought Mark – cursing himself yet again for his stupidity and the danger he had put them both in. Claire looked miserable and she'd been so happy after her shopping trip with Alison. He touched her chin. 'I know what will cheer us both up.'

'What's that?' Claire sniffed.

'Let's go online and think about where we want to relocate to. Check out properties and locations. Focus on the good things our future holds. What do you reckon?'

'I do like nosing around houses on the internet,' Claire said.

'Go on then. Fire up the laptop.'

─※─

At Alison's house, another important conversation was taking place. Jamie had baked scones and a Victoria Sponge, his mum's favourite, and was going all out and preparing a traditional English tea.

'Clotted cream too? You're really spoiling me. Good job I didn't have lunch. With everything you've made this will be enough for me until tomorrow. It's a shame Callum isn't here. He loves a scone.'

'I'll make some for his next visit at Easter. They're

easy to do.'

Alison bit into her slice of cake. 'Ooo, that's lovely! You have a real skill, not everyone can get a sponge right, very light. You must have got that from your grandmother, it's not me, that's for sure.' She noticed Jamie twisting a tea towel around in his hands. 'What is it, love?'

'What do you mean?' Jamie asked, his face all innocence.

'Something's up. All this.' She waved her hand over the food. 'What are you buttering me up for?'

'Nothing. I wanted to do something nice for you, that's all.'

'And I'm Queen Camilla. Come on, 'fess up.'

'There is something I wanted to talk to you about, actually.'

'I knew it! Spit it out then. It's nothing bad, is it?' Alison narrowed her eyes.

'No, no. At least I don't think it's bad. I'm not sure you won't though. I've been thinking a lot about my life and what I want to do with it.'

'You want to be a footballer, right?'

'No. Not anymore. All that stuff with the steroids, getting ill and everything. It's made me realise that I don't have what it takes. It was Ryan going on about how good I was. I believed him, he made me think I could do it.'

'Love, if it's what you want to do, I will support you. You don't have to give it up just to please me.'

'That's really nice of you, Mum, but I'm not lying. I

don't want to do it anymore.'

'Have you decided what you do want to do then?'

'More like, what I *don't* want to do. Don't get mad. I don't want to finish my A-levels and I don't want to go to university. It would be a waste of time.'

'Education's never a waste of time, Jamie. I know things have been tough at school lately, that's only to be expected, but once you're feeling better. Once the detox has got rid of all that rubbish in your body, it'll be different, you'll see.'

'I'm not going to university, you can't make me!'

'No, I can't, but you can't just give up A-levels and do nothing. You have to be doing some sort of training or apprenticeship until you're eighteen.'

'I've already decided.'

'Have you now. Would you like to enlighten me?'

'I'm going to take T-levels instead. They're equivalent to 3 A-levels.'

'I do know that. What subject were you thinking of?'

'Catering. I'd like to train to be a chef. I've looked into it and spoken to the careers adviser at school. She said it would be possible to drop A-levels and start the Ts in the autumn, I'd still be under nineteen when I finished the two-year course so it wouldn't cost you anything. I'd have practical experience that could lead to a job offer when I finish. And I'd be starting work without any debts. That's good, don't you think?'

'It's a plus, I'll give you that,' Alison said. 'Looks like you have it all sorted.'

'What do you think then?' Jamie looked nervous.

'As you've correctly pointed out. I can't make you go to university, and I wouldn't want to force you to do something you don't want to. But Jamie, love. Are you sure?'

'Yes, I am. I love cooking and inventing recipes. The course isn't just about cooking and the skills for that though. There's the nutritional analysis, even the business side of things. I can show you the course syllabus.' He handed Alison a booklet.

She took it and started reading, taking her time as Jamie stood nearby, watching. When she'd finally finished, she said, 'You're right. It's very comprehensive, and it's a practical alternative to A-levels. This will give you an advantage in the workplace.'

'So that's a yes? You agree?'

'On one condition. Just because you've decided you're not going to finish A-levels, I don't want you to give up on your current studies. You work as hard as you can to get AS levels as they're qualifications in their own right. One day you might change your mind about this and having those behind you would be a good idea. Will you promise me you'll do this?'

'I promise, Mum.'

Chapter Fifty-Four

'I do like that dress on you, the shade of green really suits you. You look great,' Claire said as Alison gave her a twirl and asked if she looked okay. They were back in Claire's house. She'd insisted on getting ready for the wedding there. 'It's where all my things are,' she'd argued with Mark when he'd been apprehensive about her returning. He'd stayed at the Brighton apartment the previous evening with his best man, an old school friend called Bryan.

'Shouldn't you be getting ready?' Alison asked. Claire was still in a bathrobe.

'My hair and make-up are done. All I have to do is put on my dress. I suppose I'd better do that now. The flowers are due to arrive soon so get the door if it rings, will you?' Claire disappeared upstairs leaving Alison to pace about. There was a knock; thinking it was the florist, she ran and opened the door.

'Hello, can I help you?' she said to the man outside. He was wearing a suit but despite looking smart, there was an air of menace about him.

'Just come to wish the happy couple well,' he said,

stepping over the threshold.

Caught off-guard Alison was forced to step backwards. 'They're not here, well, Mark isn't, only Claire. She's getting ready. We'll be leaving soon.'

'I'll wait. Don't worry, this won't take long.'

'Are the flowers here?' Claire called. She came downstairs wearing her dress.

'Erm no, it's…sorry, I didn't catch your name.'

'That's 'cos I didn't give it,' the man said and seeing Claire he said, 'My, don't you look a picture. Mark's a lucky man.'

At the sight of him Claire went pale. 'What are you doing here?'

'Now that's not very friendly of you and after I put on my best suit today to come and say hello.'

'Who is this man?' Alison said. She'd picked up the tension from Claire.

'Eddie. Pleased to meet you.'

Alison's eyes widened. 'You're Eddie?' She was thinking of her phone, in her bag. Where was it?

'Please leave,' Claire said.

'All in good time. Let me say my piece and I'll be off.'

'Be quick and then go.' Claire's hand gripped the banister.

'As you are probably aware, the police are not going to charge me for those terrible things I was accused of, rightly so as *I* am totally innocent. As to Ryan, well, he's going down for a long stretch after what he did to that boy, amongst other things. But myself and my colleagues aren't too bothered. To be frank, you've done us a favour. Ryan was a loose cannon, bringing unwanted attention to our…our operations. If you were worried there would be fallout over his arrest and soon-to-be conviction, you needn't be. As to my dealings with Mark, they're finished, they were once he'd paid his debt to me as far as I was concerned. Unfortunately, Ryan's mother, my sister, wanted me to look out for him. She's always spoiled that boy, mollycoddled him. So, when he came to me for a favour, against my better judgement I granted it.' He turned to Alison. 'If I'd have known what he had planned for your son, I would have never helped him. I have a code of standards, you know.'

'How do you know who my son is?' Alison asked.

'You'd be surprised what I know. Anyway, Claire, I wanted to say that neither you nor Mark will be hearing from me again. Call it a wedding present. Unless of course Mark needs another loan.' He chuckled at his joke. 'I'll let myself out.'

When the door shut behind him, Claire crumpled in a heap, shaking. Alison rushed over to her. 'Claire! Are you all right?' Unable to speak, Claire nodded. 'I'll get you a glass of water.'

Taking it from her with shaky hands, Claire drank the water. Closing her eyes momentarily, she said, 'Don't tell Mark.'

'You can't keep this from him.'

'I will tell him. Just not today. I don't want this to ruin things. And, if you think about it, it is a wedding gift, of sorts. Though I don't know how far I'd believe the likes of that man.'

The doorbell rang again and they both jumped. Looking at each other Alison said, 'Do you think he's come back?'

'Only one way to find out.' Claire went to the door and called out, 'Who is it?'

'Blooming Marvellous, the florist. I have a delivery.'

Sighing with relief Claire let the florist in and thanked them. A box containing two small bouquets within, yellow daffodils for Alison and white roses for Claire. Picking up the roses Claire said, 'They're beautiful, and to think I wasn't going to have any flowers.'

'Yes they really are.' Alison looked at Claire. 'Don't you have a headpiece to put on?'

Claire smacked her hand on the top of her head. 'I almost forgot!'

'Taxi's here,' Alison said. 'I'll let them know you'll be a few minutes.'

In the bedroom, Claire sat in front of the mirror; her hands had stopped shaking and she put on the headpiece. It was a delicate band of pearls and matched the studs in her ears which had been her mother's – something old. Looking at the bride in front of her, Claire allowed herself a smile. She was going to be happy with Mark. Slipping on her shoes she left to join Alison.

The wedding ceremony had been simple and brief, so different to the full nuptial mass of her first marriage. The guest list was significantly smaller too. Claire's brother and his family, Mark's parents, and friends from the swim club. When Claire and Alison arrived at Brighton Town Hall, Mark was there in front of its impressive façade to greet them.

'It's unconventional, but I wanted to escort you up those grand stairs inside,' he'd said. 'By the way, did you know you look absolutely stunning? My beautiful bride. Shall we?' He offered Claire his arm and they all went in.

The majestic sweeping staircase provided the perfect backdrop to the many photographs taken afterwards. Mark's mother, who was wearing a bright pink suit with an enormous matching hat, had to be tactfully asked to move aside in order that the other guests could be seen. There was much merriment as guests calculated how many people could hide behind Gwen's hat and not be seen in the photo.

Mark hugged Claire. 'Happy?'

'Yes, couldn't be more so.'

'I have a surprise for you. Strictly speaking it's not my surprise, it's the gift from my parents. There's been a change of venue for our wedding breakfast. When Mum heard it was to be in a small Italian restaurant, she said that would never do, and found us somewhere she felt was more suitable.'

'Where are we going then?'

'Patience, all in good time my dear. I think you will approve.'

Chapter Fifty-Five

'Aren't we getting a taxi?' Claire asked, when Mark grabbed her hand and led her away from the Town Hall.

'No need. It's only five minutes away.'

'It had better be, in these heels. It's chilly too.'

'Here.' Mark took off his jacket and placed it around Claire's shoulders.

'I do hope it isn't far, Mark,' Gwen said, clamping her hand to her hat as a gust of wind blew in from the sea. Then to Mark's father, 'Why haven't you offered me your jacket?'

'Because we've been married over forty years,' came the sardonic reply.

'Charming,' Gwen said. 'See, Claire, this is what it comes to.' But she smiled at her husband and gave him a gentle push.

'Follow me!' Mark said to the guests.

'Do you know where we're going?' Claire asked Alison.

'Not a clue. I'm as much in the dark as you.'

The walk took a little longer than Mark had promised but that was mainly because the group were ambling slowly, talking and laughing. 'It's like herding cats,' Mark commented. 'We're here everyone.'

Claire stared up at the grade two listed building, each window overhung with a dark green awning. The entrance had two large stained-glass doors, where a thick garland of flowers draped themselves over it and cascaded down to flank the doorway. 'The Ivy? Oh my God, Mark! We're having our reception *here*?'

'Do you like it?' Gwen asked, beaming. 'I've been here a few times for brunch and I've always wanted an excuse to hire The Tidal Room for a private function. There was never anything special enough until now.'

'Are we going in, then? I thought you were cold,' David, Mark's father, said.

The group ooed and ahhed as they looked around at the interior. The airy and art-filled room was spectacular. If they were impressed by this, it was nothing compared to the opulent décor of The Tidal Room. The ceiling mural depicted large bright fishes in a sea of blues. The walls had extravagant frescos embellished with colourful blooms. 'It's breath-taking. How absolutely lovely. Thank you so much!' Claire said to her new in-laws.

※

Mark's parents had not only paid for the hiring of the room but were also footing the bill for the whole meal. Champagne flowed in abundance and sitting next to Claire, Gwen got rather tipsy.

'I would have loved to have had a wedding like this,

but David and I didn't have two pennies to rub together when we got married. Neither did our parents.'

'It's so generous of you,' Claire said.

'Nonsense! I'm enjoying this as much as you. To be honest, I was beginning to worry that Mark was going to be single for ever. He was crushed after his divorce, totally swore off women and threw himself into his work. I was quite worried for a time, I don't mind telling you. It's so nice he's found you, such a nice woman who can speak proper English. Of course, I would have liked to have been a grandmother but one can't have everything, can one? Much better he married a mature, sensible woman.'

'Thank you.' *I think*, thought Claire. At a certain age wasn't mature just code for old?

❦

Claire stretched in the king size bed, her feet skimming the Indian cotton sheets. Mark was letting a waiter in with their breakfast. His wedding present to her had been a night in a boutique hotel, not far from the Ivy. 'As we're not going on honeymoon, I thought we could splurge on a bit of luxury for one night. Bit roomier than the apartment.'

Now seemed an appropriate time to mention Eddie's visit. 'There's nothing to stop us going back to our house if we want to,' she said, tearing at a piece of croissant and eating it.

'Really? How do you figure that?'

'I had a visitor at the house yesterday. Eddie.'

'What? And you didn't tell me?'

'I didn't want to upset you. It was a shock to me, I'll admit, but in the end it's good news.' She went on to relate what Eddie had said. 'I don't know which is the better wedding present. Eddie's announcement or the Ivy.'

'Bloody hell,' Mark said. 'That is surprising. Do you think we can trust him?'

'I think at a certain point we have to start living a normal life. We've reserved the apartment for a few more months, but then what? With the sale of the house imminent we need to get in there, get rid of some furniture and start packing. What are we going to do, commute from Brighton on a daily basis to do that?'

'When you put it like that it does make sense. And Spain? Now that it seems as though the threat of reprisals has receded, are you still up for that?'

'Yes. I want to do it. It will be an adventure. Maybe set a time limit on our stay there and reassess how we feel then. What do you think?'

'Seems fair. Plus with the way things are at work, I'd really like to get away from it all. Even if the complaint is not upheld; how am I supposed to carry on working with those people? It'll take months, years, for me to be fully trusted again, if ever. I've never fitted in anyway. I don't think a senior role, and the responsibilities that go with it, is for me. When I think about how content I was in Almería.'

'Could you go back to your previous job?'

'Nah, I already contacted my previous boss and she said she'd love to have me back but someone has got my old job and is doing well.'

'That's a shame.'

'However, she did mention a post she'd heard about somewhere along the coast. It would be a step down in some ways, but I'm thinking of applying.'

'Is it in a hospital?'

'A private clinic in a small town near Málaga. It would be fairly bog-standard stuff, but the hours would be regular and the town is nice. It's by the sea, so you could keep up with your swimming.'

'That's sold it for me then!' Claire gave him a hug. 'I'm sure we could make it work. The important thing is to be together and start living a normal life where we feel safe. Why don't you apply for the job? See how it goes?'

'I'll do that and for the moment it would be sensible to think about packing up at the house. We can spend the next week doing that, sorry it's not a more romantic honeymoon.'

'Plenty of time for nice holidays, what's important now is to start getting our lives back on track.'

Chapter Fifty-Six

For the move to Spain Claire and Mark had split the 'to do' list. Mark was to search online for somewhere for them to rent in Spain. He had already sent his job application to the private clinic. His former boss was going to be his referee and he was quietly confident that he had a good shot at getting the post.

'Are you worried that the GMC investigation is going to hinder your application?' Claire had asked.

'It shouldn't be a problem if they decide no further action is to be taken. My defence union seem to be confident I'll be okay. The fact that I was open about what I'd done and am fully cooperating is definitely in my favour. To be honest the only way I'm keeping sane is by trusting them and believing I will be cleared. I wouldn't be able to function as a doctor if I thought otherwise. Plus, I'm more than qualified to handle the role in the clinic and with luck they'll see that as an asset. What about you? When is the meeting with your line manager?'

'I haven't scheduled it yet. I'm still putting together my presentation as to how I keep my job with them and live in Spain.'

'It does seem a challenging idea.'

'I know, but I'm thinking along the lines of coming back to the UK on a monthly basis and holing up at the London office for a few days, that plus Zoom meetings. I've got to thrash out the finer details. I think I can make it workable, it'll just be convincing my boss, but they've been very flexible in the past so I'm keeping my fingers crossed.'

'How are you getting on with the contents of the house?'

'In some ways that's more complicated. If we find a place to rent and it's unfurnished, we could just load up a removal van and move it in. However, if that's not the case then I'd be best off putting my stuff into storage. Then I need to consider how long we will be in Spain and whether it would be worth transporting everything over and having to pay import duty on it.'

'It seems unfair to have to pay tax to move your own things to Spain,' Mark said.

'Yes, another unforeseen consequence of leaving the EU. It's a right pain and added bureaucracy to think about.'

'Things have certainly changed since when I first moved to Spain, back then it was all a lot simpler. I hope you end up thinking it's worth all the bother.'

'As I said, it will be an adventure. It's good to do something wild in your middle age – keeps you young!'

'Or turns you grey prematurely.'

'There's always hair dye,' Claire said, and they both

laughed. 'There is another thing I have to deal with, and it will be the worst of all of it.'

'What's that then?'

'Alison. How am I going to tell her that I'll be leaving the country? And at a time when she needs her friends around her.'

'That's going to be difficult. When will you speak to her?'

'It needs to be soon. She's always popping round unannounced and I don't want her to find out by walking in on us packing.'

'This is nice,' Alison said. She looked around the restaurant Claire had chosen for them to eat lunch. 'Out of my price bracket so it's a good job it's your treat. Very generous of you, I must say.'

'Think nothing of it.' Claire looked at her menu without seeing it, trying to decide when best to broach the subject of her move to Spain. Maybe it would be better to wait until they'd eaten. 'Shall I order a bottle of wine?'

'A whole bottle? I don't normally drink alcohol during the day. Oh what the heck! Yes, go on then.'

'A bottle of the Chablis please?' Claire told the waiter.

'Chablis? Blimey, Claire. Are we celebrating? Is it Mark? Have you heard from the GMC, that everything's going to be all right?'

'No, no. We're still waiting. It'll be a couple of

months yet, I should think.' She looked at Alison and her stomach twisted. How was she going to do this? There was no way she could sit through an entire meal without saying anything. So she announced, 'I do have news though.'

'From the expression on your face, it doesn't look as if it's good.'

'It depends on your point of view, I suppose.' Claire stopped, not sure how to couch what she wanted to say. 'The past few months have been difficult. For all of us.'

'You can say that again.'

The waiter appeared with their wine and there was silence as he poured for them. Claire took a slug of hers before continuing. 'Yes. And for Mark it isn't over yet, well, not for you either, nor Jamie.'

'I know. Just when I think he's making progress something will happen to bring him down. It's stressful. That's why it's so good to have you about. I really value the support you and Mark have given us. I don't know what I would have done without the two of you, to be honest.'

Oh God, thought Claire. Now that she'd started, she needed to continue. 'We've been more than happy to help and we'll always be there for you, wherever we are.'

'Are you going somewhere then?'

'Yes. You're probably not aware of it, I only found out myself recently, but Mark hasn't been happy here.'

'With all that's happened it's hardly surprising.'

'It's more than all the business with Eddie and Ryan. He hasn't settled in his new job and he's found being back in Britain more difficult than he'd expected. He spent most of his working life in Spain. He misses his friends, the life he had there…'

Alison looked at her wineglass, her fingers on its stem. 'So you and he are going to move there, is that it?' She didn't look at Claire.

'Yes.'

'When will this be?' Alison's jaw clenched and she still wouldn't make eye contact.

'We don't know for sure, there's a lot to sort out, but we think it will be the summer.'

'Seems like you have everything planned.'

To Claire's horror, Alison began to cry, big fat tears sliding down her face. 'Oh Alison, please don't be sad. It's not that far away and I'll be back all the time. You, all of you, can visit us whenever you like.' She reached for Alison's hand.

'It won't be the same!' Alison snatched her hand away, knocking over her glass of wine. Ignoring it she said, 'I can't believe you would abandon me at a time like this. And when I was so understanding about Mark. How could you?' Now Alison looked her in the eye and Claire shrivelled under her gaze.

'I'm sorry Alison. It's not ideal, I know. I have to think about Mark, he's my husband now. I have a commitment to him.'

'And that trumps our friendship? I see how it is.' She stood up, knocking her chair backwards. Diners nearby looked on, curious as to what was happening. 'I can't do this, I'm going.'

Claire was left on her own, stunned. The waiter appeared to take their order as Alison pushed past him. 'Will your dining companion be back?' he asked.

'No. No I don't think she will.'

Chapter Fifty-Seven

'Hello stranger!' Claire jumped as the person behind her at the Aquarium said this; turning, she saw Callum.

'Hi there,' she said, giving him a hug. 'What are you doing here?'

'Jamie and I have just been swimming. He's getting a drink.'

Claire saw Jamie at the vending machine and waved. 'What's with calling me stranger? It hasn't been that long since I saw you at the wedding.'

'Usually you and Mum see each other all the time. I've been back a week and you've not been round and I haven't heard her chatting to you on the phone either.'

Jamie joined them. He kissed Claire on the cheek. 'Hello Claire. I haven't seen you for ages.'

Claire looked at the boys. Should she say anything? Clearly Alison hadn't. 'I'm afraid your mum and I have had a bit of a falling out.'

'No way!' Callum said. 'What about?'

'Mark and I have decided to move to Spain. There are lots of reasons why. Unfortunately, your mum is very unhappy about this.'

'Why?' Jamie said. 'I'd love to live in Spain. You could go to the beach every day, it would be great.'

Claire laughed. 'You'd still have to work though, it doesn't mean being on permanent holiday.'

'But at least it would be sunny.' He looked out at the rain falling.

'She'll come round,' Callum said.

'I'm not so sure.' Claire eyed Jamie and said to him, 'Be a love and get me a bottle of water, would you? I forgot mine.' When he'd gone, she said to Callum, 'She told me I was abandoning her when she needed me most. She's probably not said anything to you, but she's finding it tough dealing with Jamie's situation. Believe me, if my circumstances were any different I would be here for her; I have been. But my life has changed and well...look, I feel awful about this. I've told her I'll be back all the time and of course you're all welcome to visit as often as you want.'

'I'll be taking you up on that offer,' Callum said.

'Anytime, we'd love to see you, all of you. Anyway, how come you're down here? Has uni finished already?'

'Yup. I did the last of my exams and headed straight here. I'll be going back in a couple of days to pack up my stuff.'

'Are you changing digs then?'

Jamie rejoined them and handed Claire her water.

'Something like that. I requested a leave of absence from my course for a year. I just got a confirmation email today. I haven't told Mum yet.'

'A leave of absence, why?'

'Because Mum and Jamie need me. I was going mad in Bristol thinking of the two of them struggling to get through this. It was starting to affect my studies. I said as much to my university when I explained why I wanted a break.'

'Your mum is going to go berserk when you tell her,' Claire said, not envying Callum that task.

'She will, but it's a done deal. Not much she can do about it now. Besides, what's a year in the scheme of things? I've got my job back at the sports store where I used to work on Saturdays. I can contribute to the household, with Mum not working I don't know how her finances are.'

'You don't need to worry. Alison has that all under control, as long as she's careful.' To Jamie she said, 'how do you feel about your big brother being home again?'

Jamie beamed. 'I think it's great. I've missed him a lot, much more than I thought I would. We've been doing loads of things together this week, I'm really looking forward to him being here all the time.'

'And I'm looking forward to being home again,' Callum said. He gave Jamie a little push on the arm. 'I've actually really missed being away from Sussex. I thought after the first year it would be better, but if anything, this second year has been worse. It will be nice to be back. Plus it will be good to see my girlfriend regularly.'

'Ah, that's who you've been missing!'

Callum laughed. 'I suppose I'd better get home and tell Mum the good news. Wish me luck.'

'Good luck. Tell your mum I was asking after her.

Mark and I were planning to have a barbeque soon, that's if this rain ever stops. You're all very welcome to join us.'

'That would be nice. I'll let her know. Come on, Jamie, you can protect me from the wrath of Mum.'

Claire watched as they walked away. They were great lads and she hoped they would take up her offer of visiting when she and Mark moved to Spain.

'Do you think it's wise to light the barbeque?' Claire said to Mark. 'Looks like it's going to rain to me.'

'One has to be ever the optimist when dealing with the British weather, if you didn't do something because you thought it was going to rain, you wouldn't do anything.'

'True enough, but cooking out in the rain seems foolhardy,' Claire said. 'It's up to you, but I for one won't be eating my hamburger out here under an umbrella.'

'You English, you've no backbone,' Mark teased.

Still laughing, Claire went back inside. Despite what Mark had said she thought it best to have a plan B, so laid the table with side dishes and drinks. Callum had said he and Jamie would join them and that he would do his best to persuade Alison to come along too. Claire still hadn't had any replies to the multiple messages she'd sent her. She wasn't picking up her calls either and a bouquet of flowers Claire had sent didn't elicit a response. She was beginning to despair of things ever being right between them. The doorbell rang. She held her breath, hoping against hope that Alison would be on the doorstep with her boys. But they were alone, and she tried to hide the disappointment she felt.

'Hi there. Come in.'

'We got you chocolates,' Jamie said as he thrust the box at her.

'And wine,' Callum said, then whispering in her ear, 'sorry, no Mum. I did my best but she wouldn't budge.'

'I didn't think she'd come but thanks for trying. Mark's out in the garden firing up the barbeque.'

'Isn't rain forecast?' Callum said.

'You try telling him that.'

Preparations got under way and the boys helped ferry food out to Mark. Jamie came back with some cooked sausages. 'It's started raining so Mark said to give you these. He's going to carry on cooking.'

Claire went out to him. 'Here, I brought you an umbrella.'

'Thanks love. Could you just hold it over me please? I need both my hands to cook.'

Claire tutted. 'This was exactly what I wanted to avoid.'

'I know, I know. Not much longer.'

'Mark!' Jamie called from the back door. 'Your phone is ringing.'

Mark gave Claire the barbeque tongs and said, 'Keep an eye on the meat, give it a couple of minutes then turn it over.'

'Don't be long.' She jiggled the umbrella into the

other hand.

'I'll be back in a jiffy.' He ran inside leaving Claire with her balancing act.

He was gone longer than a few minutes. *Where the bloody hell is he?* She was getting peeved, and wet. Mark came back and without saying anything he picked Claire up and whirled her around. The umbrella dropped to the ground.

'Mark! Careful, the food's getting wet.'

'I don't care!' He put her down and took her face in his hands, kissing her enthusiastically on the lips. 'That was my representative from the defence union. The GMC are not going to take the complaint against me any further. They are satisfied with the results of their investigation.'

Claire hugged him with all her might, tears forming. 'Thank God! Oh, that's wonderful. I'm so happy for you, Mark. For us.'

'And you know what this means?'

'You can continue practising medicine with no impediments or supervision?'

'Better than that. I can accept the job offer at the clinic. I can resign. I never have to work with stuck up Margaret again. Sunny Spain here we come!'

Chapter Fifty-Eight

With Mark's exoneration the couple were free to plan unhindered. He had handed in his resignation the day after he found out he'd been cleared. He was surprised when Marcus Beauchamp had tried to talk him out of it, saying that the NHS needed good doctors like him and that being reported to the GMC was not to be taken personally. 'You'd be amazed at how many doctors have had a complaint made against them. It doesn't have to end a career.' For Mark his wanting to leave wasn't only about the investigation. 'Maybe I'm being too thin-skinned,' he said to Claire. 'Is it too much to ask to love the job you do and like the people you do it with too?'

'I don't think so. I like my job a lot, but a good part of that is belonging to a team, having a laugh with them when you can, and feeling they've got your back. Working from home is convenient and not commuting is definitely a bonus, but I enjoy those times when I go into the office and reconnect with my colleagues,' Claire said. 'I'm so pleased my company was on board with my plan to work from Spain and go to London once a month. I would have hated having to leave my job. This way I get the best of both worlds.'

'I hope it's not going to be too much for you as well as settling in a new country and learning the language.'

'I'm sure I'll be fine. The thing I'd been most worried about was being away from Alison and now our friendship seems to be over, it's probably for the best I'm not around.'

'Still no word?'

'I've given up sending her messages. She knows where I am. At least Callum and Jamie are still talking to me. Callum says he'll keep plugging away at Alison. He's convinced he can talk her around.'

'He's a good bloke. I'm glad he'll be there for her,' Mark said.

'It makes me feel less guilty, I have to say. Now, back to packing. Do you think I need to take all my winter clothes?'

'Yes. You'll be surprised how chilly winter on the Costa del Sol can be. Remember, the house we're renting doesn't have central heating and it will have been designed to keep cool during an Andalusian summer.'

'Okay, in the case they go. It does feel odd though, packing more than shorts and a bikini to go to Spain.'

Callum flopped onto the sofa next to Alison. 'So, I hear from Claire that she and Mark have booked their flights. Do you want to know when they're going?'

'Not really. It makes no difference to me,' Alison said.

She picked up a magazine and began flicking through it.

'Really? It's not far off. You don't want to say goodbye to her and Mark before they go?'

Alison carried on reading. 'I don't think I'd be welcomed. Claire's stopped messaging me.'

'Only because you never answer her. You know this is killing her? She can't bear the two of you being at odds with each other. She didn't take the decision lightly to go to Spain, in fact she'd already rejected the idea once before, when Mark brought it up.'

Alison looked up from her magazine. 'She never told me that.'

'Because she didn't want you to think she'd be leaving. Apparently she told Mark that she didn't want to go to Spain because she couldn't imagine not living near you, seeing you or chatting every day. It's only when all this business about Mark's job came to light that she realised how unhappy he was. He'd not told her because he didn't want to upset her. I dunno, everyone being secretive thinking they are protecting the ones they love, when honesty would have been a better policy. At least everything's been sorted out with Mark though.'

'What do you mean?'

'About being cleared of professional misconduct. He heard while we were there at the barbeque. Didn't I tell you?' Callum said.

'No, you didn't. Why wouldn't Claire have said anything?'

'She probably thought you didn't care.'

'Of course I do.'

'You've got a funny way of showing it. I have to say, Mum, I'm shocked at how you've been behaving. I wasn't going to mention it, but I feel I have to now. Are you really not going to say goodbye to Claire? Lose all contact with her, never see her again?' Alison didn't say anything, she stared ahead, silent. 'Seriously, Mum? I don't get it. Claire's torn between her loyalty to you and to her husband. What did you expect her to do, ignore Mark's unhappiness because you wanted your friend on call?'

'That's a bit harsh.'

'I came back here especially to support you and Jamie. You're my family, it's important. Mark is Claire's family; shouldn't she be there for him one hundred per cent? Do you think this was an easy decision for her to make?'

Alison's lip trembled. 'No, I don't suppose it was. Do you think I've been awful?'

'Not awful. Just a bit immature,' Callum said.

'Which one of us is the parent here?'

'It's not too late to rectify the situation. I have something in mind, but I need to run it by Mark first.'

※

'You put the last of the cases in the taxi, I'll lock up,' Claire said. She pulled the front door shut and locked it, posting the keys through the letter box. The new owners were collecting a set from the estate agent. Tears threatened; she was going to miss this house even if recent events had defiled it somewhat. She'd miss

England and her life too, but there was a new one ahead of her and she was keen to start it. She wished with all her heart that Alison had contacted her, that they'd been able to fix things between them before she left, but the flurry of messages she'd left her had gone unanswered.

In the taxi to the airport Mark said to her, 'You're very quiet.'

'Sorry, it feels odd thinking I'm not going away on a two-week holiday, that I won't be coming back here. I'm a bit nervous, but I'll be okay once we get to Spain. We'll be so busy unpacking I won't have time to brood.'

'And studying.'

'Yes, did you really need to enrol me in a language school the first week I arrive?'

'It's good to hit the ground running, and it will be a way to make friends. The classes will be fun, you'll see.'

'Hmm.' Claire wasn't altogether convinced. Her previous Spanish lessons at school with the formidable Señor Lopez didn't inspire her with confidence. The airport came into view and Claire felt a fluttering inside of her, but this time it wasn't fear – it was excitement.

*

Claire looked at her watch again. Where had Mark disappeared to? He'd told her he was going to the bathroom over 15 minutes ago. Now the departures board was indicating they should go to their gate. There was a tap on her shoulder. She swung around. 'I was beginning to think you'd flushed yourself away…' She gaped at the person standing there.

'Fancy meeting you here.'

'Alison? What are you…why are you here?'

'I heard about this lovely couple who are moving into a town house on the Costa del Sol. Apparently the woman needs help with the unpacking, so I thought I'd see if I could lend a hand.'

'What? I don't understand.'

'Blimey, Claire, you're not usually so dim. I'm coming to stay for a couple of weeks to help you both settle in. Oh, and these two as well.' Callum and Jamie appeared from nowhere, grinning ear to ear. 'So what do you think? Are you all right with that or are me and the boys going to have to book into a hotel?'

Chapter Fifty-Nine

The municipality of Cala de Flores, where Claire and Mark had chosen to live, was a lively and friendly town of just under fifty thousand inhabitants. It was close enough to the airport to get there in half an hour, but unlike towns such as Torremolinos or Marbella, had fewer foreigners living there.

As they strolled along the promenade Claire said to Mark, 'It's great to think we live here now, that we're not just on holiday.'

'It'll be more believable when I start work next week,' Mark said. 'I forgot to mention, my new boss invited me to the clinic today to meet some of the people I'll be working with, then she's going to take me out to lunch. That's not a problem, is it?'

'Not at all. I've got plenty to be getting on with. I can't believe how much stuff there is still to unpack. How many boxes did we have transported from the UK in the end? Did you count them?'

'Twenty. Seems you have more clothes than you let on.'

'It's not all clothes, there are other things too. Things

we'll need to have around the house.'

'Much more in that house and it'll burst at the seams,' Mark said referring to the furnishing that had come with the rental property. The two of them had spent half a day tucking all the ornamental nick knacks and gaudy paintings into drawers and cupboards.

'We did well getting the place though. Who'd have thought from the outside the house had three bedrooms and two bathrooms, plus a good-sized space for me to use as an office.'

'The patio area is a bonus too. Aye, you get more for your buck here, that's for sure.'

'What about the WiFi? Are you going to be able to sort that today?'

'Yeah, I'll go into the Movistar shop in town and have a word. The previous tenants had internet so it shouldn't be a problem hooking us up.'

'Good. I don't think using the lobby of the local hotel for a business meeting would go down too well with my bosses.'

'I'll need it for my GA meetings too. I can't let that slide.'

'It's good you can do those online,' Claire said.

'It is, but I'll miss going out for a coffee afterwards, I've made some real friends there and my mentor has been fantastic.'

'You'll have to travel with me when I go to England for work and attend a meeting in person, so you can catch up.'

'I've already planned to do that after the summer. I

want us to settle in properly first.'

They were walking past several restaurants. 'Do you fancy a drink or something?' Mark said.

'I'd love one, but I think we'd better get back. We can't leave our guests to do all our unpacking.'

Back at the house they met Callum in the hall carrying a large, empty box. 'One down, nineteen more to go!'

'You did it already?' Claire said.

'It didn't take long. I hope where I've put all the kitchen stuff will be okay with you.'

'I'm sure it's fine. Just leave the box marked "office", I need to do that myself. Where's your mum?'

'Out on the back patio.'

Claire went out to see her. 'This is a bit of a sun trap, isn't it?'

Alison was sitting in a deckchair, her eyes closed. 'I'm not asleep, just absorbing the rays while I can. If the weather in England continues as it has been, you'll be seeing me again sooner than you think.'

'That's fine by me,' Claire said, pulling up a chair and sitting next to Alison. 'I can't believe you're here.' She grabbed Alison's hand and squeezed it tightly. 'I thought I'd lost you as a friend forever.'

'That won't happen. To be honest I don't know what's been going on in my head these past few months – to shut you out like that. I was so angry at first, then when I calmed down a bit I didn't know how to start to mend bridges. The longer it went on the more difficult it felt to contact you. I guess I was embarrassed in a way. Does that sound stupid?'

'Not at all. Pride gets in the way of a lot of things. What made you change your mind?'

'It was something that Callum said, about family. It made me remember how I was when I first got married to Gavin, how my loyalties felt divided between him and my parents. You know what my mum is like, how much time she demands of me. We were spending every weekend at their house. Gavin was getting sick of it and we had rows about it. I felt I was being disloyal to my parents by not having every Sunday lunch with them. Whenever I broached the subject of Gavin and me spending time alone, Mum would use emotional blackmail and I'd cave.'

'What happened in the end?'

'My dad intervened. He could see what Mum was doing and put a stop to it. It was such a relief not to have Mum and Gavin fighting for my time with me being piggy in the middle trying to please everybody.'

'You're right. Thank God for Callum taking the time to say something to you. He's a good son, both of them are. How's Jamie been? He seems to be a lot better.'

'His mood-swings are getting fewer, thank goodness. The weirdest thing of all is how his obsession for football has all but disappeared. He still goes training, but hasn't made the Aquarium team yet. He doesn't seem particularly bothered and I do wonder if it hadn't been for Ryan, whether he would have been as enthusiastic about becoming a footballer as he was. I'm so glad Jamie has a friend his own age. Do you remember Ishaan? The two of them are very close, they spend a lot of time together. His family are nice too and I've been to their house for dinner several times.'

'And Ryan? Any news about his court case?'

'Not yet. I don't know when that will be. I was worried Jamie would be called as a witness, but apparently there are so many other charges the police think there's a good chance he'll be convicted without testimony from Jamie. I'm just glad he wasn't let out on remand. Too much of a flight risk, so I'm told.'

'And how is it with Callum at home full time? When he told me what he'd done I knew you'd be unhappy about it.'

'I was at first. Very. But selfishly, I'm so relieved to have him around, someone to lean on, but I'll try not to turn into my mother! This is a temporary thing, just the year, then I want him to be independent of my troubles. Jamie will be starting his catering T-levels in September and he did well enough in his ASs, all things considered. It looks as though our family is getting back on track. I might consider a return to work sooner than I had anticipated, but I won't rush it.'

Callum and Jamie had hired two stand up paddle boards and were in the sea learning to use them. Jamie was pretty good but Callum's repeated falling into the water had everyone in fits of laughter. Claire, Mark and Alison were watching the antics from loungers stationed by one of the many open-air restaurants on the beach, named *chiringuitos* by the Spanish.

'Tell him to stop,' Claire said, wiping the tears of laughter from her face. 'My stomach hurts. I can't remember the last time I've laughed so much.' She looked at Alison who couldn't reply, her face creased and red. She was holding her stomach too.

Mark chuckled. 'You two are evil. And you, Alison, he's your flesh and blood.'

This only made the two women laugh more and Mark shook his head, smiling. 'I'm going for another beer. Can I get either of you something? That's if you can stop laughing long enough to drink.'

Finally calming down, Alison said, 'I'll have a lemonade please.'

'Me too,' Claire said. When Mark had gone she said to Alison, 'How are you enjoying your holiday?'

'I've had a fantastic time, it's been just what we've needed. Such a shame we have to leave. Jamie loves it here, he's so jealous you get to stay.'

'Why don't you then?'

'What do you mean?'

'Mark and I were talking about how good it's been us all being together. I know Callum will have to get back for his job, but you and Jamie don't have anything to rush back to just yet. How would the two of you feel about staying the summer? You could go back in time for the beginning of Jamie's course.' Mark returned. 'I was just telling Alison about what we'd discussed last night, about her staying.'

'What do you think, Alison? Would you like to?' Mark said.

'Of course I would, and I don't even have to ask Jamie. It's very kind but wouldn't it be a terrible imposition? You have your new job and everything.'

'Work is going very well. It's like I've been there for months already, don't worry about that. We've plenty of room and it would be great to have you here.'

'Are you sure, Claire?' Alison said.

'Yes. We wouldn't have made the offer if we weren't.'

'Then my answer is yes. Jamie! Come out of the water. I have some good news for you.'

Chapter Sixty

Claire peered out of the airplane window, looking down at the green fields so different to the landscape she had left two hours before. Once through passport control she made her way to the exit, scanning the faces of the waiting crowd.

'Claire!' Alison was waving her arm, trying to attract attention.

Claire battled through the throng of people and the two women flung their arms around each other. 'Did you have a good flight?'

'Yes, no problems at all.'

'Is this all the luggage you have?'

'I'm only here for a couple of nights, I don't need much.'

'Right oh. Let's get going. Lord knows how much the parking will cost. I got here way too early. I was so excited at the prospect of seeing you again.'

'If I'm going to be staying with you on my monthly visits, you don't have to keep picking me up. I can take the train next time.'

'You will not. It's no bother at all.'

'Let me pay for the parking then. It's the least I can do. It really is very kind of you to agree to this. I hope it won't cause you too much disruption,' Claire said.

'Having you stay with me when you come over for work is sensible. Imagine having to be in a hotel two days every month. You'd soon get sick of it. This way you have all the comforts of home, not to mention the money you're saving, and I get to see my best friend, guaranteed, on a regular basis.'

Claire had spent the day in the London office and was back at Alison's house. Jamie was out with his friend and the women had the place to themselves.

'The best thing about Jamie's course is all the wonderful food I get to eat. If he's not practising with a new dish, he's bringing something home that he made during the day. He's made us dinner, it's bound to be good. I might never cook again.'

'The sales of indigestion tablets are going to fall then.' Claire sniggered.

'Enough of that or you won't get anything to eat.'

The meal had been delicious and they lingered at the table, drinking wine and reminiscing.

'This is so great,' Claire said. 'I haven't said it before now, but that time…when we weren't speaking. It was terrible, I couldn't bear it. Promise me we'll never get to that point again?'

'I promise. It was terrible for me too. I was being too sensitive. Maybe I felt that Mark was going to take you away from me and I've wouldn't ever get to see you.'

Claire put down her wine glass. 'Not in a million years. We'll be friends forever. Come here and give me a hug, you silly thing.'

'Forever,' Alison said as she hugged her friend back.

Chapter Sixty-One

The journey back had been smooth and without incident. At Gatwick airport she had been able to finish off some work in one of the private lounges her company had thoughtfully booked. She'd been cocooned in a bubble of peace and calm. Why hadn't she done this when she'd travelled before? It certainly made things less stressful. *This is going to make the monthly commute to England a lot more doable*, she thought. Maybe she really could have the best of both worlds.

'Claire! Over here.'

She tried to find the face to match the voice and had some difficulty, mainly because Mark was hidden behind an enormous bouquet of flowers. 'I almost didn't see you there,' she said as she was gathered in a one-armed hug.

'It is a bit big, isn't it? I was shocked at the size when I went to collect them. I had said they had to be special, but I hadn't meant enormous!'

'They're lovely, thank you, but collecting me and just seeing you waiting there is enough.'

'I'm happy to meet you, and don't get used to the

flowers, they're just this once. I wanted to make sure you'd be glad to be back.'

'No danger of that. You're here, and that's reason enough for me to be too.'

They made their way to the car and despite it being the end of October the weather was pleasantly warm, and the sun was shining. A stark contrast to the England she'd just left. The motorway snaked parallel to the sea and she smiled as she looked at the blue of the Mediterranean. A late-afternoon swim already planned in her mind.

'I've made us something to eat. I didn't think you'd want to go out tonight,' Mark said.

'You're right. I've got a Spanish class tomorrow morning and I need to do my homework.'

'And you're left it until the last moment to get it done?' Mark laughed. 'Were you like this at school?'

'Pretty much.' Claire giggled. 'But the classes here are so different, a lot more fun. I'm finding it much easier, and the language exchange group I go to means I can practise my speaking more than I ever did at high school. Which reminds me. The group are planning a meal out, partners are invited. Do you fancy it?'

'Yeah, sounds good, so long as it doesn't clash with when we go out with Antonio and Carmen,' Mark said, referring to the couple that lived next door, with whom they'd become friendly.

'No, it doesn't. It's great that we've only been here a few months and already have quite the social life. And all the swimming in the sea I want. Talking of which, I was going to suggest that *you* have a lesson.'

'Ah but as you know darling, my Spanish is perfect—well almost.'

'I'm not talking about that. You promised, that when we were living here, you'd make an effort to improve your swimming skills so we could do it together, maybe go on a swim holiday.'

'You're right I did. And a promise is a promise. When did you have in mind?'

'Tomorrow is busy for me, what with my lesson, then I need to tie up a few loose ends from my trip. How about the day after?'

'Fine by me,' Mark said.

※

The beach was only a five-minute walk from where they lived, a novelty that Claire was certain she would never tire of. 'Isn't it great to walk here just wearing a swimsuit, ready to go? And look at the sea. Perfect conditions!' Claire grinned, her hand shading her eyes as she looked at the water.

'No regrets about moving here then?' Mark asked.

'None whatsoever.' She scanned the near-deserted beach. 'Look around you. We have the place to ourselves practically. No battling with stand up paddle boards today.' Kicking off her flip flops by the water's edge she stretched her swimming cap on. 'Where's your cap, Mark?'

'Do I really have to wear one?'

'Yes, you do. It makes you more visible in the sea and I want to be able to spot you. Here,' – she threw him a bright yellow cap – 'you can match the colour of the buoy.'

'I hope no one mistakes me for one.' Mark caught the cap.

'Don't worry, darling. Your head's big, but not that big.'

'Ha ha, very funny. So what's the plan for today's swim?'

'I think you're a strong enough swimmer now and you'll be able to get to the buoy. With the water being so flat today it will be easy to see, there's also the small island further out you can sight, obviously don't try and swim to that.'

Mark screwed up his eyes as he looked at the buoy. 'I don't know whether I'll be up to it.'

'No pressure. If you feel it's too much, stop and have a rest. We can always turn back, but it would be nice for you to reach it before they take the buoys away for the winter.'

'I'll give it my best shot.'

'Good! Come on, let's get going. Don't worry, I'm not going to swim off. I'll be right by your side.'

The two set off at a leisurely pace. As she'd promised, Claire stayed with Mark. She swam sidestroke so she could keep an eye on him and offer advice about his arm or leg position in the water.

'You're doing well. Do you want a breather?'

Mark stopped. 'Yeah, I could do with it.' He looked

at the buoy. 'It's still a way to go, I thought we'd be much nearer.'

'We're a little over halfway. Remember to sight every so often though. Keep the buoy in your line of vision. Lift your head a little every fourth or sixth stroke so you don't go off course. It's important if you're in the open water. Are you okay to carry on?'

'Yes, I'm fine.'

'I'm going to swim ahead and I want you to navigate your own way to the buoy, practise your sighting. I'll be watching to make sure you don't go astray. Do you feel comfortable doing that?'

Mark nodded and they swam again. Claire went ahead and was at the buoy in a matter of minutes. She waited, watching Mark. He was doing a fair job of keeping on track and she noted that his stroke had improved a lot. As he got closer, she shouted encouragement.

'Come on, Mark! You can do this!'

There was a slight current, which was working against Mark, and he struggled for the last few metres, fighting against it. Claire drifted to him and swam by his side. 'Push your arm down and glide before you raise the other one. Fantastic, nearly there, just a couple more strokes.'

Mark raised his head at the buoy, gasping from the exertion. 'Bloody hell, that was tough.'

'Hit it!'

'What?'

'You've got to hit the buoy, now that you're here.'

Mark banged it three times and roared with laughter.

'That *does* feel good!'

Claire laughed and swam over, embracing him and winding her legs around his torso. They kissed until Mark started spluttering. 'Hold on there. I may have got to the buoy, but I don't think my swimming skills are quite up to those kinds of antics.'

She released her grip on him and pulled away. 'Shame, that's something we're going to have to work on.'

'All in good time. Let me savour this moment,' Mark said, floating on his back and recovering his breath. 'I'll need a while before I attempt the swim back.'

'No rush. In fact, I think I'll swim to the island. I've been curious about what's on the other side of it.'

'Aren't you worried about swimming that far?' Mark asked.

Claire looked at him and thought for a moment. She touched his hand. 'No. I'm not afraid of what's beyond the buoy anymore.'

Acknowledgments

I would like to start out by thanking my dear friend and fellow author, Joan Fallon. She is an endless source of knowledge and advice. We share a passion for reading and at our weekly breakfast meetup we exchange novels and discuss the latest book we have read — among many other topics!

Barbara Pollock has been a constant since my writing began and has been generous with her time, reading drafts and sending me constructive and useful feedback. Dani J Norwell, another local author, agreed to read my manuscript even with the demands of a new baby, I am so grateful to her. Madeline A Stringer, ALLi member and author, kindly took the time to answer my many about the complaints' procedure for doctors.

To my 'fan club' led by Al Smith and his wife Stephanie. My friends: Catalina Cox, Kathryn Walsh and Angie Hart. My family: Dixie and Janice, the greatest in-laws you could have, Karen and Russell Tellier, American cousins who have helped spread the word!

To editor Nicky Taylor, thanks for your understanding, I really appreciate it. To the amazing and talented Lin

White, who has been responsible for seeing that this book gets published. Without her technical and editing skills, I don't know where I would be. She is a real gem!

To Ruby, my lovely dog, always there for a snuggle and walks that blow away the cobwebs.

To Dirk, my wonderful husband. His unending support and utter belief in my success continues to amaze me. Thanks for all the cups of tea and for being an author widower, taking on household duties and never complaining as I spend hours locked away in my office.

And to you, my lovely reader, thank you so much. You're what it's all about.

About the Author

Susan currently lives in County Wexford, Ireland with her husband, Dirk. When not writing, Susan enjoys walking her dog Ruby, the subject of many Instagram posts, on the local trails. In a former life she has been a bank clerk, an English language teacher, teacher-trainer and an English language examiner.

Beyond the Buoy is her second novel and part of the *Beyond the Waves* series.

Follow her on Instagram: **susan_carew_author** or

Facebook: **https://www.facebook.com/profile.php?id=61552281607524**

You can find out more about her or sign up to her mailing list by visiting her website:

www.susancarew.com

Printed in Great Britain
by Amazon